Jean-Patrick Mallinger

I0682097

Conspiracy at Kheo

Editions Dedicaces

CONSPIRACY AT KHEO

[Complot à Khéo, translated from French by Caroline Andreea Zgortea]

Published by:
  Editions Dedicaces LLC
  12759 NE Whitaker Way, Suite D833
  Portland, Oregon, 97230
  www.dedicaces.us

Library of Congress Cataloging-in-Publication Data
  Mallinger, Jean-Patrick
    Conspiracy at Kheo / by Jean-Patrick Mallinger.
    p. cm.
    ISBN-13: 978-1-77076-467-5 (alk. paper)
    ISBN-10: 1-77076-467-4 (alk. paper)

2

Jean-Patrick Mallinger

Conspiracy at Kheo

Foreword

Do you love Adventure, the one that grabs you from the first pages of a novel to the point that you can't let it out of your hands? In that case, read Conspiracy at Kheo by Jean-Patrick Mallinger and you will be delighted.

The character of the fighter tourist belongs not only on reality TV shows. Here, we are in Kheo and not in Khô Lanta, but not to play: could you imagine a tourist wanting anything else than the sun, the beach and fine sand? At Kheo, Jérôme, the tourist, did not think of basking, lazing around: he wanted an ethnologic adventure, with the pride of discovering a people reliable only on itself, isolated from the outside world... He would be fulfilled, but not as he had expected: for sure, he found himself in a closed universe, but in the middle of a community that met the worst misdeeds of a forgotten form of colonialism and dictatorship. Forgotten? Not quite! Does the human soul so easily forget its depths?

Thus, it is the reader who finds himself questioned with every page, confronted as he is in a society that is trying to save what can still be, relying on the last virtues of dying humanism. Would Jérôme manage to provide valuable assistance? Will he not be faced with the same search himself? This is a question that we will ask ourselves in the course of a plot full of twists.

We do not come out intact from such a reading... Are you ready? Then, immerse yourself quickly in Conspiracy at Kheo!

THIERRY ROLLET
Literary agent

First part

Conspiracy at Kheo

I — Destination Kheo

The Indian Ocean, Tuesday March 18, 1997, beginning of the afternoon

The helicopter was flying at low altitude. The blast of the blades rubbed the surface of the water. The sky was clear and the sea calm, a 'sea of oil', how the sailors called it. Franck, my pilot, seemed more and more nervous. 'After my coordinates, we are entering the closed zone', he told me, 'we will reach the Island of Kheo in a few minutes'. I sighed with impatience. It was a year since I had been waiting for this moment! I would soon discover a people, a corner of the world that was yet unknown to me!

Suddenly, scrutinizing the horizon, I began distinguishing a column of black smoke. 'It's not normal', exclaimed Franck, tense on his commands, 'it's bad!'

He climbed over his equipment to examine the scene from a higher point. I was worried. During our approach, we saw a sort of oil rig on fire at one kilometer from Kheo. The smoke was so dense that it projected its shadow over the rocky flank of the island and Franck decided to bypass it from a distance. Every turn gave me the impression the view toppled.

I took advantage of this high view to discover this 'place of holiday': a rocky massif in a lush forest setting, huge plantations, a large clearing with buildings from where other columns of smoke were rising! 'Damn it, it's not possible!' my pilot cried, 'it's a conflict! We're turning around and leaving, there's no question of landing there!'

I protested: 'You're kidding, I paid for my trip, I don't want to go back on your container, leave me there or I'll jump from the helicopter!'

'You're crazy, we don't even know what's going on here, do you want to kill yourself?'

'Are you afraid of a fire? I can't believe it! Do you see that beach in the north, throw me there, I beg you!'

'Yeah! O.K. for the beach, but only if there's no one there to shoot us down, I don't want to wreck my machine!'

In a few moments, we went over the magnificent empty beach, lined with palm trees. At one meter above the sand, I opened the cockpit door to throw my bag. Franck nodded furiously while vociferating. I didn't hear any of his words, for I had already taken my helmet off and detached my belt to throw myself on the sand as well. After jumping, I turned to close the door... too late, the machine was already high in the air! I followed it with my eyes to see it disappear between the sky and the sea while the song of the waves continued its tempo in the middle of the silence. Picking up my backpack, I had a strange premonition: I thought I would never leave this island!

I immediately began a long march, deciding to pay a visit to the inhabitants of Kheo. In case of conflict, it would be best if they found me before nightfall. Moreover, I had no wish to sleep outside! Scared, I had no choice but to march towards the clearing I had seen from the helicopter, since it had to be populated.

On the road, I took my first eight photos: pineapple, bananas, hives, rabbit breeding in concrete and screened enclosures, vegetable gardens... all that concerned the daily lives of these people interested me, but my main preoccupation was to meet them.

♦ ♦ ♦

After an hour of walking, I finally entered the inhabited area. I put down my bag of eleven kilos that was digging in my back to sit down for a minute. My hip was hurting me. I took out my flask and a few sips of water later, I resumed my journey.

I entered a large building site where a quarry began at the base of a cliff. There was no one. Six machines were on the site, sleeping there, unmoving. All had the same inscriptions that represented a black wheel on a red background. This wheel was hollow and empty in the center, reminding me of an alarm gear. Further away, I saw five bunkers, half buried, around which they had planted banana and eucalyptus. In the background, I clearly saw the two columns of smoke.

I took my binoculars to observe, between two units, the plain that stretched until the South beach. A row of four larger, buried bunkers barred my way. I took a stony, wide track that led to the village, crossing the cultivated fields, squared with walkways and hoses.

The village was built like a military barrack: a set of buildings around a courtyard. In the centre, a mast topped by a red flag, which I assumed was the same black gear wheel that I had already seen on the building site on the machines. This symbol was omnipresent. On the South side, the buildings were perfectly aligned, but separated to give access to the beach. Two of them were almost burnt out. The beach was arranged: an artificial dam, a pier, a covered courtyard. In the axis of the dam, the burning 'oil rig' seemed more imposing.

I advanced to the short track that overlooked the courtyard by a porch. Two hundred metres separated me from the barrack. At this distance, it was impossible to see any life form... One hundred and fifty metres... my heart was beating harder and harder... A hundred metres... I felt the bitter smell of the fire... Thirty metres... I noticed people in the courtyard through the porch, they were sitting on the ground, their eyes turned towards me!...

2 – Funny natives

According to the tribes of the neighboring islands, Kheo had a surface of 32 square kilometres, was known as a cursed and dangerous place. Oficially, it was a closed military zone and uninhabited. It's geographical position had been give to me by Franck, exofficier of the Army, friend of my dead father. He accompanied the membres of the team of a container, the 'Cirius', which moved between the islands of the Indian Ocean and Africa. Franck had become friends with these sailors with which he lived. His helicopter had its reserved place on the deck of the *Cirius*.

For a fee, this retired officer had accepted to go over the interdiction to leave me on Kheo. He didn't believe the official story, and said the place was inhabited, which excited my curiosity!

I thought to find, beside the exotism and invasion of the civilisation, a handful of natives living from fishing, hunting and pickings! The reality was quite another. The black people I saw seated in this place all had on the same combination of red with the same gear wheel listed on the back! It was shocking to see several hundred people, men, women, children dressed this way.

All this crowd was seated in front of two men perched in the box of a truck parked in the middle of the square. Seeing me come, most people turned their heads towards me to stare. I felt like a curious beast spied on by hundreds of interrogative and tired eyes. The atmosphere was heavy, but not aggressive. Some whispered in their neighbor's ear, while following me with their eyes as I was advancing toward the truck. Mothers hugged their children tightly to them, rocking them nervously. Every frightened child snuggled against an adult. In all evidence, these people were in a state of shock.

After endless seconds, I stopped at about ten metres from the truck, letting my bag slowly to the ground. If these people had wanted to kill me, I would have already been dead! A young woman was leaning against the flank of the rear wheel of the truck. She was holding a little girl who was leaning against her. Their hair was wet. A piece of wire was firmly tied around the girl's left ankle.

In the back of the truck, two men sitting against the tailboard examined me carefully. One of them, of white race, had an army green uniform, dirty and torn. A bandage covered his right eye and his face was so battered, it was impossible to give him an age! The other man, of black race, in a red overall, had to be around fifty years old. We could hear the crackling flames that finished devouring a building behind them.

The white man talked to me in a sarcastic tone: 'Oh well, news travels fast, they already sent us a journalist! Hello, Mister journalist, we saw your helicopter!'

A little surprised to notice that my camera and the binoculars hanging from my neck had made me pass for a journalist, I replied in the same fashion:

'I'm not a journalist, my name is Jérôme and I come as a tourist!'

The white man laughed: 'A tourist? It will be hard to find postcards here! My name is Athal and this is Etienne, the new governor of Kheo!' he said kissing the black man. 'Take our photos, for today is a great day.'

I took a photo of the two men (who seemed to be the leaders of this people) as well as the girl with the little one leaning against the wheel of the truck while Athal and Etienne went down from the back of the it.

Etienne spoke to all through a megaphone. 'We have a surprise guest: Jérôme the tourist, may he be welcomed

11

among us. Distribution of oil lamps in an hour in front of shopnumber two. The three families that leave tonight, come to the truck and you will eat under the covered courtyard; the others, you will eat in your respective bunkers. Interdiction to open the cold rooms until new orders, use your supplies. Don't forget it will be night in two hours... You may leave!'

Athal grabbed me by the arm, whispering: 'Go ahead, little one, photograph the inhabitants of Kheo, they are entering a new life! Take pictures.'

I politely accepted, focusing on the crowd that was getting up while talking. Then, he turned to the young girl leaning against the wheel of the truck. 'I present you Kelia, twenty years of age and her little sister Nellie, nine years, my two heroines who risked their lives participating in the attack.'

'Pleasure, I'm Jérôme, twenty four years.'

'Take a photo of us three!'

He took little Nellie in his arms and pressed against Kelia, forcing a smile from his swollen lips. This gave him a more frightening air. All three were dirty, their hair tangled. You could clearly see the electrical wire attached to Nellie's ankle. The two sisters showed a terrible air, without smiling and lifeless. Pushing the trigger of my camera, I wondered what I would do with such a photo!

Etienne came toward us, accompanied by two men with serious faces, aged about thirty years. 'Jérôme, the tourist, here are my two terrible sons: Hemerik and Fredo'.

The two men, scowling, saluted me briefly without interrupting their walk to climb into the cabin of the truck that they drove off. The place was emptying, the people busy getting ahead of the first light of evening.

3 – The infirmary

Etienne was on the verge of leaving, his megaphone under his arm. He stopped and addressed Athal: 'In fact, where will Jérôme, the tourist, sleep?'

Athal – Well…

Me – Don't worry about me, I'm used to camping in the wild, I just need a little place where no one will be bothered.

Etienne – No, not outside because of mosquitoes!

Athal – That's right, not outside. There's still a place in a bunker and the infirmary is free.

Etienne – Right, what do you choose, Jérôme, the tourist, the bunker or the infirmary?

Me – The infirmary.

Etienne – It's settled, I'll accompany you with Kelia and Nellie who will bring you water, an oil lamp and a meal tray.

Me – Thank you very much!

Athal – As for me, I leave you and I'll see you tomorrow. I had my dose of strong feelings today!

Etienne – See you tomorrow!

Me – Good night!

Etienne took my backpack and insisted he carried it. On road, he said:

'There's no danger anymore, we'll be able to sleep! The governor of Achab destroyed our chapel, as well as our electric plant, it's why we don't have electricity anymore. This said, Athal has planned it all, he says an important cargo will arrive in two or three days. Athal will help us rebuilt and rehabilitate the island.'

'Who is the governor of Achab?'

'It's a torturer who has mistreated us for too long. It's a long story with a happy ending since Achan and his collaborators died on the platform thanks to the conspiracy organized by his son Athal with Kelia and Nellie's complicity. We owe them much.'

'Athal killed his father?'

'Indeed, he's part of our family now. Here is the infirmary. Kelia, take good care of our guest, give him a single room!'

'Yes, priest Etienne', answered the young girl.

Etienne gave me my backpack and saluted me. That's when I realised he didn't have his left arm.

'I must leave you, for I have many things to do before nightfall. Well, goodnight and see you tomorrow!'

'See you tomorrow and thanks again!'

Without turning back, he raised his only arm as if to say: it's nothing! I watched him leave, his megaphone under his left arm, while Kelia opened the door to the infirmary.

We went in a big, white room, perfectly clean. Lacquered glossy white walls, white tiles, white ceiling with a white fan, white shutters... And in the middle of this spotless whiteness, a red square glass tinted in a mass of half a square meter, shined against the back wall. It represented the same gear wheel as the one inscribed on the back of the two girls!

Nothing was missing, in this modern infirmary: the furniture in chromed steel tubes, two cubicles for emergencies, a delivery room and a single room to which Kelia led me. This room was the exact copy of a hospital room: the bridge above the electric bed with its equipment, the rolling table, a standing fan, a phone on the bedside table... Because of missing electricity, nothing worked.

I put my bag on the floor, a metre away from the motionless girls who were watching me intently. I began to empty my luggage in the white closet next to the shower stall. I unrolled my sleeping bag on the bed and I wondered for how long these girls were going to stay fixed there.

Sitting on my bed, I decided to observe them as well, from head to feet. They wore dark colored boots, their red

14

combination smelling of the sea. Nellie was still glued to her big sister.

I took from my bag a box of fruit pasta that I presented to the youngest. She looked at the object without reacting. 'Take it!' insisted her big sister. Nellie hesitated, then took the entire box. 'Thank you', she said.

Impossible to make them smile, I thought. I so wanted to know their story, but I didn't dare ask.

Suddenly, they left, then came back half an hour later: Kelia was carrying a bucket of water in each hand, followed by Nellie who was holding a burning oil lantern. They left in silence with the same serious air.

After a bath in cold water, I put on a jog and lay down on the bed waiting for my meal tray. I thought I was dreaming. I was under the impression of being on another planet! All this was shocking and seemed unreal. I needed to understand. I was so confused and tired that I fell asleep in my sleeping bag until the next day!

4 — A difficult past

Wednesday, March 19, 1997

It was five in the morning when I was woken up by the purring of the engine of a truck traveling in the square. The tropical sun already illuminated my pale room. I was a little cold and most of all, hungry! I discovered, put on the service table (probably since last evening), the meal tray covered by a stainless steel cover next to a closed jar of water. The menu: vegetable soup (cold), roasted rabbit leg, pineapple wedges.

While eating, I remarked that the oil lamp was still lighted on the windowsill. Outside, voices, engines, scrapes, footsteps on the gravel in the square, people were waking up, life was resuming. This people had to take their destiny in their hands and rebuilt themselves.

♦ ♦ ♦

Around six o'clock, someone knocked on my door. Five people came in: Kelia and Nellie, always so serious, Etienne, Athal and a middle-aged woman, smiling, which Etienne introduced to me:

'Good morning Jérôme, the tourist, I present you Linda, my wife, who is a nurse.'

'Good morning Linda, pleasure to meet you.'

'How are you, my boy?' she asked.

'Very well, doctor, I'm in good health! And thank you for the wonderful meal.'

They all laughed. Kelia took my empty meal tray. She left the infirmary, following her sister.

Athal took a seat in the treatment room and Linda began to change the dressing on his eye, while Etienne proposed we go chat outside. I was impatient to know the events that would save the island of Kheo. A table and chairs had been put in the corner of the courtyard under a great umbrella. Etienne invited me to sit and said:

'You were asleep when Keila brought you the meal last evening, she didn't dare wake you.'

'Thank you… thank you for your welcome.'

'I can imagine all the questions going through your head! To tell all this, for us, is the occasion to make it known to the outside world the atrocities we have lived here because of that infamous governor Achab!'

'If I do well, are you counting on me to bear witness upon my return?'

'Why not? Achab traded with individuals of his own kind that will react how, now that all is destroyed?'

'You think Kheo is in danger?'

'Only God knows and we're counting on him to help us assume our independence. Athal knows his father very well: he has served him since infancy. As such, he is in a position to explain all activities generated from the rig. I will learn much!'

'Why is Athal desfigured?'

Etienne sighed before answering:

'My sons hit him with iron bars. If I hadn't intervened and separated them, Athal would be dead and then Achab would have killed us all! Athal came alone, without bodyguard; great mistake! We couldn't guess he came to ask for our help in organizing a conspiracy against his father! In was in my apartment under the mechanical workshop where Hemerik and Fredo work, when I head the assault.'

'But why such violence?'

'It is best to wait for Athal's answer. He'll join us as soon as my wife finishes his care.'

Waiting for Athal, I noticed the activities in the square. Under a large covered area, the women were washing clothes while singing, others were peeling whole bowls of fruit and vegetables. In the background, in the south, men loaded the remains of the two buildings that had burned in the bed of a truck with a mechanical shovel.

Some children, like Nellie, were playing and running around the pole on which the red flag and black logo still flew. I noticed they had few toys: a bicycle, a ball, two hoops, two jump ropes...

Kelia brought us a a tray with drinks: five glasses and a jug of mango juice. Athal came at that moment and sat down next to me, while Kelia served us. Etienne asked Athal:

'Explain to Jérôme, the tourist, why Hemerik and Fredo hit you.'

'Well... it's more than twenty years ago, Etienne and his people got tired of being abused by my father, so they went on strike. At that time, I was nine and my father didn't yet have a helicopter. He only moved by boat. He embarked me with him and two of his men to fetch Etienne, Linda, Hemerik and Fredo. He wanted us to 'negociate' on the rig.'

'His men bound our hands to the pipes beneath us, it happened in one of the premises under the technical platform', followed Etienne, 'a workshop used as a torture chamber. They cut my left hand in front of my wife and sons!...'

'To stop the bleeding', Athal continued, 'they used a blowtorch! I still remember the smell of burnt! I wanted to get out, but my father ordered his men to retain me. I vomited. My father wanted to make 'a man' out of me, capable of taking a scene of torture! They made me whip Hemerik and Fredo, aged ten and eleven then. To finish, they released Linda to rape her in another room. One of these men was the rig's doctor, and he loved to make unhealthy scientific experiments. That evening, he just made an injection to each of the victims to put them to sleep. They were then swung on the beach during the night. As for me, I spent the rest of the evening under the shower, fully dressed. I didn't eat anything for two days, it made my father laugh!'

Athal stopped his speech to sip his mango juice.

I was uncomfortable seeing Ettiene's stump put on a table next to the pitcher. I couldn't finish my glass. Kelia, who had finished hers, called her sister to pour some more.

Athal continued his story:

'After this, there were never other signs of a strike or contestation… until yesterday! The reign of my father and his collaborators is over!'

◆ ◆ ◆

Athal got up and invited me go with him to take a little tour on the sea with my camera. Leaving the table, I crossed eyes with Kelia. She smiled to me for the first time. I was dazed by what I had just heard, but decided, at the same time, to know more.

5 – Racism and despotism

We arrived at the pier where a strange inflatable boat was moored, which Athal called the *Zodiac*.

'This inflatable boat of twelve metres long', he told me, 'I designed and had it made on the continent. Officially, it was destined to take a team of four workers that had to sand and repaint the metal structure of the platform. Unofficially, it had to allow the slave staff to escape the final blast of their workplace.'

We climbed aboard this big boat. We went over a motor and a kind of small tank to access the front. Athal turned a small handle and the boat immediately advanced in silence.

'Great electric propulsion', proudly exclaimed the man, 'it starts on the first try without pulling a launcher and it's very quiet. During work, this gasoline engine, in the middle, activates a compressor for pneumatic tools and paint gun. It recharges, at the same time, these batteries that power the propulsion for the return of the workers at the end of the day.'

♦ ♦ ♦

We found ourselves a few meters away from what remained of the platform: an immense tangle of wire mesh, two hectares of forest steel tubes bent in all directions. It resembled the squeleton of an enormous animal, collapsed on itself. All this inert mass of scrap still seemed so terrifying that I wouldn't risk coming to prowl during the night! A thick vapor still stood gaping the bowels of that awful carcass. The heat of the fire had twisted everything, not one element was straight and an indefinable burning smell emanated from the fog. Athal stopped the electric motor of the zodiac, which stood still and then began telling me about his past:

'This is what my dog life resembles to: a fiasco! I was born on this damn platform! I tried in vain to satisfy my father's wishes, but for him, I never rose to his expectations. When I did well, it wasn't enough, when it was really well in his eyes, it didn't last long. I wanted to blow it all up and make them all go with me. This conspiracy, I began mulling it over four years ago. The last straw was when I realised everything had died inside me, even the sexual desires were diverted, my reasoning, my way of thinking... I was incapable of having my own opinions, I needed my father's advice in everything. His approvall was vital! He led me, he wanted to mold me after his image. The only way to escape from his hold was to lead him into my suicide.'

'But I don't get it, you're still alive.'

'It's true, because of Kelia and Nellie. They took part in the attack.'

'How so?'

'You'll ask them.'

'I would never dare!'

'You're wrong, Kelia is strong. She dared resist my father who abused her so! She'll tell you herself how she intervened on the platform just before the explosion. She remembers it well!'

'So be it. But tell me, where are Kelia and Nellie's parents?'

'Euthanasia. They died of radiation while manipulating a radioactive waste barrel that had a defective closure.'

'Radioactive waste? Here?'

'Of course. Didn't you notice the bunkers at the top of the island? They are destined to store the radioactive waste. My father, through finances, wanted to rid the rich countries of that fiflth. He declared Kheo and its surroundings 'close military zone', and with this, he was at ease. Who could have taken an interest in a godforsaken island in the middle of the Indian Ocean, filled with harmful waste to the health and nature? This worked for everyone and especially my father who could traffic unknown in international waters!'

But I thought that the bunkers were arranged for living in!'

'That's right, the five at the top are arranged, but the big four that are the most buried contain radioactive waste of high-level activity and long life. They come from industrial countries that use nuclear energy for civil and military purposes.'

'And the arranged bunkers, what was your father's reason for building them?'

'My father hasn't led anything here for four years, I was responsible for all the island's logistic. To win his confidence, I made as if to play his game, by treating the people badly. Listen to what I told him:

"Father, you have a lot of work leading your numerous affairs on the continent and everywhere in the world, so give me the direction of Kheo. The deep sea air deteriorates the metal platform, it's a work for the personnel on the island, I'm going to put them to work, those niggas!"

'You didn't speak with your father on familiar terms?'

'I didn't, and I had to call him "father", not "dad". He thought himself a general: "the governor of Achab". He couldn't tolerate any familiarity. He called "niggas" the people here. He didn't hesitate to give me over the affairs of the island. He gave me his account number the next day. Since then, I began working, I had free hand. For him, Kheo was of the least importance than all his other current affairs.'

'What type of affairs?'

'My father was leading a vast mafia empire of international scale: all kinds of trafficking, drugs, weapons, pimping..., '

'You talked of euthanasia regarding Kelia and Nellie's parents…'

'Right, we finished with incurable or too old patients through Linda, it was one of the methods used to adjust the

21

demography of the island. Like this, we avoided the population from getting to big. You have, without doubt, noticed that there are no elders here.'

'You say Linda killed the sick?!'

'Yeah, Linda gave them the pills we ordered her to give. At the infirmary, there's not much, just enough to heal a wound. In case of disease, she immediately had to let the doctor on the platform know, by communicating the diagnosis of the patient and especially his identity. According to the patient's age and the severity of his illness, we sent her the appropriate medicine: to heal or kill him. The pills to heal and the ones to kill had almost the same appearance, even color and packaging, but for sure, they didn't have the same effect!'

'But Linda didn't notice anything?'

'No, and she still doesn't know, we made her believe the death of her patients was natural, certainly caused by an unknown germ in a drink. People died following a simple fever or malaria attack! Concerning Kelia and Nellie's parents, their prognosis being committed, euthanasia was the only solution. According to my father, killing a nigga was no more serious than killing an animal!'

'And what was the other method of 'adjusting' the demography of the island?'

'Beautiful young girls were sent to different countries for prostitution and never came back. Kids were sold for international adoptions and organ trafficking transiting through African orphanages with the complicity of local authorities and O.N.G cans. My father used to say: *"I will never understand why white people are so stupid as to pay handsomely for small niggas, they don't lack pets, for sure!"* For him, everything was ok to gain money! Not surprisingly, the population hasn't increased for twenty years. Adjusting the demography was my main occupation. I had made a computer file mentioning the identity, age, professional competence, the measurements, the registration number of the 1326 people living here. I know everyone. Know that I deliberately forgot to add the twelve births that occurred in the past four years. My father suspected something and began to distrust me. He thought I was too condescending towards his farm of niggas as well as...'

'Stop! It's unbearable, let's change the subject please!'

'Yeah? As you wish.'

'I heard Kelia call Etienne "father". Is Etienne a priest?'

'Yes, everyone here calls him this, we consider him a sort of spiritual leader. He teaches the Bible and the Christian values, things like this. I noticed the belief of these people had a "positive impact on their mental balance". I concluded that this irrational escape by adding a hint of comfort and adequate food, could make this small world more malleable and efficient at work! It's with this kind of argument I convinced my father to authorize me to build a chapel we called "of religious trinkets" and a station for electricity production to improve living conditions in Kheo. I was so hoping to establish a friendly relationship with the people. Big mistake! They are too wary of the son of a tyrant!'

'Why do the people here speak French so well? It's not their native language.'

'Absolutely not! When my grandfather took over Kheo in 1939 for colonisation, he established boards and mercenaries to reduce the people to slavery and force them to speak French. We publicly whipped those who continued jabbering something other than French: efficient way to make the people lose their mother tongue. Everyone today expresses themselves with literal French. Nothing is known of the slang and idiomatic expressions. My grandfather and father did everything he could to destroy the identity of these natives to properly handle them. Dressing them all the same, with this awful combination of red was part of his programme. This people has always been isolated from the world. Schooling was well under control: no illustration in teaching materials. The courses were reviewed and corrected on the platform before introducing it in the classroom. Despite this fierceness to destroy the local culture, there's something that not even my grandfather and father managed to take from this people, it's their faith in God. Bibles and song books were burned at various times, but there always remained a Bible stashed somewhere! The teacher has even managed to copy one!'

'The two burnt buildings on the island, were they the chapel and the electrical plant? All this was sponsored by your father. How did he do it? Did he send someone to start the fire?'

'No, he just sent two missiles from the platform. It was equipped with an anti-air defense. The governor's small universe always had to be protected from outside views. Well, he never had conflicts, no one cares about this place that isn't even on most marine charts!'

'Uhm... I can't stand this smell of burnt anymore, I would like to go back to the coast, please!'

'Right, but do you want to take some photos of the platform?'

'Understood, I'll take five while we're moving away, like this, you'll have more angles.'

'It works. Anyway, I want to go back, my head is pounding, I hope Linda has some sedatives.'

The *zodiac* circled the carcass and took the return course towards the land.

6 – In the mouth of the wolf

During the return course, I observed Athal. His deformed face gave me the impression that he was unmoved and impervious to events. I found him to be jovial or vulgar, or cynical! He was visibly disturbed, he spied my reactions each time he told me something dramatic, like measuring the gravity of his own words. Turning off the motor he said:

'I wanted to take you to visit the tower of the island in the *zodiac*, but I would rather save gasoline and I don't know the autonomy of the batteries…'

'It doesn't matter, we can visit it on foot, I love walking, I used to go hiking when I was a student.'

◆ ◆ ◆

Back at the square, Athal asked me to photograph all the people present during their activities. I made him understand that it was embarrassing for me to take photos of people in the middle of their work. He assured me that the people would be pleased, then he left to go to the infirmary.

I began focusing on the twenty something women that cooked under the large covered patio, facing east. The place was divided in two by a big, concrete work table containing sinks, ovens and hobs above which was fixed a huge fan of galvanized steel. Among those who were peeling fruits and vegetables, two were carrying babies on their backs with a cleverly crafted device from elements cut from red suits! I thought these newborns were part of the dozen children Athal hadn't inscribed in his father's statistical evaluation.

The opposite courtyard was practically empty. Hundreds of bowls and metal meal trays were stacked on some tables for lunch. In the background, bins for laundry could be seen. Further away, fifteen men were cleaning the perimeter of the chapel, where only a pinion could still be found. On one of them, a steel cross remained intact, of about two metres high, last trace of this place of cult.

The teeth of the dipper from the shovel driven by Hemerik scraped noisily on the concrete floor, while the other men threw with bare hands all the blackened rubble from the path of the machine. There also, some smiles were immortalized. Hemerik remained serious, shaking his head once to mark his approval, and his brother Fredo gave me a quick little friendly grin. It was a good start, I felt the need to see this people happy and completely free of its past. These people fascinated me, because of their courage and interior force, the more I knew them, the more I loved them!

The photo session lasted an hour and had begun to seriously dent my film stock, so I decided to return to sit at the table especially placed for me in the morning in the courtyard. I saw Kelia, Nellie, Athal, Etienne, Linda and three other people that I didn't know yet, going to the same place. When I wanted to sit, Ettiene introduced a man and two women to me:

'Jerome, the tourist, this is my brother, Nicodeme, schoolmaster and his two assistants Mado and Rose-Marie. Mado is Nicodeme's wife and Rose-Marie is my son's, Fredo's wife.'

'Delighted, I see the whole family is busy!'

Everyone greeted me with a nod, smiling. Etienne continued:

'Jerome, the tourist, I have a job to ask of you...'

'I'm listening.'

'This morning, we took out all the tables from the biggest classroom in order to fit in 112 students aged 10 to 14 years. This afternoon, I would like you to introduce yourself and answer their questions. Is it ok?'

'I'll gladly do it... but what kind of questions?'

'You know well we're cut off from the world. These children need to know what happens outside their native island. I'll help you start the dialogue with them, Nicodeme, Mado and Rose-Marie will be there as well.'

'That works. At what time does it begin?'

'At two o'clock.'

My glass of mango juice was still on the table, someone had covered it with a saucer to protect its contents from insects. Kelia and Nellie were sitting astride a bench, one behind the other. Kelia began making braids with her little sister's hair. Athal asked her to tell me about the last minutes of the platform. She didn't hesitate in answering:

'Monday morning, I was assigned to work on the platform with the day staff. I spent my day helping the cleaning ladies and in the kitchen. In the evening, the governor's men didn't let me go on the *zodiac* to return on the island with the others, they locked me and tied me in a workshop below. Tuesday, a little after noon, they made me eat a bowl of soup, they untied me and made me take a shower on the floor above. In the bathroom, there was a dress on a hanger. They told me: *"When you'll finish bathing, you'll put this on."* I didn't want to put it on and after the shower, I got out with my usual suit. They were furious. They dragged me to an upper floor, right before the governor in a big room. There were lots of paintings and lights and instruments. The man who dragged me told the governor: *"She didn't want to put the dress on!"*

At the same time, two other man entered coming down the staircase overlooking a dock outside. They had Nellie and brought her close to the governor as well, next to me. They said: *"Sir, this little one came alone in the shuttle, she had this letter on her!"* The governor, after reading the letter, ordered to lock and tie my little sister in the workshop where I had passed the night. Nellie was crying and I shouted: *"Let her go!"* The governor pulled my hair back so hard, that I found myself sitting on the ground and he screamed in my ear, blowing the smoke of his cigar: *"It's not the niggas that make the law here!"* He pushed me with his foot. I saw my sister leave, held by the two men, she was begging me to go look for her. The governor screamed: *"This filthy race managed to contaminate my son with religious trinkets! I'll massacre them all! Arm two missiles! Impact point: the chapel and the electric plant... You! Don't stay planted there! Search the shuttle and bring me everything it contains, there's a box that interests me! And you, take this bitch to my room and bring her dress, I'll take care of her later!"*

While they were dragging me on the stairs towards the governor's apartment, I heard one of his men call him: *"But Sir, regarding the missiles, your son is no doubt still on the island and...*

I know, he betrayed me, if he comes out alive, I'll go snatch his guts myself! Execution!"

Once in the room, the man threw me on the bed. He squeezed my neck and he said: *"Listen well, little bronzed, when the governor finishes with you, it will be my turn, do you understand?"* He threw the dress in my face and got out, slamming the door.

The room was huge and luxurious. I heard two explosions on the side of the island. Through the window, I saw two fires, I got out of the room to go look for Nellie, but the man who had thrown me on the bed was standing guard and he pushed me back inside, closing the door.

It was then I decided to set the fire. I searched everywhere, bed tables, furniture hung above the bed, cupboards... I found a lighter beside a cigar box in a drawer of the desk. I gathered everything that could burn on the bed: clothes, couch cushions, documents, papers... and I set fire. I took a wet towel from the bathroom to cover my nose and I waited behind the door. The whole room filled with smoke. A siren began screaming. The one who was standing guard opened the door while shouting: *"Fire!"* I took advantage that he was taking a kind of big red bottle from a wall in the hall to run. I went down the stairs, while crossing the governor's men who were running the other way. I thought they were going up to help their colleague put out the fire. I passed really close to the governor, who had remained alone. He was just opening a big box while screaming: *'Get this out, get this out... it's gonna blow... hurry, where are you going, you bastards, get this box out!'*

In the panic, no one gave me any attention anymore and I went in the workshop below where my sister was tied. As I didn't manage to undo the knot of the wire surrounding her ankle, I used a saw like the one Hemerik and Fredo use, and I cut the wire. I opened a hatch on the floor and jumped into the water under the platform. We found the *zodiac* attached nearby by a carabiner. While moving towards the island, we heard various explosions...'

'Yes, and we were very scared', continued Nellie, admiring her first braids in her pocket mirror, 'we even believed the governor was shooting at us!'

'Athal was waiting for us alone on the pier with the binoculars. My sister jumped in his arms, which surprised me a little, for I knew nothing of what had happened on Kheo. We were terrified, Athal couldn't manage to calm Nellie down! He repeated: *"It's over!... It's over!..."*'.

Athal remained silent, with an absent air. Etienne and Linda had listened to Kelia's story with much attention, like it was the first time. Their existence had changed in a few minutes, the girls had almost died.

I took advantage of this pause to ask Athal:

'What was this story with the shuttle, box and letter?'

'A chance out of three that this worked, and it did!

At the beginning, I had to attach the boat with the bomb under the platform on the night of Monday to Tuesday, to make it explode with me, on the inside, a suicide attempt of sorts. Only, I didn't think Kelia would be retained on board the platform and I had to change my plan with Hemerik and Fredo's help. Besides the 150 kilos of explosives strewn around the motor and the boat's tank, I added a detonator that activated only by turning the contact key. A hidden switch under the dash replaced the function of this key. We had also placed in the shuttle 120 kilos of explosives, a veritable delay bomb! A timer was to set the explosion off at the end of four minutes after the opening of the lid for the box to activate. When everything was ready, Tuesday, a little after noon, I sent Hemerik and Fredo to join the others in the bunkers and I installed Nellie at the helm of the boat, forbidding her to touch the contact key. I told her: *"Once you get there, stop the engine with the help of this button behind the dash, give the letter to the governor and wait for your sister to be brought, do you understand?"*

'Athal didn't want to come with me!' cried Nellie, caressing her braids.

'No, for if I had returned to the platform, my father would have tortured Kelia and Nellie to death to punish me. So I sent Nellie alone to bring the bomb to my father. In the letter, I wrote this: *"Father, will you accept this loading of sapphires from Madagascar and accept it in exchange Kelia and Nellie's release."*

I observed everything with my binoculars. What happened inside the platform, Kelia just told it. My father sent men to take the box from the boat. Supposing this box had really contained a treasure, my father wouldn't have released the girls only for that. He was too dishonest to respect a change. So he activated himself the timer by opening the box, but I had arranged a screen indicating a count down of a minute! When my father's collaborators saw the explosion would take place in less than a minute, they ran towards the helicopter, leaving my father alone with the bomb. I had it programmed to explode at the end of the four minutes. Thus, Kelia and Nellie had time to escape in the *zodiac*. The helicopter also could have escaped, but it only had 8 places for 14 men! They fought to climb aboard! I don't know where my father was during the first explosion, the most important thing was to see the girls escape in the

30

zodiac. I don't know if the boat exploded before or after the box. The third explosion brought forth like a geyser all the water in the swimming pool. Everything scorched. I saw the helicopter climb into flames just before it exploded. The rotor activated the furnace like a ball fire! It was a hellish racket that echoed into the quarry! The rest you know, since you came to join us.'

'When I think you dared sent this little Nellie all alone, with all those explosives! She and her sister could have died several times!'

'I didn't have any other choice. By going to the platform, I condemned the girls to death. They had a chance out of three to make it out: being killed by my father, being killed in the attack or survive by running. Like you see, they survived.'

'It's God that allowed them to make it out', Etienne concluded. 'Bless him!'

7 – The colors of democracy

At meal time, Athal left for the infirmary with Linda. But the nurse came back alone to join us to eat.

'Where's Athal?' asked Ethienne.

'He had a panick attack', answered Linda, 'he wants to isolate himself in a bunker, but I don't have any antidepressants to give him.'

'Poor boy, we must pray for him, I'll go see him as soon as possible. After giving thanks.'

After giving thanks, Etienne wished us bon appetit. We ate soup, grilled fish and a banana, everything served on a platter the girls brought us. The crowd, having come back from the fields, was sitting in the courtyard and under the covered area to have the meal. We thanked God by a song.

Those who worked too far inside the island were eating where they were.

'Kelia and Nellie are always with you?' I asked Etienne and Linda.

'They live with us', Linda answered, 'they sleep together in one of the rooms in our apartment.'

Some children, amazed to see a white eat with black at the same table, looked at us from a distance. After the meal, each went back to work. The girls cleaned the table and separated: Nellie stayed in the courtyard with the others, while Kelia went to take care of a rabbit breeding that she was in charge of. Waiting for two o'clock, I played ball with the little ones in front of the school. They were very amused and surprised that I could play their game.

♦ ♦ ♦

At "H" hour, the whole class waited for me in silence, the children standing, flanked by Rose-Marie in the back, in the left and by Mado in the back, in the right. Etienne joined me, when Nicodeme, in front of the blackboard signaled us to go in. After the greetings, the pupils had permission to sit down, the boy on one side, the girls on the other. Rose-Marie and Mado remained standing with their arms crossed. Etienne vainly tried to initiate the dialogue:

'Who wants to ask the first question? Come on, you all know Jerome, the tourist, he's been with us since yesterday, he comes from the continent.'

It's true that these preteens were indoctrinated, for them, I was a white stranger with blue eyes and light brown hair, belonging to the "superior race", a ruler who mistreats, who requires, who punishes... and even if they had seen me play and communicate with some of them, they still needed to hear the priest's reassuring voice to untie their tongues. A boy raised his finger to express in an academic French the first of a long series of questions: "How is the place where you live on the continent called?... How is your governor called?... How is your flag?..."

Not easy to locate France without a world map. A world that was reduced to some islands around Kheo, faced with a grand, mysterious continent from where refueling sometimes came by cargo ships.

Regarding the governor, I held a course of civil instruction, I suddenly had the urge to actively participate in the detoxification of this generation! Etienne, visibly satisfied of my established connection with the schoolchildren, made me a discreet sign before leaving to rejoin Athal. The teacher invited me to use the blackboard. I began by drawing the French flag, but there was only white chalk, as white as all the walls in the buildings on the island!

I willingly gave my drawing the same sizes as the red glass square with a black symbol still hung above the table (there was one in every class). I wrote "blue" in the first rectangle, and "red" in the third one before coloring in white the one in the middle under the children's watchful eyes (and the present adults!) that didn't understand why this national symbol wasn't on my back, like theirs was. I told them this:

'In my country, which is a republic, we don't have a governor, but a president of the republic. He doesn't lead alone, he is surrounded by a certain number of advisors. We also refer to France as a democracy, that is a government of the people, by the people, for the people. The citizens choose themselves their leaders by elections.'

Then, I drew a diagram to represent the workings of the constitution: executive power, President, Prime Minister, state ministers, deputy ministers, state secretaries, legislative power, national assembly, senate, parliament... to not complicate the explanation more, I avoided broaching the theme of political parties. So many people to lead such a country! It must be said that with a population that surpasses sixty million inhabitants, the surface of France (comparing it to that of Kheo) should, according to them, occupy three fourths of our planet.

My clothes intrigued them. It wasn't the same I had on when I first came and others could be found in my bag! With what, then, resembled a French citizen's uniform? I wanted to show them photos of landscapes and daily life of my home country and suddenly, I realized that by leaving for good the accommodation rented by my parents, I had emptied for the last time the mailbox. I had found an advertising review of about thirty pages that I had kept in my backpack. I told the teacher I had to go look for a newspaper in my bag to be able to continue my explanations. Going to the infirmary, I met few children, for the most part were clinging to the school windows to watch us.

◆ ◆ ◆

At my return in the classroom, the excited pupils talked noisily, but the two women imposed silence and the meeting continued. My newspaper called: *Extract from the spring-summer 1997 fashion* slowly made the tour of the classroom under the vigilant eyes of Mado. These young readers were surprised to see so many clothes with so many colors. They asked the significance of the numbers and the letter "F" inscribed on the photos. They had no money on the island and I had to show them the role and power of money in my country and everywhere in the world. I took out of my wallet a bill of one hundred francs, as well as some yellow and white coins that Nicodeme hastened to slip into a transparent bag that he gave to the students.

Discreet laughter and whispers accompanied the fashion brochure. They guffawed at the sight of these models with white skin that some outfits let show nude legs and arms. Also, sunglasses could be seen, hats, pumps with strange, delicate high heels... I had never seen such

34

enthusiasm for a simple advertising that I would have gladly thrown in a bin!

Liberty, equality, fraternity. France revealed itself to them like a huge paradisiacal country in which you could individually lead your life, dress like we wanted and chose who led our country. Agriculture, industry, energies, distribution... these children that drank my words were interested in everything, with an amazed look. They took me for a great teacher, an inexhaustible source of general culture. They even asked me if I was a member of the French government!

The advertising review remained in the girls' group, fascinated by the multicolored dresses, while the money stayed in the hands of the boys.

◆ ◆ ◆

At five o'clock, everyone went out of the classroom. The crowd, having come back from the fields prepared the activities of that evening. I had taken my money back, but the advertising, all crumpled continued to attract new looks from adolescents and adults, gathered in the courtyard after the work day.

Nicodeme accompanied me until my table and remained seated near me. He asked if it was possible to continue my explanations for the teenagers the next morning, according to priest Etienne's wish.

'Of course', I answered, 'and I'll visit the island tomorrow afternoon with Athal.'

While we were chatting, I heard Mado order the girls in the courtyard to give me back the advertising review and it was Kelia who brought it, followed by Mado.

'You can keep it', I told her.

'Thank you!' she said, delighted and smiling.

'Thank you in her name', added Mado.

They moved away and the girls' group formed around them.

♦ ♦ ♦

At dinner time, the whole place was filled with oil lamps and the crowd was sitting on the ground, thanking God with a song that resonated even under the courtyards. At our table, Linda and Athal were missing. Etienne explained that his wife had left for the bunker to take Athal to eat, as he was not yet recovered.

Hemerik came to give the report of the works of the day. After which, the ones for the next day had to be planned.

'Tomorrow', indicated Etienne, 'you'll dig the foundations of the new chapel outside the village. You'll first help me trace the perimeter according to the plan Athal drew last night. As we don't need fish right now, you'll order the fishers to resume the manufacturing of concrete blocks, Athal calculated the necessary quantity...'

'Athal is a criminal like his father and you're always busy planning with him!' *(Silence)*

'What is the meaning of this? Athal always acted with his father's constraint and you know it! Today, he turned, he's beginning a new life.

'How can you forgive this?' cried Hemerik, grabbing his father's stump, 'who will give you your arm back, God or Athal?'

'That's enough', Etienne suddenly folding his mutilated arm said, 'shut up!!'

'You don't like hearing this! You decide everything with that white beak and you find this normal? I tell you we do not negotiate with Satan's son! A murderer like him has no power here!'

'Exactly! He has no power here because I'm the governor of Kheo and I decided Athal will be a member of

36

our community, if you like it or not! Athal changed his attitude and you would do well to do the same!'

'I don't trust him. White people are all the same!'

'Calm down. We'll talk about this again with your brother and your mother.'

'Count me in!'

Hemerik moved away in a rage. His father, with a desolated air, made excuses:

'I am very sorry. I hope this conversation wasn't too shocking. My son never really thought when he said: *"White people are all the same"*.

'Don't worry. Your families have suffered greatly and I understand his reaction.'

'There's no question he'll sleep with his rage. May God help me talk to him this evening.'

♦ ♦ ♦

Linda, Etienne, Kelia and Nellie and me took our first dinner outside together, at the light of an oil lamp that attracted mosquitoes. We were the only ones not eating on the ground. I was so welcomed by these people that I felt at home. I had known them less than a day and I had the feeling of being one of the family!

♦ ♦ ♦

Back in the infirmary, I slept in my quiet room, thinking a lot about Athal and Hemerik. I strongly hoped for a reconciliation. I turned off my lamp. The tropical night seemed more profound and dark than the one in my native country. Sleep took me gently.

8 – A free people

Thursday, March 20, 1997

At five in the morning, I was woken by the light of day and the noise outside. I went out of the infirmary at six to avoid Kelia bringing me a meal tray all the way to my room. Outside, people sitting on the ground were finishing their breakfast. Others were getting ready to leave for the fields. Those who carried bags and baskets, had taken a place in the truck bed. The children were playing and talking, waiting for the hour of class, reserved for teenagers that morning.

Kelia, Nellie and Etienne came to join me at the table with the meal trays and greeted me. Kelia then went to school. I noticed the rolled advertising brochure that went out of her back pocket. Her sister followed her. The priest, alone with me, explained that the girls hand already eaten and that Linda would come in a moment. All this small group waited for me to breakfast with them. They treated me like a son.

Soon after, the nurse brought good news concerning Athal: he was better and thought to come among us at noon. I was in a hurry to ask other questions. I asked how Hemerik had reacted the night before at the family reunion.

'Well', Etienne assured me, 'we prayed together and even if our son hasn't yet seen Athal again, I think he is on his way to reconciliation. In any case, he has shown us his wish that it be so.'

'Yes', Linda added, 'but we musn't hurry him. Hemerik is like that, he gets annoyed easily, but he's not stubborn, we can reason with him.'

♦ ♦ ♦

After the meal, Nicodeme remained alone with me, waiting for class. He talked to me about his young audience, aged from 15 to 21, reaching 90 people. There were married couples among the older ones. He confided his eye problem that got worse with time, to such a point that he could barely write at the blackboard. His assistants helped him correct the homework and prepare the classes.

♦ ♦ ♦

At eight o'clock, the meeting started in the same conditions as yesterday. Kelia was seated in the first row, her precious advertising review on her knees. Etienne introduced me and the first series of questions began. The jobs, the studies, manners, customs, leisure... Not easy to answer without risking to make a caricature of the French citizen. Like for the younger ones, the civic course impressed them. The diagram with the functioning of the republic had remained on the blackboard, which made my task easier. Kelia accepted to pass around her fashion magazine, which most girls already knew. The money circulated as well. Young adults questioned Etienne on the possibility of someday going to France. Mado and Rose-Marie wanted to know the women's occupation on the continent.

♦ ♦ ♦

Around eleven o'clock, all this small troupe followed me to the courtyard. In groups, they talked to me, like extending the course.

♦ ♦ ♦

Athal appeared a little before noon. He was looking better and confirmed our project of visiting the island after lunch. I was thrilled to see him again. He asked me to go take my camera and the morning ended like this: Athal photographed me with other people. Alone or in a group, everyone wanted to appear with me on film, like I was a star!

◆ ◆ ◆

During lunch, no one was missing from my table. The atmosphere was relaxed. The people sought the shade of covered yards or ate along the walls that housed them against the sun.

Suddenly, we saw Hemerik and Fredo each pushing a wheelbarrow on each side of the square. They unhooked them in the rooms, all the square red glasses representing the black sign, symbol of governor Achab. When the wheelbarrow were full, they pushed them in the middle of the square at the feet of the flag. Athal whispered in my ear: 'Prepare your camera, my boy, I really think the two brothers are preparing us something!'

Fredo went in search of a sort of pole on the top of which was hanging a burning, opened oil lamp, to let the flame out. He gave it to his brother who was waiting, leaning against the mast. The two men had ripped the sleeves of their suits to reveal their bare, muscular arms. They had also fully shaven their heads. There was complete silence in the moment when the pole approached the lamp to the flag, which caught fire immediately. While the black wheel gear was deforming and disappeared in the fire, a huge roar went up from the crowd, a victory cry that made the whole island tremble and made me shiver from head to foot!

Hemerik got out a square of red glass of his wheelbarrow, tinted in the mass and waved it high. The object shined in the sun. He turned on himself to show it better to the crowd before violently launching it against the metallic pole. Then, it was Fredo's turn...

In all, about thirty plates exploded in contact with the pole. We all got up to sing a song of thanks to God! Linda gave the tone to start the song. Hemerik and Fredo happily trampled in rhythm the pieces of glass scattered on the ground. In one leap, Athal went to join them in their dance! What an intense moment!

On my first day on the island, I had found a people in a state of shock. On the second day, they resumed their activities without really realizing their new condition. But on this Thursday, March 20, and through this symbolic gesture, something in the invisible had taken place: a rupture, a page of history had just turned in the hearts and I was the only witness in the world to live it directly. Slavery was abolished forever in Kheo!

9 – Warnings

Lunch lasted more than usual that day. The fish, the fruits, the vegetables, the sun… all seemed new and better! Athal took our photo.

Peacefully, everyone then resumed their activities and the afternoon passed slowly. The time was not for big projects yet, but there was a need to taste the present, to appreciate this freedom so new. Only Etienne anticipated, planning the reconstruction of the island with Athal's ideas.

Etiennne wasn't a mystic and passive priest, outside of reality, but he was pragmatic and providing, like a shepherd looking after his herd. He defined himself like the governor of Kheo, he behaved himself, at the same time like a spiritual guide and a leader. The people, too used to submit to an absolute and arbitrary power, didn't decide anything by itself. A completely new situation had to be managed in urgency. This priest and his wife were totally committed to it, like a father and mother ready for everything for their children. They were once the servants of governor Achab, against their will, and charged with executing a dictator's orderes. In this new day, only God was their guide and advisor.

◆ ◆ ◆

Athal and I were the last to leave the table. We took the gravel path by which I had come on the first day. That moment already seemed far away in my past! The road climbed until the bunkers and then got lost in the quarry. Everywhere, men and women worked in the plantations. Athal explained the functioning of this site:

'When my father decided to build these bunkers, I bought all these machines that are in the quarry: a charger, a shovel equipped with a mechanical chipper, a crusher, a strainer, a truck bucket, a concrete plant... I wanted to make construction materials by using the raw materials on the island, like this rock we reduced to pebbles to make concrete. Like this, we save the sand of the beach reserved for mortar. Only the cement is imported.'

Between the bunkers, we heard the engines of the machines. We entered the quarry. Hemerik, in the cabin of the enormous concrete mixer, beckoned us to approach with an authoritative gesture that scared me a little. Further away, men were preparing row molds for concrete blocks.

We climbed in the cabin by a metallic ladder. Hemerik, seated before a command dash saluted us by raising his hand without even looking at us. Taking his usual gruff air, he addressed Athal:

'Athal.'

'Yes.'

'I had a talk with my father last evening. I noticed he has a lot of esteem for you. I don't see things his way. For sure, you have eliminated your tyrant of a father, but know that this doesn't make a hero out of you.'

'Far from me the idea of considering myself a hero.'

'My father made me understand you are not responsible of your father's abuses towards us. You were manipulated since your childhood and I promised to forgive you with God's help, for it is beyond my forces. Since I was born, I was maltreated, tortured, we have never known anything else. Your father mutilated mine, he raped my mother... and it's not all...'

Hemerik activated a command and concrete fell into a tray under the machine. Men approached with their shovels to take it.

'I heard you know all of us here: age, sex, family situation, measurements, skills, serial number and what not!'

'Yes.'

'You must know I am single.'

'Yes.'

'Did you know Maryse?'

'Uhm... I don't think so...'

'I knew her: her age, the color of her eyes... she was my fiancée! Eight years ago, your father made her go to the damned platform from which she never came back! I assume he raped her on board before sending her to one of this prostitution networks on the continent. What do you think?'

'I'm... I'm sorry...'

'Not as sorry as I am! You see, it's difficult to forgive. Not only did he steal my childhood, he also stole my love. It's my whole existence that's been destroyed by your father, and unfortunately, I'm not the only one! Now that you have free reign and you're seemingly well-intentioned, you'll contact the authorities of the countries on the continent and hire whom you will to find all those who were deported. You will not leave Kheo as long as you haven't completed your mission!'

'I don't intend to run from my responsibilities.'

'You see', continued Hemerik turning to his speaker, 'my father prevented us from committing a sin by killing

43

you when he intervened in your favor. He's a priest, he loves everyone and forgives everything, while I, I do not have the charisma of a priest who only counts on divine justice. As such, waiting for this justice being fully exercised on each of us, I will personally oversee that you dedicate all the days left to you to live to repair the damages made by your father and his collaborators... at least, what can be repaired!'

'I spent four years trapping my father, I will dedicate all the time needed to continue this way. I will assume everything that will happen after him!'

'It's the least you can do. Now, gentlemen, if you'll let me, I have work to do. Have a nice walk!'

We went down the ladder followed by Hemerik who joined the fishers who were making concrete blocks. Fredo was emptying buckets with pebbles with a charger by the opening at the top of the concrete plant. We greeted all these men before plunging into the coolness of the forest without saying a word.

10 — Confessions

After a few minutes of walking on the road that continued to climb, I dared ask my first question:

'You just said to Hemerik that you spend four years preparing the attack, why not try to inform this people? Etienne, for example, he would have undoubtedly listened to you.'

'I already told you Etienne was too scared of my father and to encourage him to collaborate with me, I voluntarily surrendered myself to his sons!'

'You knew Etienne's sons would hit you and you purposely went to meet them for them to mark your face at the risk of dying?'

'Yes, I did nothing to defend myself despite my martial arts experience. Presenting myself to them, alone and without weapons, I was sure they would jump me. That was part of my plan. I had a chance out of two to survive. If they had killed me, my father who still ignored this conspiracy, would have avenged me and killed three quarters of the population. As I lived and I was disfigured, I left Etienne with no choice!

When I regained consciousness at the infirmary, Linda was at my bedside crying. She began treating me. I didn't know my eye was punctured and my father didn't know I had left the platform. Etienne was turning in circles like a bear in a cage. I think he was praying. I imposed my plan: *"Etienne, you have to help me prepare an attack to finish my father. Your sons must help me make a bomb. I have it all planned. The people must take cover in the bunkers. You have to help me now!"* I saw him hesitate, he was scared. He answered: *"It's too risky, your father will kill us all!"* *"Listen to me well, Etienne, you either collaborate to help me kill my father, or my father will kill you all, starting with your sons, not to mention the tortures that will follow their deaths. They dared beat me! They're condemned!"*

I heard Linda cry even harder. Etienne was looking for a solution! He said: *"Let's suppose I tell your father about your project of hurting him, maybe he'll let my family and I live..."*

"Not a chance, he'll believe me more than a nigga like you! I will not leave this infirmary as long as you don't decide. Anyway, I will never return to that platform! Think well and fast, every minute counts and my father doesn't know I'm here. When he'll learn, it's not going to be pretty. Believe me, you have no other choice, Kheo's fate depends on your decision, the future of your people is in your hands!"

"That's not true! It's in God's hands. If it his will that the governor dies, I can't oppose, but first, I must talk to my people!"

"I advise you to hurry and to do it discreetly. Gather all behind the bunkers, out of sight of the platform!"

An hour later, he came looking for me to tell me that the people wanted to hear me behind the bunkers. Once there, be loaned me his megaphone to explain my project to everyone, but many were afraid. Hemerik started screaming: *"It's a trap, he's looking for an excuse to hurt us! He's like his father, a manipulator!"*

'Etienne defended me by trying to show that I had taken great risks in coming alone among them and that governor Achab didn't need an excuse to oppress the people! The crowd ended up accepting the priest's advice. Everyone left in the bunkers during the rest of the afternoon. Etienne and his two sons helped built the bombs.'

'That mustn't have been easy, Etienne's sons hate you!'

'Yeah, they didn't stop repeating to their father that they didn't trust me! But they helped me anyway. The situation was past the point of no return.'

'How did you manage to get enough explosives to attract your father's attention?'

'I had a stock of explosives to detach the rocks in the quarry. My father had no reason to distrust.'

'No one saw that bunkers were being made?'

'Negative. These bunkers were supposed to stock the last arrival of radioactive waste that we had stored on the sea in the North of the island. For this, we used a fishing boat during four days.'

'On the sea? But it's dangerous, at what distance from the beach?'

'A hundred meters. The barrels rest at 30 meters on the bottom of the sea and are perfectly sealed. The water would absorb the eventual radioactive leaks, if there are any!'

'It's crazy! Salt corrosion can endanger and provoke site contamination much faster than you think!'

'Bah, we'll go get them out now that we're out of danger. Still, this weekend, we might receive the visit of the mafia!'

'If I understood well, no one on the platform thought of checking that this radioactive waste was put in the bunkers!'

'No, my father wouldn't have risked it, he wanted to avoid all contamination!'

'Etienne accepted to involve his sons in the preparation of a bomb. It's surprising, it could have been a consciousness problem for him being a priest!'

'Yeah. This is why he hesitated. For him, an attack was a murder, a grave sin. He then understood that it was self-defense. If I asked for his sons' help, it was in order for them to take action against their tormentor. I am the instigator of this conspiracy, but them, at present, are as responsible as I am.'

'In fact, it's like you trapped everyone!'

'We were all trapped by my father. It was the only way to end it.'

'Linda said you had panic attacks. Still, you should feel better now that you're rid of your father. And this people is saved, it's great, isn't it?'

'It's true, but I'm incapable of rejoicing for other people's happiness, I have no compassion for anyone! I would love to have good feelings, but I only feel pain, a mix of disgust of myself and guilt. I wish I were never born, or being in someone else's shoes, who has a child's innocence! I can't accept my past. When I'm too ill, I suffocate and I have panic attacks, I would rather die…'

'Death is not a solution!'

'Yeah, I know. Etienne says only Jesus can deliver me from this prison. According to him, by dying on the cross, Jesus took the world's sins with him. His blood had the power to erase all sins, even the bad ones, like mine! But

I don't see how this could happen to me! I clearly see Etienne is trying to evangelize me!'

'Of course, he's a priest.'

'All this is really pretty, but I continue to gnaw inside, and I ended up rebelling against my father, the idea began one Saturday, four years ago. Guests who had come from very far had moored their yacht against the platform to celebrate with my father who made me stay with them until late in the evening. This group of degenerated partygoers had brought a few prostitutes. They wanted to have "fun" with them all night aboard the yacht. The last servants had finished their tasks and went back to the island on the boat. While I greeted all these good people to go to sleep, my father, dead drunk, mumbled: *"A surprise for you, have fun!"*

When I opened my room, I felt a smell of cigarette. A prostitute was sleeping on my couch. Without saying anything, I closed the door and sat on my bed. The woman, lightly dressed, then came to rub against me to excite me. I showed no reaction, so she got worried and backed away. I signaled her to go back to my couch. I knew she didn't speak French. She got vexed and looked at me askance by crossing her arms. Some dollars from my pocket quickly consoled her! I made her sit without smoking close to an hour before sending her on her boss's yacht. I was at the same time disgusted, irritated and shameful. For the first time, I realized that even my sexual urges were deregulated. I finally dared to reconcile with my father's overwhelming influence on my life and the damage of my being inside! My only model was the one who created me. It was in that exact moment I decided to conspire against him… four years ago.'

'About creation, you never told me about your mother.'

'My mother left my father for good when I was five years old, she couldn't stand anymore the bad company he kept. He was violent and he cheated on her.'

'He cheated? He met other women on the platform?'

48

'Affirmative. Other times, my parents lived on the island. After I was born, my father's fraudulent affairs were increasingly successful, which allowed him to modernize his universe. On the platform, he had luxurious apartments built, a big pool in the middle, a bar, a small cinema, a fitness room, a dojo… He wanted to impress his guests, mockers like him who loved to humiliate those who were not in their clan. According to them, a woman was an object of domestic pleasure. We can sometimes use her to procreate! When my mother saw all these delinquents being more frequent in the passing of their weekends at her home, and most of all, those prostitutes alone with her husband, she had enough and she left.'

'She left you alone with your father? And how did she leave?'

'A billionaire accepted to take her on his yacht one Sunday evening while I was sleeping. I'll let you guess my reaction the next day. My father had no more restraint in his fornications from that day on.'

'I just can't imagine your mother abandoning you at the hands of that monster!'

'Still, it's what happened. I don't hold a grudge anymore, there isn't a person who could live with such a person, it's understandable. And if she had tried to take me with her, my father would have hired an army to find her, eliminate her and take me back! But, I'm afraid I'm boring you with all my stories!'

'Uhm… No, since it's me asking all the questions. This said, I think it's best not to stir all this sad past!'

Absorbed by our conversation, we walked slowly. At the end of the path, we saw the light shine through the fruit trees and eucalyptus. We came to a green clearing surrounded by pens in which rabbits in captivity leapt. We heard Nellie and Kelia behind us, they were pushing a small cart containing cans of water. We stopped our walk to give the girls time to join us. They were laughing, amused at seeing two white men planted in the middle of their daily occupations. I asked Kelia to let me push the cart, which she accepted, puffing. I made Nelia sit in the front of the vehicle, against the containers, then we continued on our way. Kelia asked:

'Jerome, the tourist.'

'Yes.'

'Are you not tired?'

'No. Where do you go to draw water?'

'We will soon arrive at the wells. It's there we take the water from for the rabbits and to water seedlings between the pens.'

'Is it Hemerik and Fredo that made the cart?' I asked, noticing the tubular structure and bicycle wheels of the small trailer.

'Yes, Jerome the tourist', replied Kelia.

'Please, just call me Jerome in short, ok?'

'Ok, Jerome in short!'

I didn't insist further, promising myself to formulate my request better next time!

At the same time I heard a woman's voice call me:

'Mister Jerome the tourist, could you come to the school? Mister Nicodeme sent me to look for you.'

I recognized Rose-Marie, Fredo's wife. Athal told me to accept. I left him the cart, and while we were going down, I turned for a short moment. Kelia's look crossed mine. A smile and she disappeared in the shade of trees.

II — A new life

Rose-Marie seemed without breath. Why would Nicodeme want to see me? The reason must be important to make Rose-Marie run like that! She answered without even waiting for the question. She told me that Nicodeme needed me to sort the books and course packs formerly prepared by the staff of governor Achab. The schoolmaster wanted to teach his students in the way of teachers of a democracy. I was a little surprised, but also happy to feel useful!

On road, we crossed a cultivator driven by a man who was taking a perpendicular track to our direction. 'He's going to turn the new earth', explained Rose-Marie, 'he cut a portion of the forest and burned the soil to enlarge the area for cultivation.'

◆ ◆ ◆

Seeing us arrive, Mado shouted to her husband: 'They're here!' Books and course packs were piled on tables aligned along the length of the class! Mado, impatient, was waving her pen to write my remarks following her inventory, while the schoolmaster thanked me for accepting to come.

'I'm not sure how useful I can be in such a thing', I told Nicodeme, 'I'm not a teacher!'

But the man paid no attention to my words and invited me to sit down and begin my work. Most courses had nothing bad in them, but the subjects taught weren't very diverse: French, math, biology, agriculture, fishing, apiculture, mechanics and technology for the boys, sewing and cooking for the girls. Well, obviously, nothing about world history or geography. All these works were bound the same way: the black symbol on a red background on the cover above the title, some rare black and white illustrations. These unattractive books gave no motivation to learn!

I also found a moral book which boasted the wisdom and generosity of governor Achab. According to this text, the people were presented like a big family, placed under the divine protection of the benevolent governor. The latter showed himself anxious to modernize the island and meet everyone's needs. We could read a series of commandments, a clever mix of Bible verses and popular proverbs. I didn't hesitate for a second: I tore the book in front of Mado who cut the title from her list before tearing her pile of books. Nicodeme came closer to understand: 'It's the moral book that we eliminate!' cried Mado. 'I suspected that!' answered the schoolmaster. Did they really need me to make this gesture? And what of the other books? In these classrooms, they only taught what was useful for the good functioning of Kheo and the platform.

Nicodeme, Mado and Rose-Marie were waiting, sitting in front of me. They put me ill at ease. I decided to propose we go out in the courtyard together, apparently so we could organize the course. In reality, I was hoping to see Etienne or Athal come toward us. I contended myself to explain the functioning of the French school system: kindergarten, primary, secondary, higher education... the different diplomas that I knew and my anecdotes during exams. I tried to follow the course of their training. It's like this I learned that Nicodeme had taken courses given by a doctor or an engineer on the platform. They were the ones who prepared the statements for the examinations to test the knowledge of the adolescents ready to start work. After completing the tests (which are always passed in the absence of their teacher), the two women collected the copies and sent them to Achab's men who especially oversaw the students that day. Nicodeme had to stay on the platform during all the period of testing. It was better for this only teacher the results of the exams were good! The doctor and engineer moved to the island only to interview students that were finishing school.

♦ ♦ ♦

Athal came, pushing the cart in which Nellie was. Her sister was following. All three were cheerful and tired.

Some groups of people were going back home as the evening approached.

Athal told me: 'Don't worry for all these old books, I ordered new ones with school materials, felt pens and computers. Three containers will arrive tomorrow.'

'We're going to have to make some place to fit everything', remarked Nicodeme.

'Affirmative', answered Athal, 'I suggest you put all Achab's series in the local incinerator, it's the only fit place for them!'

As soon as these words were spoken, the teacher and his two collaborators got to work using Kelia's cart! Nellie and other children joined the three adults to help them accomplish this task that seemed to delight everyone!

♦ ♦ ♦

Athal and I went back to our table to talk.

'A lot of work for tomorrow', I said.

'Yeah! Etienne will come soon to organize all that', answered Athal sighing. 'I'm counting on you to help me manage all the affairs of Kheo!'

'Me?'

'Affirmative. This people needs us.'

'But I can't stay, I have to go back to France to return to my job at the end of March.'

'So what? Your employer can't replace you?'

'Uhm... yes, but...'

'You would leave Nicodeme all alone to teach with his eye problem?'

'But Athal, what are saying? I'm French and...'

'And what? You imagine the French authorities will come looking for you here?'

'No, but...'

'Stay with us, do it for this people who needs you!'

'Athal, what do you know about me?'

'Excuse me for insisting. You, no doubt, have a family that awaits your return.'

'No. My past isn't prettier than yours.'

'You could have managed my father's affairs, those that are legal.'

'Legal affairs? They exist at *Achab industry*?'

'If you stay with me, you'll never miss for anything. In Mexico, my father's bank is still there. Me, I only know the world through the Internet, but you, you're smart and you know the customs on the continent. You'll be very useful for our community. You could even help me manage my father's fortune!'

'I have no experience concerning financial management. Besides, this bank must contain dirty money. Doesn't it bother you?'

'No, but we can clean the dirty money by giving it to the poor!'

'It's your point of view. I have responsibilities in France, I can't just leave everything like that!'

'As you wish.'

Kelia served us drinks and sat next to me. She opened her precious advertising review. Athal continued.

'You said you had a difficult past? Tell me.'

'My father and mother both died the same day I was twenty-two years old. Me, who thought being an orphan was more difficult for a child than for an adult! I lived with them. They financed my studies, they were proud of me. We were doing well. I was dreaming of being an ethnologist, I wanted to become Doctor of Ethnology: a youthful whim. I have always loved the people, this is why I love to travel, I'm curious by nature. I have always wanted to know people's lives, their customs, their religion... Last year, I spent my first leave in Africa with the Pygmies. I was accompanying a humanitarian mission. I took lots of photos. I would have wanted so much to show them to my parents.'

'Why did your parents die?'

'Killed in a car accident. I was with them that day, driving the car. My father was on the passenger seat at my right and my mother was sitting behind him. My father died instantly. My mother went into a coma and she died that evening at the hospital.'

'Good parents with you during all your childhood. What a thing! I haven't known that!'

'I survived with the right hip dislocated.'

'The cause of the accident, bad weather?'

'No, a truck crossed the line to cut our way, I turned to the right to avoid it and that's how I slipped on the aisle. The car hit a power pole sideways.'

Kelia seemed moved while listening to my story. She was an orphan as well. We at least had this sad point in common!

'And after, what did you do?' continued Athal.

'I lived alone in the apartment my parents rented. After several months of education, I ended by giving up my studies. I felt guilty!'

'Guilty of what? It's the driver of the truck that's really guilty, not you!'

'I know, it's exactly what my psychologist said.'

'In fact, what did the truck have with you?'

'The driver was drunk, but this didn't stop the police from removing my driving license for a year!'

'But why?

'Because I left the road to avoid the truck, that's what I'm guilty of. According to traffic laws, I'm not allowed to move away from the road. I should have hit the truck to save my license!'

'And you would have been dead with your license still valid. What's with this?'

'Maybe I would have been dead, but my parents alive.'

'Yeah, and you would have left the most miserable parents in the world!'

'Yes, well! Today I'm the unhappy one, I miss them so much. They were Christians. They would have been happy that I'm interested in God's things, but I wasn't pressed to convert. I wanted to make my life, discover the world. I wanted to believe in the Man. My parents were so involved to the point of giving everything to humanitarian projects. I didn't understand why God allowed them to die. At first, I was even irritated against him.'

'If you're irritated with God, it's prove you believe!'

'Obviously! I heard talk about God since a young age, I can't not believe in him! But we can believe God exists without really committing. Today, I see things more calmly. I notice that people who have really felt something about God are different. They have an inner force, a hope, solid beliefs. Why would they act, pretending to be happy? Today, I'm in the mood to know this God they love. If God revealed himself to them, why not to me too?'

'It's logical. I also said this to Etienne. As we'll all leave one day, why not die happy?'

'My dear Athal in all his fineness!'

'Yeah. You had good parents who loved you, it's normal you miss them. Me, I don't feel all these beautiful and big feelings. I would love to know this Jesus who relieves pain, I gnaw too much internally! Etienne will surely explain how to do it... After the accident, what did you do?'

'Once healed, I found a job at a printing house. My first savings went to a trip to Africa. This year, I decided to come here.'

'To discover the people of Kheo! Tomorrow morning, we'll receive three containers. We'll built an Internet station to get in contact with the world again. We'll gather all the families to organize the search for deported people.'

'If they're scattered all over the planet, it's not going to be easy to find their traces!'

'I know. If you would only accept to stay and help me!'

'Athal, we already talked about this, you know I leave on Saturday morning!'

At these words, Kelia interrupted the reading of her review to observe me. She then left to take care of her sister, while Athal continued to share his projects with me.

'I'm thinking of reselling my father's jet, stationed at Mahe airport. I would love to treat the people in poor health.'

'You're thinking of Nicodeme's eye problem?'

'Yeah, and also of Etienne's hand. Today fitted dentures exist .'

◆ ◆ ◆

The evening meal was a privileged moment where our usual table was complete. Joy lighted every face, even that of Hemerik, who had come to give the daily report to his father:

'We finished digging the foundations for the room. I stored the top soil on top of the crops. We made enough blocks to erect the casing of the sole. Will you need us to unload the containers?'

'No, there are enough people. It would be best you continue your site before the rain starts. Just leave us the truck to unload the containers.'

'Understood. Actually, is it normal we always eat the same meals?'

'Yes, so we'll finish with what's in the cold rooms! Everything will go back to normal when electricity will be back. One of the containers has a turbo generator.'

'Good. Good evening to everyone.'

Hemerik walked away through the crowd that was eating. The light from the oil lamps made the skin on his shaved head and his nude shoulders shine.

◆ ◆ ◆

The meal was over. The families went to their rooms on the floors of the buildings. One by one, the lights disappeared in the thickness of the tropical night.

Kelia remained alone in front of me. The flame of the two lamps on the table shone on her cheekbones and dark pupils and almond eyes stared at me one last time.

'It's late', she told me, closing the pages of her advertising review, 'I'll clean and go to sleep. I put three buckets of water in front of your room. Good night.'

'Thank you Kelia, good night and see you tomorrow!'

◆ ◆ ◆

Going into the infirmary, I noticed Linda occupied with putting drops in Athal's injured eye. He, with his head thrown back, a yellowed old book in a sorry state in his hand. They were both in full conversation about the words of God. They talked without paying me any attention. I understood Etienne had borrowed Athal his bible, who had the habit of confiding in this pastoral couple to express his suffering. He questioned the nurse:

'I would really love to have your faith. I already read a Bible on the platform four years ago. My father had taken it from one of you and I recuperated it before burning. Actually, I read it in hiding.'

'You were searching for the truth, no doubt.'

'Yeah, but I didn't understand how you could be so happy despite everything we made you live.'

'Our happiness doesn't depend on circumstances, but of our relationship with God. Our reason for being, it's Jesus's love that lives in us.'

'But how can you be sure he loves you? Just reading this in the Bible?'

'Not only. When we read his words at first, we decide to believe in his love and he, God reveals himself in our heart. First we believe and then God reveals himself, confirming what we read in the Bible.'

'I only feel guilt and disgust! Redemption, the new birth, the battle of the flesh against the spirit... I understand none of this. You, you can lives these things because you're not as bad as I am!'

'False! We're all sinners and whatever the nature of our sin, the Bible teaches us that: *"Where sin abounds, grace overflows"*. The blood of Jesus erases all our sins, if not, what would his sacrifice have been for?'

'But you, you're innocent!'

'Of course not! We're all born in sin, even if we haven't stolen or killed. Because of the original sin, we're all guilty since birth! Sin separates us from God and the day when we decide to believe and see Jesus again as our personal savior, something wonderful happens: we ask God's forgiveness and we automatically go to his presence, this isn't make believe, you have to live it! We receive this indescribable supernatural peace. It's written: *"Christ's peace surpasses all intelligence"* Don't try to understand, just feel!'

'I would love to feel this peace so much!'

'Stop underestimating yourself. God loves you just as you are! If you don't love yourself, how could you receive divine love? Let yourself be loved by God and the Holy Spirit will do the rest in you! And hold the lamp higher... stop moving, I'm trying to clean this remaining eyelid!'

'Today, it hurt more than yesterday, especially when I read this Bible, it made me cry!'

'You cried? I notice mister Athal has feelings, it's not what you had us believe!'

'Yeah, but I didn't know a pierced eye could still cry... and it stings!'

'Pierced or not, I would like for it not to become infected.'

◆ ◆ ◆

My friends had left. Left alone in this infirmary, I couldn't fall asleep: when you wash with cold water, it wakes you up! The conversations of that day came back to me. All Athal's projects: equip Kheo by bringing material, reestablish an Internet connection with the world, finding all the people who had been deported by Achab, refloating radioactive waste containers... I was stunned by the magnitude of these projects, not to mention their realization...!

From now on, Athal wasn't looking to escape his responsibilities, by coveting his own death, he was determined to put right all his father's hateful acts. I was worried thinking about the personnel from the platform waiting for the helicopter near Mahe airport! How would all those people react? They were just finishing their week of leave before starting two weeks of work according to the rotation of posts required by the regulations. These men had all their families living on the continent and the islands around. Not to mention the mafia trafficking with the governor. These four days of radio silence would finally alert them and send someone to Kheo!

It seemed to me that the inhabitants weren't really aware of the potential danger weighing over them. Without doubt, they put their belief in God. In this regard, when I heard Etienne and Linda talk about God, I thought I was hearing my dear parents! Same expressions, same vocabulary, same arguments, same Bible, same testimony... same God. The writing of this Bible had the same effect everywhere. A people cut off from the world, therefore, knew nothing of the countless religions and alleged widespread truths on the planet. Its only reference: the Bible.

12 – Worrying tomorrows

Friday, March 21, 1997

The third night of my stay was the most agitated and the worst. I woke up around six in the morning following a nightmare. In the dream, we were all busy waiting for the arrival of the container carrier. The sky was menacing and darkened by huge black clouds that were mixing with the morning mist. Suddenly, a strange light came from the carcass of the platform, like some projectors come alight! I observed this phenomenon with my binoculars. Athal and Etienne were close to me. "How is this possible?" I asked Athal, "is there electricity on the platform? I thought everything had burned!"

'And how everything burnt! Give me your binoculars, I have to see this!'

We saw countless floating debris at the surface that the waves brought to us. Among the waste, Athal recognized human remains, pieces of bone and burnt, decomposed flesh: "It's my father's body!" he cried. At the same moment, the silhouette of a ship coming towards the island loomed on the horizon. All the people of Kheo gave shouts of joy behind us, a joy that didn't last, for Athal recognized through my binoculars, a war ship ready to attack us. He immediately told Etienne who shouted to the people: "It's governor Achab's military fleet! Everyone take cover! Run!" We ran towards the bunkers. While I was running, I heard a click behind me... and I woke up, sweating, on my sleeping bag! Athal and Linda had just entered the treatment room.

♦ ♦ ♦

Contrary to previous days, the morning, as seen from my window, was very gloomy and cloudy, which made my white room even dimmer! After refreshing myself with water from the third bucket, I joined my two visitors, still deep in discussion. Athal had the same position as the other day, Bible in hand, and Linda put a new dressing on his eye, smaller than the ones from the previous days. He called me:

'Hello, Jerome the tourist! Did you sleep well?'

'Not really, but it's time I woke up.'

'One could say you're worried, isn't that so?'

'I had a nightmare, that's all.'

'Come, we're going to eat.'

'I'm coming.'

I pulled the upper part of my track suit over my T-shirt before going out. Hemerik's men went to their site, while others waited for the arrival of the three containers. Etienne was organizing the work. We took out tables and chairs from the school to align in the courtyard and big notebooks to record everything. Some people were singing under a cover.

I suddenly noticed Kelia and Nellie run towards me, they had probably been watching me for a while. They greeted me and proposed we go look for my breakfast. What eagerness, I thought! Nellie asked in a supplicating tone:

'Jerome, the tourist, come with us, we'll take care of the rabbits. The pastor knows!'

'Uhm… yes, if the pastor has nothing else for me to do.'

'Great!'

Thrilled, the little one ran to announce my answer to her sister, while Athal and Etienne approached me.

'Good morning Jerome', said Etienne, 'slept well?'

'Not really, I dreamed that the island was victim of a military attack commanded by the Achab governor!'

'Eh? I don't believe such a war will come, rather an economical war!'

'Actually', Athal continued, 'we may be faced with creditors who'll want to recuperate the money we owe them by pressuring the personnel from the bank in Mexico.'

62

'Really? In that case, let the bank give these people back what your father owes them and let's not talk about it again!'

'It's not that easy! These mobsters won't be happy with just that. As soon as they'll hear of my father's death, they'll take over the bank to cut us off! The resources of the island aren't enough for us to live self-sufficiency, we must begin with the continent.'

'So? What's the solution?'

'We would have to transfer a part of the funds in your account in France, supposing you have one.'

'My bank account? But...'

'You don't have one?'

'Yes, of course I do, just like everyone else, but is this legal? How much do you want to transfer?'

'There's nothing illegal in depositing a few million francs in an account belonging to a French citizen!'

'No... I don't want to be involved in this, this dirty money isn't mine!'

'This money, my father gained by exploiting the people of Kheo, by selling their lives and their flesh. We must act quickly while the employees of the bank still think their employer, Achab, is at the helm. Afterwards, I won't be able to do anything and the outside world doesn't know about us.'

'Sorry, all this is too complicated for me.'

'So be it. Remember, you could have had half of this sum for your personal use! You could have, for example, bought the printing house in which you work and hired your boss! *(Silence)* I'm kidding!'

'I would love to help you, I love you all, but not like this. Why not try to make an alliance with a country on the continent in order to benefit from military protection and a logistical assistance?'

'In exchange of what? What country would want an island without resource and interest? We couldn't even develop tourism because of an alleged radio-toxicity that would panic the whole world!'

'You want to say that the radioactive waste doesn't pose any danger?'

'Zero risk doesn't exist, but I guarantee that once stored in a safe place, these products will remain inert.'

'Especially those that are thirty meters on the sea bottom in the North part of the island!'

'The lifting of these barrels is one of my priorities.'

Etienne nodded his head in sign of approval. Kelia brought me breakfast prepared in an European style: coffee, honey, fresh bread…

'Fresh bread?' cried Athal, 'the lucky guy, Kelia cooked him bread! Where does the flour come from?'

'A little remained for the worship supper on Sunday', Etienne answered, 'I gave it to her. She prepared the dough last evening!'

Kelia smiled and they all watched as I ate that good bread, still warm. They had already eaten an hour earlier, something that didn't taste as good as this! Etienne bent as if to whisper something:

'Friday is when we change the rabbit's litter and I usually help the girls with this task, but I have to stay here to receive the container carrier. So I appointed someone to replace me, but Kelia refuses this proposition and insists that you help her in my place! Do you agree?'

'Gladly, especially as this delicious bread gave me strength!'

Everyone was quiet as I spread honey on a slice. Complete silence. A little embarrassed, I decided to ask questions to Athal:

'That symbol, the black gear wheel on red background, what does it mean?'

'My father was a technology passionate. It was like an idol, the key to social and political success. Technological and scientific progress, results of hard work were, according to him, the ornament deserved by a people, a proof of superiority. He admired those who worked hard to make their country triumphant by exploiting those weaker. He claimed that neglecting modernism always drives a nation to ruin. He saw black people in underdeveloped countries as ignorant beings, lazy and inferior. That gear wheel represented progress, the future, power and superiority... and what else do I know?'

Silence again. This insulting answer put me even in a worse position! I regretted my question, that still, didn't cut my appetite. I quickly thought of another question: "Who evangelized the island of Kheo?"

Etienne hurried to answer:

'As far as I know, Kheo would have been evangelized by British missionaries at the end of the 19th century. They would have left us with written Bibles in the Malagasy language. As soon as Achab's father came to colonize our island in 1939, he began by destroying everything concerning Christianity and imposed a dictatorship in which learning the French language was mandatory. As such, our people was bereaved of the words of God until 1972. That year, as we were praying to God without pause for him to send us the Holy Writings, a French cargo en route to the island of Maurice, made a forced stop on the North side of Kheo. Surprised by a cyclone, those sailors had to interrupt their voyage to repair a few damages. Among the crew, a Protestant pastor offered us a dozen Bibles written in French with some songbooks. We gave fruit and honey to these people around a fire camp lighted on the beach! After six hours they took to the sea again. Achab never found out about it! Praise God!'

The sky was glum, like the one in my nightmare. Also, after having thanked my interlocutors, I wasn't sorry to go away in the girl's company! My meal finished, Kelia cleaned the table and everyone went their way.

13 — The rabbits

Nellie was waiting in the cart, seated against a trash can filled with peelings.

'Nellie', cried Kelia, 'you're exaggerating! Go down immediately!'

'No, I like to be pushed!'

'Leave her', I told Kelia, 'I can push.'

Everyone was getting ready for the arrival of the containers. In different buildings, they were arranging, they were making space. Women were cleaning three cold rooms while singing.

We left by the porch toward the deserted plantations. The screeching of the cart tires sounded on the pebbled path. In the distance, we could see the foundations for the new chapel. The men were laying the first blocks. The girls were delighted to share this grey morning in my company. I confess that I was equally enjoying this moment. I had the chance to go into their daily lives, knowing that my stay on Kheo was coming to an end. Kelia began the conversation:

'Thank you for accepting to help us.'

'Don't mention it, and thank you for the bread, I thought to understand you prepared it especially for me!'

'Yes, and the pastor said it was a good idea, I made the dough last evening.'

'I know. What will my work consist of?'

'You'll have to remove the manure from the pens to store a little further away. I'll mow the grass for food and Nellie will put clean hay as bedding.'

'I see everything is well organized!'

'Do you raise rabbits in France as well?'

'Yes, but I never saw industrial breeding. The rabbits I have seen are in small numbered overlaid cages.'

'Overlaid cages? Do they resemble small buildings made to the size of the rabbits?'

'You could say that.'

'How strange! You, the French, don't live in a community, even your rabbits have individual houses!'

The plantations, the bunkers, the site with its machines, the quarry, the forest... everything seemed different under the greyness of the sky. The inclination of the road was higher in the forest. Kelia asked:

'The slope is steep... Do you really not want Nellie to go down from the cart?'

'Don't worry, when I'll be tired, I'll ask her to get down.'

'The bad season is approaching. I don't like this time of year when people die!'

'What? What are you saying?'

'Every year, in July-August, it's disease time. Aren't there any diseases in France?'

'Yes, but we treat people as soon as possible!'

'Here as well, but the treatments to protect us aren't always efficient.'

'What treatments?'

'Every year, at the beginning of the disease season, the doctor on the platform and his team organize a mandatory medical visit at the infirmary for each inhabitant. They take our measurements to make us suits. The doctor made us swallow vitamins and injected us with vaccines.'

'And despite all this care, some of you die, is that it?'

'Yes, they say certain season viruses evolve quicker than the vaccines. This explained the deaths.'

'And you, you're worried about the next *"disease season"*?'

'Yes, because today we don't have a doctor anymore and Linda doesn't have any medication, vaccines or vitamins...'

'Kelia, you must know the truth: there was never a *"disease season"*. Governor Achab lied to you, he was trying new recipes to make you sick!'

'Are you talking about the vitamins and vaccines?'

'Exactly. Athal told me everything, those criminals were using your bodies to test new experimental substances.'

'But why? What were those substances for and why were they so dangerous to the point of death?'

'Drugs are chemicals, they are made to heal, but they can provoke adverse reactions that we call "side effects". Scientists must limit these effect while conserving the maximum efficiency of the product.'

'Products meant to be sold on the continent, I assume!'

'I suppose, but I don't know to whom. Achab did whatever he could he get rich. I even think he made cosmetic products and chemical weapons in the laboratories on the platform. You served as guinea pigs for these experiments.'

'What are guinea pigs?'

'Small rodents, laboratory animals on which we try treatments to know if they're dangerous for humans or not.'

'Are you trying to tell me that all those who died were poisoned?' *(Silence)*

Kelia stopped walking and turned her back to me. She was crying. Not knowing what to do, I stood there unmoving for a long time. Then, I decided to carefully lay down the front of the small cart to approach Kelia gently...

'You're lying', she said, 'it's impossible! The pastor would have told me!'

'I'm sorry, Kelia. Etienne didn't have the time to tell you everything.'

She went further away to lean against a tree, she seemed crushed. I followed her, and after a long hesitation, I dared put my hand on her shoulder. She suddenly turned to cry against me. Nellie, who had no doubt followed the entire conversation, got down from the cart (that turned to the rear) and came to snuggle against her sister who continued to evoke her memories, in a trembling voice, interrupted by sobs:

'When the vaccined people weren't strong enough, they went into a coma. They were transported on the platform as soon as their state was signaled. We had to move quickly to avoid contamination. At the end of a few days, they died and their bodies were incinerated on place to avoid an epidemic.'

'This explains the absence of a cemetery on the island.'

'Were they really poisoned?'

'They weren't falling into a coma. Actually, Achab put them to sleep with drugs to be able to dispense with their bodies in the laboratory. The incineration erased everything after the experiments.'

'When I think that my aunt and uncle had the same fate five years ago! My aunt was eight months pregnant!'

'A pregnant woman gave them placenta! You have been manipulated for fifty years. It was a way of slowing the growth population of your people! I'm sorry to tell you all this, but…'

'You did well, I would have found out one way or the other.'

She took a step back, drying her eyes and said:

'Let's leave! We must hurry while there is still dew, the grass is easier to mow when wet.'

Nellie went into the cart and we walked in silence until the clearing bordered by the enclosure of rabbits.'

This is what surprised me with this population: these people were capable of rapidly going over their sorrows, like death was only a passage. There was this wisdom of going over the hardship of life without abandoning their word, nor being destabilizing by dramatic circumstances. Etienne said: *'We're cut off from the world here, we only have God. But in God, we have everything!'* The hope and faith of this community seemed unshakable. I, the son of Christians, felt really small next to them!

Along the way, hay was drying on a thirty meters fence, stretched horizontally. We walked until a hidden cabin behind an enclosure at the shade of trees. Kelia opened it and gave us tools. The door wasn't locked. There was no key and no padlock on the doors of the buildings on the island!

Each tool had its place. Three pairs of black rubber boots were carefully lined. The girls took theirs and gave me Etienne's boots, a little short for me! Kelia sharpened her scythe with alarming rapidity, the smallest mistake and...! As for Nellie, she handled the fork with ease from her nine year old height! My task consisted of gathering the old litter into a bunch behind the enclosure using a wooden wheelbarrow. A city dweller like me had never done this kind of work before and I found the situation rather comical! I would have loved to see myself in a photo with my scraper, my fork, my broom and my laborer too short boots! If someone had told me that one day I would collect the manure of rabbits on an island in the Indian Ocean...!

As soon as I finished cleaning a cage, Nellie put fresh hay. There were eleven cages, containing a dozen rabbits each. Kelia brought fresh grass in the lattice feeders accessible through hatches. The girls used, each in turn, the same cart to carry hay and grass. The soil of each cage was lightly inclined, permitting flow of manure and rain. The rabbits could take cover under a metal sheet, suspended a meter above ground, in the middle of branches. Each cage was numbered.

My work was done after about two and a half hours. After which, I put away the wheelbarrow and tools in the shed, while the girls finished putting the grass and hay.

Boots removed, tools put to right, cabin closed and all three of us were busy tying our shoe laces at the same time, a foot on the side panel of the cart. My walking shoes had a principle of lacing identical to that of their boots.

70

Nellie took place in the cart and we left quietly towards the village.

'Who kills the rabbits?' I asked Kelia.

'Me. I kill and cut them on place. After, I give them to be cooked or freezed, according to the community's needs.'

'Are there other breeding like this one?'

'Of course, a dozen, managed by other families. There is also poultry. All this part of the island is reserved for breeding.'

'Why here?'

'Because of the rugged terrain. The plantations are more in flat areas.'

'It's logical.'

'This afternoon, we'll come change the water of the troughs. I'm in a hurry to see what they'll get out from the containers. I would have wanted my parents to see this so much, they who have only known Achab's oppression! They died last year. I still remember their irritated hands because of that poisonous dirty chemical!'

'I know, Athal told me everything. A barrel of radioactive waste badly closed, your parents ignoring the danger when they touched it.'

'They hadn't the right to wear that white suit that the people on the platform wore to get that barrel! They would have still been alive today!'

'What white suit?'

'When my parents were contaminated, Linda warned Athal via radio. Three quarters of the poison had been deposed by the truck in front of the last bunkers. We didn't know those barrels were dangerous. Athal told us to stay away. Men from the platform, completely protected by that funny suit grabbed the damaged barrel with special tools to arrange them in the first bunkers that were already filled.'

'The most buried bunkers?'

'Yes. My father and mother, unconscious, were transported on the platform, from which they never returned. It was the worst day of my life! Athal ordered something unbelievable: he asked that we threw the rest of that waste in the sea, in the North of the island without being seen. We would have said he had taken that decision without his father knowing!'

'Certainly, he already anticipated what would come.'

'He dreaded a conflict. He then asked we arrange the bunkers by storing a few days' worth of food. At that time, we were asking ourselves about what kind of conflict he was talking about!'

'Especially as there never was one on Kheo.'

'Maybe Athal couldn't take his father's cruelly towards us.'

'For sure, and no one among you doubted Athal was acting in your favor?'

'No. It's true we had seen the island modernize in the last three years: running water, electricity, cold rooms, machines to make concrete buildings and for agriculture... but we thought they were to indirectly serve our enemy's interests!'

'When did you know Athal managed everything independently of his father?'

'Since he started being the only one to speak to the pastor by radio.'

'Before this, was it Achab in person who gave Etienne orders?'

'Yes. In addition, he came once a month by helicopter with his son and a few armed men to see the residents. Sometimes, he flew over the island to show it to his guests.'

'Athal didn't do the same?'

'No. We saw him come two or three times a year by boat. He was accompanied by armed guards.'

'And the only time when he came alone, Hemerik and Fredo jumped him!'

'No, they didn't jump him, they hit him with metal bars!'

'It's a way of speaking. So the radio that Etienne always used still exists?'

'Of course, it's in its housing above the mechanical workshop where Hemerik and Fredo work. But it was cut at Athal's request just after the attack.'

'That's understandable, he wanted to cut all contact with his father.'

'The first white man I saw without weapons, except Athal, was you, the day you came to the courtyard! You approached Athal and the pastor who were standing in the bed of the truck. You stopped right in front of me and my sister. You greeted us, leaving your bag on the ground. We all thought you were a journalist!'

'Yes, and I must confess I was really scared. I didn't know you and you could have taken me for an enemy!'

'I immediately knew you were a good person.'

'Thank you, I was so well received, I will never forget that day!'

We slowly walked down the flank of the island. Among the plantations, we saw Fredo and two other men reconnect all hoses temporarily used to supply water to the sanitary building. Not being able to use the original electric pump due to the lack of electricity, they had installed another one with a thermal engine on the well.

'Look', Kelia told me, 'they're putting the watering like before. It means we're going to have electricity! I can't wait to see the things in the container.'

♦ ♦ ♦

The courtyard resemble a huge market. Several hundred people of all ages were coloring notebooks with felt and colored pencils!

Nellie jumped out of the cart and ran with her big sister to join Mado and Rose-Marie behind the rows of school tables serving as a counter. The two women were responsible of the distribution and took care to give the materials to each resident according to Athal's directions. He was managing, with Etienne's help, the flow of products that were coming by truck from the pier where containers had been placed one behind the other.

To not disturb all these seated people, I put the cart against the porch wall. I heard the conversation of the couple seated closest to me. The man worked on a coloring book and was busy filling with blue a giraffe's silhouette. His wife asked:

'Why are you putting blue on this animal?'

'Because I love this color.'

'We don't know this animal! You can't know if it's its true color!'

'It's a giraffe. It's Athal who told me. Giraffes live somewhere on the continent and I decided to color it blue.'

'I'm sure this color is not the right one!'

The man replied in an irritated tone:

'The real color of this strange animal doesn't matter, I do what I want with what I received. You have the same thing as me, don't you?'

'Yeah, but that's no reason to do whatever you want with these felts!'

'It's not nothing. I do what I want, like in a democracy!'

◆ ◆ ◆

Etienne invited the crowd to leave the premises with his megaphone, because of the works. The place emptied and I took advantage to cross with the cart. The excavator driven by Hemerik and the truck led by his brother went under the porch. The mast on which the red flag of Achab had once floated was torn and the cup of the excavator dug a hole in the ground.

Etienne approached:

'Ah, Jerome the tourist! All went well with the girls? Are the rabbits well?'

'Yes, they're all well and alive!'

'Thank you for your help!'

'It's fine. But tell me, these works in the courtyard...?'

'It's an idea of my son Hemerik, he absolutely wants to build a cross in the middle of the courtyard for our Sunday mass! It's not important, but he insisted. He can't conceive a place of cult without a cross!'

◆ ◆ ◆

At dinner time, the school tables were used to eat. All my friends were there: Athal, Hemerik, Fredo and his wife Yvonne, Etienne and his wife Linda, Nicodeme and his wife Mado. I was sitting between Kelia and Nellie.

The women who were filling the cold rooms hadn't had time to cook. They put baskets with fruit and dry pastries on the tables.

That morning, no one had worked on the plantations. Only the people responsible with breeding had been absent to take care of their animals. The fishers remained at Hemerik's service.

After the prayer and song of thanks to God, the organizations of afternoon activities was decided at my table. Kheo had to obtain its energetic independence as soon as possible. As was his custom, Athal had everything planned: solar panels from Europe, wind turbines from Canada... Hemerik wanted to know and decide everything with Athal:

"*Hemerik* - All roofs will be covered with solar panels, even that of the villa!

Athal – Yes, we must distinguish which panels produce electricity and which ones enable water heating.

Me – A villa? Where?

Etienne – On the West flank of the island, Achab and his father lived there before the construction of the platform. But today, this building is in ruins! What are you going to do with it?

Kelia – Athal visited it the day he came with us. He wants to repair it to live there and put the radio station.

Etienne – Really?

Athal – Yes, the room upstairs is still functional, it's big enough and well placed to instal part of the Internet equipment. I'll need help.

Hemerik – Half of my team will go with you. Remove everything by truck to the quarry and then take turns with the wheel tractor and trailer to the villa.

Etienne – I assume you're going to build the cross with the other half of your team, right?

Hemerik – Exactly! Fredo will join us on the platform as soon as he'll finish connecting the generator.

Fredo – We'll have electricity in an hour!

Etienne – You're going to the platform? What for?

Hemerik – We're going to recuperate segments of metal beams that are not twisted. I saw pieces that are straight and will serve us for the cross and the roofs of the building in construction. The welding torch, hoists and slings are already loaded on the fishing boat.

Etienne – Still, that place is unhealthy, it's not right to work where a lot of people lost their lives. We must consider that place as a cemetery and respect it as such!

Hemerik – A cemetery? Our cemetery for all, is the ocean, where our ashes are thrown, you know this very well. The dead have no need for beams, while we, the living, we need to build the cross and the roof of the future church!

Fredo, talking to Athal – You'll need help to make the connections for your station?

Athal - Yes, I'll let you know when all the gear is in place.

Fredo – The gear?

Athal – It's a word that means 'material' in popular language.

Nicodeme – There are many unknown words to us in French!

Athal – These words belong to the popular language that isn't used on Kheo.

This is how lunch was: exchange of ideas, ambitious projects with the courtyard on a long term. I was happy to see Hemerik and Fredo work with Athal, yesterday's enemy! Right now, they were deciding everything together to such a point that Etienne seemed to lose control of the situation!

Towards the end of the meal, children were playing around us, exploring open boxes containing musical instruments. Hemerik seemed particularly interested in a drum that he placed behind him before lunch so he could take it later. He asked Athal:

'I would really like to pound on these drums. Could you show me how it's done?'

'This is a drum, you hit it with drumsticks.'

Three children came close to touch the instrument. Hemerik continued:

'You'll not touch this, if else, it's on you that I'll bang!'

Frightened, the children went away while Etienne fixed his eyes on his son who said:

'I'm kidding!'

Nellie had quickly finished eating to be able to continue her coloring. Kelia was deep in thought and Linda asked her:

'Kelia, are you ok? You didn't eat much!'

'I'm… I'm a little tired.'

'No, there's something troubling you.'

'Yes, I'm thinking about disease season. Jerome told me everything!'

A silence interrupted the conversation. Linda spoke after a minute that seemed like an eternity to me:

'I know, Kelia. We all found out that many of our loved ones have died poisoned due to those horrible experiments of governor Achab. And the worst of it is that I administered it, without knowing, that poison to all our sick ones. They died shortly after on the platform! How do you think I feel? Every night, I see their tense faces in pain!'

Etienne put his only hand on that of his wife's:

'Achab is the only culprit, you always wanted to treat the people. God knows all this and he will reward each one according to his deeds!'

'Listen Kelia', cried Hemerik, 'no one will dominate us here! It's over!'

Hemerik's words imposed a new silence:

Kelia – Does everyone here know?

Etienne – No, I'll speak about it on Sunday.

Athal – The crew from the container carrier won't hold their mouth for long after seeing the platform destroyed. We have to move quickly to get our supplies as long as we're still in charge!

Nicodeme – Hold their mouth?

Athal – "Hold their mouth" means keeping a secret. This cargo is one of the only ones authorized to come here. My father paid for the silence of these sailors who were close to the personnel of *Achab industries* on the continent. The crew that must return to the platform will soon understand why the helicopter doesn't come for them!

Etienne – You're right… Let's get to work!

14 — The villa

The women cleaned the tables and the flow of products coming from the containers took over once again. They unpacked, sorted, distributed, put away... The sun made a first showing. At Athal's request, I took a new series of photos. Then I fell asleep on my bed for two hours.

♦ ♦ ♦

Nellie knocked at my door to invite to go work with her sister at the rabbit quarry! I noticed the girls didn't want to make do without me! The pain from my hip being gone, I gladly accepted.

Outside, the activity was still as intense. Hemerik and his whole team were welding sections of component beams for the future cross. Teenagers were wearing the same outfit as Hemerik and Fredo. They had no more sleeves on their red suits and their heads were shaved. They wanted to help the pastor's sons with an eagerness that compelled admiration! They were about to brush with drain oil the base of the cross to put in concrete. Hemerik gently asked to wait until the metal cooled down.

Nellie took her place in the cart in front of the empty containers. Kelia deeply thanked me for having accepted the invitation and then we left towards the heights of the island! On site, children came to greet me, showing me their brand new bicycles:

'Hello, Jerome the tourist! Look, we received a new bike!'

'Yes, thanks to Athal who knows everyone here!'

'Was it him who made all these beautiful things come to us?'

'Absolutely, think of thanking him!'

The little boy, a bit surprised at my answer, turned towards his companion and gave an approving smile before running, skidding on the gravel. The whole troop followed him towards the porch.

♦ ♦ ♦

During our walk, Kelia began asking me questions, sometimes embarrassing, interspersed with thoughtful silences:

'Are there dramas like the ones here in your country?'

'There are all over the world.'

'People like Achab, they exist in France as well?'

'They do, but people like Achab can't act freely.'

'Because France is a democracy, I suppose.'

'Yes, and mostly because there are laws and justice that ensures the application of those laws.'

'Laws resembling the commandments of the Bible?'

'There are some resemblances, but these laws are written by people that don't mention God's name.'

'How can you live without God?'

'Kelia, you react this way because you believe! Certain people don't have faith, which by the way, is a gift of God. It takes time to become a believer in our society, people have the choice to believe or not in God. Believers and non-believers must live together, while respecting each other and the laws of democracy.'

'And if someone tried to act like Achab, what would happen?'

'This person would be immediately stopped by representatives of the law.'

'So there are no crimes in France?'

'Unfortunately, there are. Criminals manage to harm their fellow citizens, but they end up getting arrested. In France, there are courts, prisons, magistrates, policemen, all kinds of people who try to bring order for everyone's sake. If man were naturally good, all this system would have no reason to exist!'

'I know we're all fishermen. But I don't understand Achab's behavior. He acted like there was no choice between good and evil! When he kept me on the platform and tied me in that dark workshop where I spent the night, I truly thought I was living my last hours of my human existence! I thought of my parents who were waiting for me in the sky. Achab and his people were stronger than me, they had the power to abuse and annihilate me. I found the strength and daring to resist because my sister was in danger. When I saw her being dragged on the ground like a vulgar bundle of rags, I did everything to rescue her! It was unbearable. This feeling dominated over my fear and my own suffering.

Today, I feel no resentment towards this dictator but rather a deep disgust. How can other people crush others only to serve their egoistic interests, motivating that we're an inferior race? Besides, they acted as they would live for eternity on Earth!'

'Kelia, first of all, you're not an inferior race, then you won't be able to understand this behaviour if you won't admit that people can live without God. Individuals like Achab respect no laws: nor those of men, nor of God. But I assure you now: non-believers aren't all killers!'

'Before Athal's intervention and your arrival on our island, I truly thought white people were all unbelieving criminals!'

'It's understandable, your people has always lived under this dictatorship.'

'You're a Christian at least, you don't resemble Achab's people!'

'I still don't consider myself a Christian. I have a few steps to enter the ranks of the people of God.'

'But you're a believer!'

'Yes, but thinking God exists isn't enough to be a Christian, I have to commit myself by giving him my life and making this commitment through baptism.'

'I didn't know you weren't christened. I received mine a year before my parents' death. I was 18.'

♦ ♦ ♦

We crossed in silence the rabbit's clearing. Nellie, still seated in the cart, in front, was humming to the rhythm of my steps.

Kelia continued to question me:

'You must leave tomorrow? Wouldn't you like to live with us on Kheo?'

'I... I don't know if I could adapt to this new life here. I have a job at a printing house in France, my boss awaits my return at the end of the month!'

'A boss?'

'Yes, a boss, like a team leader, he leads a company. I work for him in exchange for a salary.'

'A salary, you're talking of the money you showed us in school?'

'Exactly. In my country, this money is essential to life. It allows us to dress, live in a house, eat.'

'I remember all your explanations on this subject. I would really love to see your house. Is it big?'

'I don't have a house. I was living in the apartment my parents were renting. "To rent" means borrow for a sum of money. As this place was too big and expensive only for me, I gave it back to its owner before I came here. A colleague accepted to keep my furniture in his garage while waiting for my boss to find me a smaller place for me to live.'

'Your boos really takes care of you.'

'Yes, he's an extraordinary person, if all bosses were like him!'

'You're leaving tomorrow, you're thinking of coming back when?'

'In a year, during my next leave.'

♦ ♦ ♦

82

I still didn't know this side of the island. At the end of the narrow road, a huge stone wall formed the edge of a well around which three women were working. The oldest, holding her container full of water balanced on her head, was waiting for the younger two to fill theirs. They burst laughing when they saw me push the cart transporting Nellie and the containers.

'Jerome, the tourist,' whispered one of them.

After exchanging greetings, amused looks and smiles, they left in another direction. I decided to sit against the wall to rest. Nellie came down from the cart and she took charge of filling the containers. Kelia explained that the three women took care of poultry raising.

I noticed an old metal pipe coming out of the well and plugged into a niche stone among the bushes about ten meters away. Kelia immediately explained:

'There was once a pump there to deliver water to the tank of the villa of the governor.'

'The villa in ruins of which Athal talked about?'

'Yes, it's really close to here. Do you want to see it?'

'If it's possible, I would!'

'The access is a little difficult, but it's possible. Nellie, leave the cart there, we're leaving for the villa!'

The dimensions of the villa were obviously huge, at the measure of a dictator's madness: forty meters long and thirty feet wide! I found the architecture a little simple: two roof sections that ended in a gentle slope of carved stone pillars sheltering narrow terraces on either side. Under the front sprocket, a longer terrace must have once dominated the sea when the garden was maintained! In extension of the rear sprocket, the first floor was standing as a tower and only occupied a quarter of the total area of the villa. It's through the front openings we entered this sinister remains. There was much light at the ground floor, for two thirds of the roof corrugated sheets were missing, exposing the beams and joist frames in decomposition. Kelia explained that

Fredo and Hemerik had taken those sheets to make shelters for the rabbits and poultry.

Debris littered the marble floor, the window panes had disappeared. Vegetation invaded everything. Lianas, cactus ... vines wrapped around pillars and rafters.

The back was even more sombre but in a better state, sheltered of the heavy rains. Under this still intact roof area stood a carved wooden staircase leading upstairs. Nellie went up first and opened the door to the main room, even more somber. Behind the dusty window panes, closed shutters slightly left the light of day filter. A large canopy bed had been forgotten there.

'This is the room of Achab's parents', indicated Kelia while her sister climbed on the bed to jump on it.

'I also think it's the place where Athal wants to install his radio station and Internet.'

'That's right... Nellie, stop jumping on that bed!'

Kelia, wanted to show me the landscape but had trouble opening the window and tried to remove the blocked shutters. I tried with her and during the maneuver, the shutters eventually fall off and tumbled to the ground floor.

'Sorry!'

'It's nothing', she answered, 'everything must be redone in this house!'

The light of the evening invaded the room where the creaking of the springs of the bed on which Nellie happily jumped resounded. In the background, among the trees, we saw a sort of rusty tank perched on top of a metal support.

'It's the water tank', Kelia reminded me, 'it's where the pipe you saw is plugged. Fredo and Hemerik recovered all the valves from the property.'

Then, turning to her sister, she raised her voice:

'Nellie, stop jumping up there! It's disgusting!'

'No way', answered the breathless little girl, 'for once, I have the chance to jump on a bed!'

'That bed is rotten! Too bad for you if you pass through it!'

Under the child's feet, the old mattress of four meters produced a cloud of dust that clung to the rays of the setting sun.

Kelia closed the window and invited me to leave the room, warning her sister, still occupied with jumping:

'We're leaving! I suppose you'll spend the night here since you love this bed so much!'

The woman went downstairs first, faster than me because my hip was feeling sore again. She turned towards me and noticed my grimace of pain. She took my hand and didn't let go until we left the property. Nellie bounced off the floor boards to join us.

Kelie pushed the cart charged with containers full of water and prohibited her sister to settle there. She asked on the road:

'What do you think of this villa?'

'It's big. It was certainly built under constraint, with stones cut by hand!'

'Without doubt. I have always seen it uninhabited.'

'Achab didn't need it anymore since he lived on the platform. He forbid you to get close?'

'No, he couldn't care less. But none of us wanted to live there. Too many bad memories!'

'I understand.'

'The garden is unattended, only the parcel containing the hives is maintained. Bees continue to give honey to our community.'

♦ ♦ ♦

We arrived at the clearing with rabbits. The water troughs were emptied on seedlings and then rinsed and filled with fresh water from the containers. Once the work was done, Nellie hastened to take place in the cart, but Kelia strongly opposed:

85

'No, Nellie! We'll walk all three, Jerome's hip is hurting, go down immediately!'

'I'm tired!'

'We're all exhausted! You weren't tired when you were jumping on the bed!'

After a long hesitation, Nellie abruptly went down and threw herself against her sister, mumbling:

'Dad and mom are waiting for us in the sky…'

'Nellie, why are you telling me this now? You're not going to do this kind of crisis every time you're upset!' *(Silence)*

Kelia continued in a low voice: 'Nellie, I don't like yelling at you, but you have to understand that this situation is as difficult for me as it is for you. You're not the only one on Earth who suffers. Jerome also lost his parents!' *(Silence)*

'You're going to push the cart yourself, in front of us. It's empty, light and the road descends until the village. Do you understand?' *(Silence)*

The little girl moved away from her sister, looked at me briefly with a confused air and then started walking in front. Kelia continued to talk to me while holding my hand:

'I'm sure Athal, Hemerik and Fredo will built an installation to simplify this water collection.'

The girls sang an old song that I'd heard in the church my parents attended:

I need Thee every hour, most gracious Lord;
No tender voice like Thine can peace afford.

I need Thee, O I need Thee; Every hour I need Thee;
O bless me now, my Savior, I come to Thee.
I need Thee every hour, stay Thou nearby;
Temptations lose their power when Thou art nigh.
I need Thee every hour, in joy or pain;
Come quickly and abide, or life is in vain.
I need Thee every hour, most Holy One;
O make me Thine indeed, Thou blessèd Son.

I'm thirsty of your presence, divine chief of my faith:
In my huge weakness what would I do without you?
Every day, every hour, oh! I need you,
Come, Jesus, and stay near me.
Enemies from the shadows roam around me:
Overwhelmed by their number, what would I do without you?...
During the stormy days of darkness, of fright,
When my courage weakens, what would I do without you?...
Oh Jesus, your presence is life and peace,
The peace in the suffering and the eternal life...

When I was younger and unbelieving, I thought Christians were people a little naive and weak, their God being a shortcut for explaining the unexplainable and also a way to escape responsibilities. The Bible was for them the only truth, destined for "brainwashing" and their songs allowed them to "self-condition" themselves! Me, a French citizen, born in a materialistic, mercantile and Cartesian world, had yet received a Christian education. Father and mother fully engaged in the church and in the social work connected with it, I was born between "two pages of the Bible", according to an expression used in the religious environment! This hadn't helped me choose the "way that led to the sky"! But the dramatic events I lived in my youth, especially the premature, brutal death of my parents, had made me think about the meaning of life. Rather than continue to seek all faults and errors of Christians in their attitudes, I recognized a true positive impact of the word of God on the human race!

The people of Kheo, which evolved in isolation away from the geopolitical context I knew, had this disconcerting faculty of appropriating the divine promises. These believers, who had no past filled with religious wars and great philosophical thoughts, knew how to make their faith live. They simply believed, like children. They made me want to resemble them, to talk to God!

But with my hand in Kelia's, I only heard her vibrant thin voice that sang and made the light between the mandarin branches dance. Her sweetness, her delicate attentions towards me, the contact of her hand… all this began to melt my heart!

15 – The last evening

We went out of the shadow of the forest, passing between the truck and the tiller and its trailer, still and silent. A tarpaulin covered the truck loading: probably the computer equipment to be installed in the villa. Hemerik's team, surprised by nightfall had probably decided to hand in tomorrow the transportation of the valuable "stuff"!

Crossing the porch, Kelia let go of my hand. For the first time, I heard the hum of the generator. Electric lights lit across as the evening advanced. On site, the crowd bustled around a white cross, nine meters high. Men were finishing a small resealing of a trench on the floor of a building that started and ended against the concrete base at the foot of the cross. The girls left me while I was advancing towards Hemerik and Fredo. As soon as he saw me, the last one told me proudly:

'Good evening Jerome, the tourist! Did you see? I installed a laser beam at the base of the cross to light it up all night! It can flash and even change color! Does this also exist in France?'

'Uhm… I haven't yet seen a laser beam light a cross, but this kind of illumination exists and it's used in concerts and other festive events.'

'Turn this off', ordered Hemerik, 'there are enough mosquitoes that stick to the fresh paint!'

Next to the cross, on the right, men were covering with a hood a stage they had made with pallets, of blocks and form boards. Hemerik explained that all the community was preparing for Sunday, the first cult celebrated after Achab's disappearance.

Everywhere, children were running. The meal trays began to circulate and, as was the custom each evening, the crowd sat on the ground for dinner, after having sang to God:

Since the Master of glory has come to rescue us,
Since it's enough to believe so he'll heal us,
Let us trust in his grace: To all he said: "Come and believe!
I died in your place, died on the cross!"
Just a little suffering, fighting and work,
Then, delivery will come and the joyous day of rest.
I want, oh my loving Father, live for you now
Until the end of my life... Yes, forever!

♦ ♦ ♦

I sat so well between Kelia and Nellie! Tiredness took over me. I didn't dare think this was my last evening with them!

Dinner finished, Kelia remained alone at my table to talk to me. As I was exhausted, I didn't understand the subject of her monologue, but the sound of her voice was nice and slightly dominated the hubbub of the crowd. When she saw my eyelids close several times, despite my efforts to stay awake, she put her hand over mine saying:

'I'm going to leave you, I see you're tired. Good evening and good night!'

'I... good night', I answered a little confused.

I decided to go to my room. The seated families were taking time for sharing. Some were praying, other were singing in the glow of a powerful projector placed above the porch. Neons placed on all the facades of the buildings illuminated the courtyard.

Going in the main room of the infirmary, I noticed Linda trying to bandage the foot of a boy sitting on a berth. She explained:

'He wanted to follow the adults jumping from the top of the podium: sprain!'

'Poor little guy! If you want, after treating him, I can carry him to his room.'

'No, thanks, I'm going to notify his father to come get him.'

The child, with tears in his eyes, was looking with fascination as his ankle and heel were slowly disappearing in the endless white strip coming out of the skilled hands of the nurse.

'What a day', said Linda, 'the children were very excited and a little left to themselves! The adults were too busy! And you, how are you? Tired, I suppose?'

'Tired, but happy to be with you all! My leaving tomorrow won't be easy!'

'You like it here with us. The girls have changed since they have been walking with you!'

'How come?'

'Since their parents' death, they isolated themselves from other youngsters and didn't talk. While now, thanks to you, they're smiling and talking again!'

'I didn't do anything and I didn't know they weren't talking. We mentioned our memories. Maybe it's because I lost my parents as well.'

'Maybe. It's important to share our joys and pains.'

'I think your community is living a wonderful moment of liberation, you can breathe now that Achab won't ever be able to harm you again!'

'Breathe?'

'Uhm... it's an expression that means not being tormented, to no longer suffer oppression.'

'Yes, we're breathing! And you, you need to sleep!'

'Yes, indeed. I wish you a good night!'

'Good night, Jerome!'

For the first time in Kheo, I took a good shower with hot water, while the neons flooded with light all the whiteness of the infirmary. Once in bed, I fell asleep without reading and without a lullaby!

16 – Destination Mahe

Saturday, March 22, 1997

It was about five thirty in the morning when I was woken up by choral singing. Through the window, I noticed twenty people all ages standing on the platform. They were singing under Nicodeme's guidance, facing the rising sun. I knew this song and interpreted thus with four voices and without music, seemed more taking and solemn.

I put my things in my backpack. I was in a hurry to see the girls and the whole family before my departure. I rolled my sleeping bag and went out of my white room.

Outside, the crowd sitting on the ground, was finishing its breakfast. I stopped in front of the group of choristers, next to Nicodeme. In the place of the desk, the teacher had installed a brand new synthesizer. He had written with a marker the name of the notes on each key! He then explained that thanks to this instrument, they could finally sing the songs as they were written in their original tone. At his feet, an open briefcase overflowed with partitions, methods of learning musical theory and... ten pairs of glasses! Athal had really provided everything, according to the needs of each! Moved by the beauty of these voice, I listened motionless the whole song:

O the deep, deep love of Jesus, vast, unmeasured, boundless, free!
Rolling as a mighty ocean, in its fullness over me!
Underneath me, all around me, is the current of Thy love
Leading onward, leading homeward to Thy glorious rest above!
O the deep, deep love of Jesus, spread His praise from shore to
shore!
How He loveth, ever loveth, changeth never, never more!
O the deep, deep love of Jesus, love of every love the best!
'Tis an ocean full of blessing, 'Tis a haven giving rest!

'We're ready for tomorrow's worship', declared Nicodeme to his choristers, 'good day!'

'Have you all already had breakfast?' I asked the teacher.

'They have, we didn't. We were waiting to eat with you.'

'Thank you, I'll take this occasion to take a photo with you.'

'What time are you leaving?'

'Franck, the pilot who accepted to bring me here, gave me as meeting hour nine o'clock.'

'Where? On the North beach?'

'We haven't settled an exact location, but I saw a rocky plateau at the top of the quarry. It's a visible and uncluttered place, without vegetation. Franck will find me fast!'

'Come, let's go to the table, the girls have seen you. They warned the others.'

All had waited for me to wake up to share this last breakfast with me. Athal had sunglasses that were hiding his bandage. After prayer, they asked me questions regarding my professional life, my projects. They wanted to know who would see my photos in France. The girls ate little and listened attentively to my answers.

Nicodeme gave a big envelope to Athal and one to me. They contained a hundred children's drawings which we circulated from hand to hand. Those destined to Athal were toys and scenes from the middle of unpacking of the objects from the containers. Some illustrations had brief messages:

92

"Thank you Athal for my beautiful bicycle... Thank you for all your presents... Thank you, I love these toys... Thank you for my colorful pencils... Thank you Athal for the containers, you are welcome among us... Athal, we love you, we pray to God your eye will heal... Thank you Athal for the beautiful things for school..."

The drawings meant for me represented me while pushing the cart transporting Nellie! The girl's face was redder than her suit, mine was as white as snow! I saw myself sitting at my table, I recognized Etienne with his cut hand, Athal as white as me with his eye bandage, Linda and the others, as well as the crowd seated on the ground, smaller. On other drawings, I was a little shocked to see myself standing with my backpack between two buildings in flames! In others, the platform on fire was in the background, while I was still alone with my backpack and my binoculars! I was asking myself how certain young children could interpret the fact that I had entered their history just after an explosion. I read these messages:

"Have a good trip Jerome the tourist... Welcome to Kheo Jerome the tourist! Come back whenever you want... Come see us again with the helicopter Jerome the tourist... Have a safe trip to the continent Jerome the tourist... Have a nice journey to your beautiful country France, Jerome the tourist... Jerome the tourist, have a good journey back to your democratic country... Goodbye Jerome the tourist..."

◆ ◆ ◆

After the meal, I asked Athal to take photos of me with them until the end of my film. The girls made it so they would always be in the field of vision of the camera! Then, came the terrible moment of goodbye! All formed a circle around me, Etienne prayed aloud and sang a song. Hugs, smiles full of emotions, words of goodbye... When kissing

Kelia, I had great difficulty restraining my crying. Nellie didn't want to let me go:

'Don't go', she said, 'stay with us!'

'I would love to Nellie, but it's impossible, I'll come back next year, I'll bring you a present from France!'

I wiped with my thumb with a tear rolling down her cheek. Linda whispered in my ear:

'Since she lost her parents, she can't take separations anymore!'

'Me neither!'

Walking boots, backpack, binoculars… I returned in direction of the porch by which I had arrived four days earlier. The crowd, resuming their activities greeted me. Some gave shouts, others applauded… each one wanted, in their own way to say goodbye to Jerome the tourist! Children strolled with the bicycle around me.

The girls accompanied me until the quarry without saying anything. I had the impression they walled up in their sad silence as before. They observed me while I climbed the cliff to wait on top of it.

It was eight and a half when I found myself at the top of the quarry where I had decided to wait for the helicopter. 'Half hour earlier', I thought, 'Franck is very punctual. It would be better to prepare to be on time!'

After putting my backpack next to a rock, I took a tour of the plateau to admire the view with my binoculars. I scanned the horizon. Beyond the plantations, I recognized the girls' silhouettes. They were slowly returning to the porch.

The one whom I would miss the most was decidedly Kelia. Realizing this, I noticed I had fallen in love with her. I had to leave her and not see her for a year!

I decided to go sit on the rock next to my backpack. I needed to think, to make decisions and fight against anxiety. I was very determined to come back to Kheo later on. I wasn't upset anymore against God who had taken my parents, I wanted to truly meet him, give him my existence. I had to get closer to the Christian friends of my parents. I was sure I would be welcomed in their church! I also thought about going back to my workplace, my colleagues, my friends to whom I would show my photos. I tried to imagine my future home.

Nine and a half. No helicopter. Franck was, no doubt, late. I was paying attention to hearing an engine purr. I heard the one of the tiller down the cliff. Life continued without me in Kheo and I fought against the anxiety that was trying to overwhelm me. I found my single orphan solitude burdensome.

Ten and a half. Still no helicopter. I began to worry. I regretted not having understood Franck's last words at the moment of landing on the north beach the day of my arrival on the island. Why had he been so upset? What was the real reason of his worry? Did he know Achab's mafia?

Eleven and a half. Still nothing! This didn't seem like Franck, who always honored his commitments. The sun warmed with all its strength the stones of the cliff.

The unbearable wait made me lose control of my thoughts. The images of my past, the day of my car accident came violently: after the shock, I regained consciousness for a moment, to see pipes and devices placed around me that were dislodging the plates to release me. My ears were ringing. Between firefighters that were busy working near me, I saw a stretcher further down, on which my father was lying. There were no traces of blood on him and his face was peaceful, like he was sleeping. I didn't know yet that he was dead. I vaguely heard one of the men say: "*broken*". I learned later on what that word meant: "having a broken neck", in the firefighters' jargon. My mother wasn't there. An ambulance had already taken her to a hospital where she died that very night. I never saw her face again!

I was tired of rehashing these bad thoughts. Also, I had the vivid desire to speak to God and to "get it off my chest" like I had never dared to do it before. I expressed my distress to him, my weariness, my mediocrity, my weakness facing events. I had the impression of having God all for myself, that he was listening to me, consoling me. It was a wonderful, new moment for me! The love of Jesus wasn't simply a religious word, but a reality! I don't know how long this lasted. I was euphoric, waves of joy going through me.

Noon had passed by about twenty minutes! I heard the dry grass being trampled on behind me: the girls had come for lunch. I was delighted. They took a seat on each side of me on the rock, like we were at a table. Nelie talked first, while Kelia took out provisions from a big basket:

Nellie – We didn't see any helicopter come for you.

Kelia – That's why we thought we could eat with you.

Me – You thought well, thank you! It's with joy I accept your invitation!

Kelia cut a piece of fresh bread slices to make sandwiches with honey. I observed her hands and noticed a piece of string adorned her wrist. I was moved. I wanted to stay with her so much! She gave me a first sandwich that I gave to her sister. We ate in silence. Thermos of coffee, water, mango juice... nothing was missing.

The picnic finished, Nellie asked for my binoculars to better admire the view. Kelia didn't seem in a hurry to go down.

'Athal and his team have finished setting up the Internet materials in the room of the villa', she told me, 'they're unpacking everything and making the connections.'

'What they did do with the old four poster bed?'

'They threw it out the window!' *(Silence)*

'Kelia...'

'Yes?'

'I'm going to give you a mission.'

'What does this mean?'

'This paper, you're going to give it to Athal.'

'What is it?'

'It's my account number in France. Athal will understand.'

'I'm going. I'll leave you the drink, if the helicopter is late, you're going to need it!'

'Thank you.'

She embraced me and called her sister who gave me back my binoculars.

I sighed seeing my friends move away.

The hours passed slowly. I observed the comings and goings of the people who unpacked, put away, distributed... tirelessly. The third container had been opened. From time to time, I looked at the horizon: still nothing.

How could Franck have forgotten? No, it was impossible! A last minute delay for sure, a breakdown, an unscheduled task was the cause of his delay! I thought him worthy of confidence. In the end, I knew him little. Who was he really? Why did he know where Kheo was found? He was so proud of telling me of this island unknown to the public!

In the square, I saw entire boxes of clothing. They had pulled the curtains from the windows of the two classrooms. The school had been transformed in changing rooms. The red suits gradually disappeared, giving way to multiple colors: pants, skirts, dresses, belts, ties (to which no one knew how to tie the knot), caps, hats... Despite my binoculars, the great distance didn't allow me to recognize the identity of the people. I saw a woman run after someone who was taking her flower hat from her head and putting a cap in place! That someone must have been a man to whom they had given by mistake a woman's hat!

Five o'clock soon! "It will be dark in an hour", I thought, "Franck never pilots during the night!" He had to pick me up when his container carrier, in route to Mauritius, would follow the boundary of the restricted area...

While I was complaining, I suddenly heard someone approaching behind me. I turned and saw a woman wearing a long, orange dress without sleeves. Her hat was lined with flowers. I recognized Kelia with her big basket that she put next to me! She was radiant and happy, she was dancing before me, hopping and twirling... She was shining!

'Look', she told me, 'we opened the last container, I received a dress! It's the first time I wear a dress! What do you think?

'I... it suits you!'

'Jewelry as well!'

She came closer, tilting her head to better show me her big, large earrings shaped like gold rings. Rings, watches, bracelets... The piece of string was gone from her wrist.

'Take a photo of me!'

'I... don't have any film left!'

'Too bad. Look at these funny shoes', she exclaimed while putting her big basket on my knees, 'I can't stand them!'

At the bottom of the basket, I saw a pair of new high-heeled shoes! She continued:

'I wonder how do the women on the continent walk with these!'

'These shoes aren't adapted to move on the pebbles of Kheo! The women on the continent walk on pads or sidewalks.'

'What are sidewalks?'

'Smooth, hard surfaces, black or bluish in color.'

'Hard like the concrete of the bunkers?'

'Exactly. But actually, your sister isn't with you?'

''No, she stayed with her friends. All the girls want to see the dresses they're going to wear.'

She took a seat next to me on the rock. She got out her advertising review that she perused slowly. Then, she put it in the basket and snuggled against me by extending her legs. She looked at her bare feet, exceeding her dress and she asked:

'Jerome!'

'Yes...'

'If I don't put those funny shoes, my outfit won't be complete. Do you think it's right?'

'Now this is a question! You do as you feel. The important part is that you feel ok!' *(Silence)*

She removed her hat and snuggled against me. Her head on my right shoulder was so close that her tresses touched my cheek. It was troubling, my throat tightened and my heart beat faster and stronger!

Gently, my right arm slipped behind her to enclose her. My hand closed over her bare arm. She trembled, for the tropical autumn breeze enveloped us. I was boiling inwardly. I was still hesitating: I dare... I dare not... I dare... I dare not... I dare! I turned towards her. I had never seen her face so close: her almond eyes, her dark skin. Her hair smelled of hay and her lips had the taste of honey! During our embrace we heard the distant engine of the helicopter. Horrified, she moved away from me suddenly, while shouting:

'You're going to leave! I want to leave with you! I want to live with you, in your beautiful country. You'll teach me the common language!'

'But Kelia, it's not that easy. You don't have a passport.'

'A passport?'

'Kelia, why did you hide your feelings towards me?'

'I didn't dare. I knew you would leave, and we're so different!'

'You're raving! We don't care about our differences, I love you too! I have suffered too much with the death of my parents, I don't want to be separated from those I love anymore!'

'Then let me leave with you!'

'Kelia, listen to me, here's my plan: Franck won't leave again this evening, the night is too close. He'll sleep here and we'll leave together with Nellie tomorrow morning. We'll find a solution, Franck knows a lot of people!'

I barely had time to finish my sentence that she launched to the base of the cliff making big signs with her hands to attract the pilot's attention. But the machine was delaying in flying over the remains of the platform. I watched it with my binoculars.

'Don't tire yourself, Kelia, it's still too far away to see us. I wonder why it's staying there for so long. For sure he doesn't believe that I'm going to wait perched on scrap pieces of platform!'

A few long minutes later, we finally saw it come to the island.

'He saw us', Kelia cried, 'he's coming towards us!'

'I don't think he sees us, but he's coming towards us for sure!'

Through my binoculars, the device seemed abnormally big. It didn't resemble Franck's usual helicopter. I finally understood that my pilot had changed the aircraft. This one was of a dazzling white. The light of the setting sun reflected in it.

'Surprise!' I told Kelia, 'Franck changed helicopter! Damn Franck, I believe him capable of redeeming a military machine and repainting it white for his personal use! This time, he saw us!'

While I was putting away my binoculars in my bag, I heard Kelia screaming while running towards me:

'Jerome! Jerome! Look! It's not your friend Franck!'

The device was like suspended at a hundred meters from us. It turned on itself, revealing its white flank in the middle of which a bright red sliding door opened. I recognized the mark of... the black gear! Two soldiers in combat gear pointed their guns at us. I was petrified. Instinctively, I turned around to protect Kelia. Behind me, the enemy was approaching at about thirty meters away. The air being moved by the rotor, lifted around us a stinging cloud of dust. The advertising review and the hat with flowers flew far away towards the top of the trees. The deafening hiss of the turbine forced me to shout to my friend:

'Don't be scared, whatever happens, we'll stay together!'

I placed the palm of my hand over her eyes wet with tears. Her arms were around her body to keep her dress, she was waiting, trusting and immobile, leaning against me, like she was abandoning her life to me. My last thoughts turned towards God. I closed my eyes and held my breath, dreading the first burst of the machine guns...

Second part
The island of Kheo, the Indian Ocean

I – The enemy's return

After endless seconds, a loudspeaker screamed at us: 'Hey, you two there, return immediately to the place of report, I want to see everyone down there... execution!'

Without even turning around, I grabbed Kelia's hand to drag her to the shadow of the trees. Distraught, we went down the cliff, running and sliding at breakneck speed until the bottom of the quarry where we met Athal, Hemerik, Fredo and Etienne who were coming back from the villa. Breathless, we all exchanged stunned glances. Athal screamed: 'Follow me... quick!' We ran to take shelter between two bunkers. Athal pushed us against a wall and hastened to tell us:

'Listen, we don't have much time. Don't interrupt me! I know that guy, I think it's Eglon, my father's accomplice. He should in no way know the truth about the events at the beginning of this week, or else he'll kill us all and replace us with African labor. We'll have to bluff.

'*Etienne* – Bluff?

Athal – Yes, it means to lie. I have to make Eglon think that I still have the situation in hand and I'm governing Kheo in place of my father. You must play my game by showing yourselves submissive and obeying orders. I'm sorry if I'm going to be tough on you, but I have to seem as severe as my father.

Hemerik – You're going to treat us like your father did to please those torturers?

Etienne – Let him speak, he knows how to handle those people!

Athal - No one will be abused. Have faith in me. I was born on the platform, I grew up among them, I know their way of thinking, their ways. If you'll do as I tell you, I promise you Eglon and his people will leave the island in a year without having hurt anyone.

Fredo – What will we have to do?

Athal - Lots of little things to spoil their life using their method of lies. It will be enough to follow my recommendations to the letter.'

As the aircraft was approaching, its roar echoed increasingly within the walls of the bunkers. Kelia, frightened, grabbed my arm.

'*Athal* – Pastor Etienne, we don't have time, I need your approval now!

Etienne – Yes… starting today, we're going to do everything you'll tell us until these criminals leave. But how can we be sure they're going to…?'

The loud speaker interrupted Etienne and his words: 'You there, niggaz, what are you waiting for? All to the place of report! Move it or I'll fire into the pile!'

'*Athal* – Don't be afraid of anything and follow me to the square!'

During our run, we continued our conversation.

Athal told me:

'Officially, you're a new recruit named Maximilien, chosen by my father. I'll present you like an agent charged with surveying all the inhabitants with which you're going to live. You'll sleep in the infirmary and you'll eat with the pastor's family like usual. You'll come to the bunker each day to make your report and convey my orders to the pastor.

And if Eglon will ask questions about my past and my alleged relationship with your father that I never knew…?

I'll answer in your place. You'll be respectful towards him calling him "my colonel". Be discreet with Kelia. If Eglon finds out you have an affair with her, he's going to be distrustful and…

It's obvious, I'll do nothing that could put us in danger!

There are going to be various sites to manage in the next days and I'll make it so you'll be able to be alone with her several times a week.

Thank you, but all this scares me. I'm not in the habit of talking to this type of individuals.

You're my agent chosen by my father, you're directly under my authority and I'm governor of Kheo, don't ever forget that. With this title, I'm superior to colonel Eglon and to all his group of morons. I forbid you to talk to them without my authorization.

All right, I won't forget!'

Crossing the plantations, we saw two other helicopters land close to the foundations for the future hall of worship.

Breathless, we arrived with difficulty at the entrance of the porch, sheltered from the looks of the soldiers. Kelia, still clutching my arm, was slowing me down due to the contact with the pebbles on the road with her naked feet. Athal took this moment of pause to give us his last instructions:

'Hemerik and Fredo, you're going to join the others and you're going to cover with tarps the cargo that still remains in the square. Kelia, you're going to see your sister. Jerome and Etienne, you stay with me and you're going to let me talk to Eglon. Take a desolate and dismayed air.

That's not going to be hard!'

Kelia embraced me one last time before going out from the porch. I looked, with a heavy heart, while she disappeared in the crowd.

Twenty eight men in combat gear and fully armed, entered the square, passing over the area of the former chapel. They all had a red armband representing the mark of Achab. One of them, at the head of the group, was wearing a cap. I guessed it was colonel Eglon. Everyone was waiting on their feet and in silence, having regrouped in ranks. The enemy group stopped while Athal, Etienne and myself walked towards him at a decided pace. Athal removed his glasses to reveal his bruised face. He whispered: 'Above all, don't say anything, let me talk to them!'

2 – Return to power

The man with the cap was in his fifties and a little wrapped. His face was flabby and pale. Jowls pulled the ends of his lips down giving him a haughty air. He kept himself straight like an i, his head back slightly. His eyes, dwarfed by thick, rectangular glasses, seemed to watch everything with contempt.

Athal – Ah! My colonel, here you are finally! What a mess! We have been victims of an attack!

Eglon – Athal? Is that you? But what in the name of God happened here? How come an attack? Where is your father? What happened to you?

Athal (taking a desolate air) – Sadly, my father didn't survive, he and the rest of the personnel perished on the platform. Missiles, at least four, everything exploded! We couldn't do anything!

Eglon – Missiles? Launched by whom? Did you see anything? Where they cruise missile?

Athal – No, short-range missile from a submarine close to the coast.

Eglon – But how could it approach here without being spotted by the radar on the platform?

Athal – I don't know anything. I only know that my father had engaged in electrical work that day. Maybe the panel instruments were disconnected at the wrong time. While I was heading towards the platform on boat, I saw two missiles go towards the island, making two buildings explode. Everything happened very quickly. Two other missiles reached the platform, making everything blow! The breath of the blast capsized the shuttle and sent debris fully in my face... my eye is fucked! I was ejected and Max picked me up with the *zodiac*. The shuttle sank.

Eglon – Fuck, it's not possible! Who are these sons of bitches who dared do that? And you father who saw nothing coming! I can't believe it! Did you see the submarine?

Athal – Yes, I had just enough time to see the silhouette, but I couldn't read the inscription, I was hurt... *(Silence)*

Eglon (putting his hand on Athal's shoulder) – I understand my boy... your father... my best friend... we knew each other since our childhood. He would be proud of you... A submarine!... But who?

Athal – Come, let's sit at that table over there.'

Etienne and I remained upright, ready to receive orders. The soldiers formed a circle around us. One of them kept a big dog of a German shepherd breed in leash. The people, neatly arranged, were still waiting in silence.

'*Eglon* – I see you haven't lost any time, I saw three containers at the end of the pier.

Athal – They're empty. My father had suggested to modernize the island several months ago and I ordered material that we have just finished arranging.' *(Silence)*

'*Eglon (staring)* – Missiles... everything is fucked... but who, dear God, who could have done this?... Nothing else since Tuesday? No sign of the enemy?

Athal – No, everything became as before.

Eglon – Nothing will be as before! Achab isn't here anymore, and those sons of bitches who could come back at any moment. We have no protection now!

Athal - Actually, I did arrange bunkers for you and your men next to mine. It's less comfortable than on the platform, but we'll be more secure.

Eglon – The bunkers? And the nuclear waste?

Athal - Everything has been moved to the sea in the north.

Eglon – You made all this in four days?

Athal - Uhm… yes, and it's not all, we even began installing Internet in the old villa!

Eglon – Damn, with you, the niggaz don't have time to be idle!

Athal (talking to Etienne) – You may leave, the report is finished, each go back to his functions!

Etienne – Very well, Sir.

Eglon (talking to one of his men) – Gontran, tell your pilots to separate the helicopters, the enemy not being identified, we'll be on alert!

Gontran – As you order, my colonel, but… where do you want to put them?

Eglon (in an annoyed tone) – I don't care! I just want them separated. You can see well they're too close, if one of them takes a missile, all three will blow!

Gontran – Yes, my colonel, but at what distance?

Eglon (starting to scream) – One at three hundred meters north, one at three hundred meters south, one a three hundred meters east! In the name of God, is it clear?

Gontran – Very clear, my colonel, at your orders my colonel!

Eglon - Camouflage net on each device! Move your ass, it will get dark soon!'

The people's activities resumed in the square in the usual hubbub. Tarps were placed on the outside boxes that remained, dinner was prepared, the premises were arranged with showers. Behind us, the soldiers unloaded trunks from the helicopters that the pilots were starting for the last maneuver. Eglon remained seated, prostrate and lost in thought. One of his men brought a trunk, an opened bottle of rum and two cups he then placed on the table. As I was still standing next to Athal, he made me understand with a little nudge that I needed to pour the drink in the cups.

'*Athal* - My colonel! *(Silence)*

Athal - My colonel!

Eglon – Yes.

Athal - I would like to see my father's last files to know his projects.

Eglon – Pft! What for? No platform! Look, they're in the trunk.'

Athal opened the trunk that contained notebooks with large spirals and computer disks. He took a notebook from his pocket on which he began to write, turning the pages of the notebooks. Eglon resumed some color after drinking half the cup. At the same moment, as the night was beginning to fall, the outside lightning came on. The lasers of the metal cross erected in place of the flag, lit up the court, which did not fail to get the officer out of his torpor.

'Hey, but what's this? You replaced the flag with this ridiculous cross? And you let the niggaz do this?'

Athal continued to examine the documents spread on the table without replying.

'*Eglon* – And where did the red suits go? Since when do black women wear jewelry? This is nonsense!'

Athal - My colonel, you noticed, I don't use the same methods as those of my father. But as you yourself said just now, I don't let this people be idle, the end justifies the means! *(Silence)*

Eglon – Still, giving jewelry to niggaz is like giving jam to pigs!

Athal (in an annoyed voice) – And your men, are they volunteers perhaps? You give them tobacco, alcohol, they're fed, housed, highly paid...

Eglon (raising his voice) - Thank goodness we give them all that! They're not niggaz! You father, he approved your methods?

Athal – My father trusted me, and I intend to continue the mission he gave me according to my methods and until the end of my days! I dare hope you'll be up to the task to resume the affairs of governor Achab with the same efficiency!

Eglon – Easy to say, everything's fucked! No more work tools! Qualified personnel, engineers, chemists, lab people, workshops, everything went up in smoke! I put three million dollars in that fucking platform! And today, nothing! With what will I resume Achab's affairs? What will I tell my clients?

Athal – Calm, this island is at your disposal. We'll adapt the infrastructures.

Eglon – How?

Athal – My colonel, I have also lived a very difficult week, I'll tell you my plans Monday morning. It's time to go to the bunkers.

Eglon (talking to me) – And you, Max, what post did you have on the platform?

Athal – My father recruited him to second me in the logistic organization of Kheo.

Eglon – Really? And what was he doing on the cliff with a black woman?' *(Silence)*

Athal stopped writing and tore a page from his notebook which he placed in his pocket.

'*Athal* – That black woman was posted on the cliff as a sentinel. She was charged with surveying the horizon and alert Maximilien as soon as she saw a boat or an aircraft approaching, which she did when she saw your helicopters!

Eglon – You even have negro sentries here?

Athal – Yes, so what? No need to be a man to be a sentinel and serve as a target for the enemy!

Eglon – In any case, your second and the black woman had a funny way of monitoring the horizon! I saw them glued to each other. Without doubt, one of your new methods that...

Athal (irritated) – Eglon, you're beginning to be troublesome with your remarks, take care of your mercenaries as you see fit and let me lead my personnel. The situation is complicated enough already, so spare me your thoughts! You either accept to work with me, or you get the

110

fuck out of here, taking your gorillas with you! Message received?

Eglon (finishing his cup) – Yeah… it's ok!... We will not argue with each other because of niggaz! Have a drink!

Athal – I must warn you as well that a virus is around the island. If one of you has the smallest health problem, you have to tell us. The bunkers are equipped with a reservoir of six hundred liters of bleach, chemical toilets and central drinking water. The lighting is connected to batteries.'

Athal started to drink his rum. I took advantage to talk to him discreetly:

'My backpack is still on the cliff.

Ask Fredo to go get it, he has a flashlight. Prepare eighteen meal trays for the colonel and his staff. The meal will take place in the bunkers… And also a little meat for the dog.

Yes, Sir.'

When I was about to leave, Athal slipped a piece of paper in my hand that he got out of his pocket, without doubt the torn page from his notebook. As I walked away, I heard the two men getting up from the table. Athal wanted to accompany the enemy troops to the bunkers. I was eager to read the paper away from prying eyes.

3 – Cohabitation

I found myself alone in the middle of the crowd looking for pastor Etienne's family. I got close to a lighted place and unfolded the piece of paper Athal had slipped in my hand. Here is what it said:

'Jerome (don't forget your name is Max) when the 18 meal trays will be ready, ask Linda to accompany you with her sons in the truck to serve the colonel's men in front

of the bunkers. Tell her to pour a laxative in three bowls of soup from three trays randomly selected (avoiding mine!).

Be careful with your behavior in front of these strangers! When you're with me, serve me like a servant. When you're alone with the people, let them serve you. Don't accomplish any chore yourself. Be discreet with Eglon's mercenaries. They need to know the least about us. If you must answer them, be vague and use their vulgar language. Don't forget you're officially employed by my father.

Tomorrow morning, after breakfast served at seven o'clock in front of the bunkers, I'll come see the pastor to indicate the sequence of operations.

Courage and have no fear. We have defeated my father together, we'll defeat Eglon as well, as I have a plan to make him run from here! Eglon is only a small fry without consequence and his men are stupid!

Show this paper to the pastor before destroying it!'

I saw Etienne, Kelia and her sister come towards me. I had just finished reading the note. Without saying a word, I gave the paper to the pastor who read everything in his turn.

'*Etienne* – I understand! Nellie, go look for Linda in the infirmary. Kelia, go look for Fredo in the workshop. Go to the kitchens!'

Fredo stopped the truck in front of the yard where the women were preparing the meal. As every evening, the crowd sat on the ground, sang and thanked God before eating. Men passed between groups wearing pots full of fish soup, while Fredo and Hemerik loaded two at a time in the truck which had the arches and the tarpaulin unfolded for the occasion.

'*Linda* – Is everything ready? All the dishes are there?

Fredo – Everything is there. Get up, I'm leaving!

Etienne – Leave until the soup doesn't get cold! The girls and I will wait for you at the table.'

During the few minutes on the road, Hemerik, Linda and me sat on the edge of the boards, grabbing the hoops. Hemerik had on the red suit without sleeves. His mother was wearing an apron in black and gray stripes over her dark blue dress. It was the first time I saw her dressed like that. She winked to calm my anxiety. Fredo made a maneuver to set the back of the truck to face the main opening of the bunker.

The soldiers chatted and waited outside, bags and weapons placed on the ground. The dog, tied to a tree about thirty meters away, didn't stop barking. Fredo joined us in the dipper.

'*Fredo* – Athal is still inside, he's no doubt showing the place to Eglon!

Hemerik – There's no question of waiting for them, the soup will get cold!'

Linda began to give bowls, covered biscuits, fruit and cups on trays and gave them one by one to Hemerik who filled the bowls with soup. Fredo, kneeling in the back served the hungry men who had immediately approached us. I was holding an electric lantern, making light over the trays, following their movements.

The mercenaries had noticed me and began to taunt me while sneering. I was in no mood to answer.

'Hey, Max, have you been on Kheo for a long time? *(Silence)*

Max, answer, don't keep silent. Are you still in civilian clothes? Don't you have any weapons?

Me – No need for weapons to be obeyed!

Oh! Max the menace has no need for weapons! What authority!

Hey Max! Will you introduce us to your lady friend, we saw you with her on the cliff! Is she good? *(Silence)*

Maxou, don't be silly, answer. It looks like you live with the negroes. Aren't you scared at night?

Max, come have a drink after your service, we'll talk!

Me – Thanks. Sorry, but I don't have time.

No time? Hey guys, Max the menace has no time!

Of course, he's too busy banging all the little bronzed girls on the island!'

While they were still talking, Eglon and Athal got out of the bunker. Linda had just poured the contents of the third pouch of laxative in the seventeenth bowl of soup. Hemerik whispered to his mother: 'Miam-miam, the good sou-soup for the morons, like Athal would say!'

The colonel who had heard the last mockeries of his men started screaming:

'Gontron, gather!

Yes, my colonel!'

The men quickly put their trays on the ground and got in line.

'*Gontran* – Platoon... on your ranks... fixed!

Eglon – Listen to me well, you fuckers, business is going mad, it's not the time to piss me off! The first one that pisses me off, I will send him with the next cargo to Dar es Salaam! Is it clear? *(Silence)*. I give you two hours to unpack your things and get settled. Curfew twenty-two hours to five o'clock in the morning. Gontron, I want two guards on duty around the buildings with the dog and a guard on the bunker roof! Guns, night vision, radio, infrared binoculars! Post a guard at the entrance of the bunker! Execution!

Gontran – At your orders my colonel!

Eglon – Any questions? *(Silence)* Tomorrow morning, wake up at six o'clock!... Dismissed!'

The men gathered their trays and entered the bunker in silence. Eglon and Athal came to look for their meal at the back of the truck, Fredo being already at the wheel. I took the chance to ask Athal one last time:

'Mister Athal, what have you decided with the washing up?

Everyone keeps his tray, we'll return the dirty dishes to you tomorrow.

Understood. Do you need anything else?

No, we'll send someone if we need anything. You may leave. Nobody outside during curfew!

Alright, till tomorrow Sirs!'

Eglon had already turned his back to me and walked away with his meal tray. Athal, who seemed satisfied with my replies winked, turning away himself as well. Fredo started the motor. Hemerik grabbed the flashlight that I was still holding.

'Give, he said, I'm going to look for your backpack. Where is it?

On the cliff, on the top of the quarry.

Where you were waiting for the helicopter with Kelia?

Yes, maybe you'll also find her basket. Don't you want for us to wait for you here so we can take advantage of the truck?

No, leave, I'll come back on foot!'

He jumped from the truck that was already moving and disappeared into the night. I was left alone with Linda seated in front of me. She assured me I had talked well and that all went according to Athal's wishes. Obviously, she had complete confidence in him and said she was determined to apply his instructions to the letter.

The truck stopped in the yard a few meters away from the porch as to not bother the people who were eating. After all the tough emotions of the afternoon, I went with joy at my usual table. The inhabitants of Kheo ignored the enemy who watched over them a few hundred meters away. They were confident and sure of the future defeat of their invaders!

I entered into a new life of fear mixed with joy: fear of these armed criminals, fear of being taken prisoner and being held hostage on this island… and happy of staying with Kelia with whom I was in love. I observed her discreetly while she poured soup into bowls. She was glowing, her orange dress cheered by the lurid clarity of the neons. Nellie was helping her sister by imitating her gestures. She was wearing a similar dress, pink, a red hat and red ballet flats. Straddling the bench to come sit next to me, Kelia let show her usual dark boots!

'Here he is, Linda said to her husband seeing her son Hemerik arriving, you can say the prayer!'

Etienne prayed while Hemerik put the backpack and Kelia's basket behind us. He gave me a piece of paper that Athal had given him during his return when he passed in front of the bunkers. I read it out loud:

'Tomorrow morning, after the service at breakfast at seven o'clock, tell Fredo to get the truck ready with the back facing the door of the cold room in the middle.

Hemerik should choose six men to dig a square hole of five feet on the side and two meters deep. Evacuation of the rubble by emptying the buckets in the truck. The works will begin during the service. Towards ten o'clock, Eglon and some men will go near the platform in the zodiac. Two soldiers will stay on duty on site. When Fredo will see me with the two guards next to the generator, the pastor will take the chance to explain the situation to all, the noise of the engine of the generator will prevent the guards from hearing, and I will explain the instructions concerning the production of electricity. I warned Eglon that urgent works will be made in front of the cold rooms. I will tell you later what that hole will serve us for. Have faith and may God bless you! Until tomorrow!'

'A hole? For what purpose? Asked Fredo.

You'll see, answered his brother, Athal knows what to do.

It's sure that he knows what he's doing! I know three who will remember their first night!

They're going to have a stomach ache, Linda added, maybe they'll need some medicine!'

Everyone began to laugh.

116

This is how the first day ended, in the bad company of Achab's servants that I thought never to know! I went back to the infirmary, unfolded my sleeping bag. I was fully engaged in a new history that was beginning...

4 – The resistance was organized

Sunday, March 23, 1997

It was around six o'clock that I woke up. Like usual, I was the last to arrive at the table for breakfast, where all my friends were waiting for me! Kelia, seated next to me, quickly kissed me on the cheek, while the pastor began saying grace.

Surprised to see that everyone had their red suit on, I asked Kelia. She answered that all the inhabitants will wear their most beautiful clothes on Sunday for the nine and a half service! On the table, still warm bread, boiled eggs, honey, fruit, milk jugs and coffee. (Milk powder and coffee was imported on the island). Evidently, the Sunday meals were richer than those of other days!

As yesterday and according to Athal's instructions, I accompanied Linda and the two girls to the truck for the service of our enemy in front of the bunker. The soldiers, less talkative and boastful than before, came with their trays to look for their bowl that Linda filled to the ladle of milk or coffee depending on the choice of each. Some hadn't yet finished getting dressed and moved slowly with their belt resting on the shoulder... Eglon and Athal, still in deep discussion came the last, without saying anything.

♦ ♦ ♦

Towards eight o'clock, when I was in my room, busy looking for suitable clothes to go to the service, I heard Athal, Etienne and the two girls enter the main room of the infirmary. Athal closed the door behind him checking that the two guards that accompanied him were far enough away in the yard.

'Hello, he said, here is what awaits us: Eglon wants to use all the arable land to produce poppy!

Hemerik – But, it's impossible! No more pineapple or vegetables? What will we eat?

Etienne – Shut up and let him speak!

Athal – No panic, we'll import fruit and rice from Madagascar. All this is temporary, we absolutely must cooperate. I managed to convince Eglon to not deforest, deforestation would endanger our freshwater supplies. So we'll free all the lots and organize a consolidation by eliminating the aisles in the middle and recalculating the surfaces. To assess their size, we'll take into account the number of members of working age in each family.

Fredo – And the poppy seeds, where will you look for them?

Athal – They'll arrive with a new cargo in a fortnight when we'll finish our orders.

Hemerik – What orders? We're still waiting for material?

Athal – Of course, you'll go measure all the openings and the roof of the villa that will be entirely renovated to make Eglon's general headquarters before becoming ours when Eglon and his mercenaries will have left the island. Awaiting that day, we'll have to work for them, while I'll work on their conscience!

Hemerik – And the hole in the cold room?

Athal – Officially, this excavation will be for a technical room that actually has no reason to be under ground level, but which will allow access to a secret room dug under the slab of the cold room.

118

Fredo – A room that will serve for what?

Etienne – But let him speak, he would have certainly continued to explain!

Athal – This room will contain a computer connected to the Internet and linked to Eglon's computer in the villa. I will finance the works. The fact that we will do the renovations ourselves will allow us to discreetly install cameras and microphones to be able to better spy Eglon and trap him!

Fredo – The works in this secret room, how will we do them without being seen?

Athal – You'll see. I had asked you to choose six men, is it done?

Fredo – Yes, they're installing the jackhammer as we speak!

Athal – Perfect! They should begin immediately. In a little over an hour, they will have finished making noise and the service will be able to begin in silence.'

♦ ♦ ♦

At nine o'clock, the six men in red suits stopped the jackhammer. They leaned against the back of the truck to breathe fresh air, looking at the dust falling on the threshold of the door of the room containing the five cold rooms. Outside the walls of the buildings, we saw Eglon and three of his men head towards the pier to get to the platform in the *zodiac*. The other soldiers who had stood guard overnight were resting or playing cards in the bunkers.

♦ ♦ ♦

Nine thirty: the beginning of the service. I vainly tried to recognize Kelia's face among the women. I already missed her, I would have wanted her to be at my side!

119

The opening song sung by the choir (directed by Nicodeme) immediately plunged me into a deep joy, I was taken by an intense emotion, I felt loved and protected by God whose presence was so palpable in the middle of his people. My value scale rocked, the disturbing circumstances in Kheo, the permanent threat of Eglon and his men suddenly appeared to be insignificant...

People, come and may we hear everywhere your solemn hymn!
What joy we will spread, and we will say to the Lord:
How terrible you show yourself, Lord, in everything you do!
The enemy, invincible for a long time, comes down for peace.

People, let us always bless God's glorious name,
And the world resound everywhere of his praise:
It's him who guards our life, and surely leads our feet:
It is he who gives infinite grace, securing us from death...

The preaching of the pastor was based on the Christian's ability to endure adversity by the grace of God. Etienne was not content to invite us to love and serve our enemies as suggested by the Word of God, but he put in value the notion of letting God himself resolve our situation as we obey Him. He cited several verses:

'*My friends, don't take revenge yourselves, but let God's anger act, for it is written: It is I who must do justice; it is I who will give each its due, but here is your part: If your enemy is hungry, give him food, if he's thirsty, give him to drink. It would be like putting hot coals on his head and the Lord will give him to you*'... '*When a man's behavior is agreeable to the Lord, he will even reconcile with his enemies*'...

Then came the moment, between two songs, when the speaker interrupted his narratives to explain the new situation on Kheo while Athal occupied his two guards near the generator: 'Don't worry about the presence of colonel Eglon and his men, Athal has a plan to make them leave in less than a year without violence nor mistreatment. During this time, of occupation, we'll have to devote our work to poppy cultivation. We will import all that is necessary concerning food. We must obey Athal and Jerome who simulate complete complicity with Eglon...'

The message was brief. The crowd had trust in its pastor and didn't show any sign of worry. The service resumed its normal course. Etienne pushed the preaching even further by inviting the people to pray to God to bless our invaders!

The service ended with a song sung by the choir and taken by the whole crowd with a power that made me shiver from head to foot. The people rejoiced as Eglon lamented at the foot of the burned carcass of the platform!

♦ ♦ ♦

Towards noon, the crowd dispersed, the families came back together to organize the meal. The whole place got covered with a multitude of multicolored rectangles: bath mats, towels, sheets... Most inhabitants wanted to have lunch seated on the ground in their most beautiful Sunday clothes!

Around one o'clock, Linda, her sons and myself went to serve our enemies. Athal was already with them since an hour ago. Eglon and his men stayed for the whole afternoon near the bunkers. One of the mercenaries, the biggest one of all, was playing with the dog throwing him a piece of wood that the animal caught in flight. The others were loitering around, were walking in small groups, talking and smoking. Eglon and Athal were seated on folding chairs on the roof of the bunker. Sitting facing the sea, they exchanged their project ideas, calculating and taking notes.

As for me, I was only in a hurry for one thing and that was leaving my usual table to run in the woods with Kelia! After having eaten, she was in a rush to clean the table to go put on her red work suit. Her little sister Nellie preferred to keep her beautiful dress to go play with other girls her age in front of the school rather than accompanying us with the cart with cans.

That afternoon, Kelia and me passed a lot of time giving food and drink to the rabbits as we slipped several times in the grass to embrace one another!...

As the lily among the thistles,
So is my beloved among the young women...
(Song of Solomon, Chapter 2, verse 2)

5 — New sites

Monday, March 24, 1997

Hemerik and Fredo formed the teams to accomplish all the tasks according to Athal and Eglon's directions. Officially, my mediator role consisted in surveying the different sites, making reports to Athal and communicating his orders to the pastor's sons. My post allowed me to sneak everywhere, both in the bunkers among the soldiers, as well as in the buildings of the people. Going to see the three men appointed by Hemerik to take the measures of all the openings in the villa, I took the opportunity to stop at the rabbits' clearing to spend some quality time with Kelia between two pens!

Everywhere, work went well. A trench was dug perpendicular to the door of the cold room in the middle to end up on an unused well. This was supposed to receive water foe washing and deicing all coolers of the cold rooms. This device was perfectly useless and unjustified! Athal had planned this to make the works last in front of this building and allow the six diggers to get rid of the debris they got out from below the slab to throw into the freshly dug trench. The teenagers who had shaved their heads and who still accompanied Athal, stood guard in turn to warn the diggers of a possible approach of the soldiers. Each time the trench was full, Hemerik came to empty it in the truck with the help of the mechanical excavator. No one found anything strange in this maneuver! Eglon's men would have never dared to criticize the work essential for the proper storage of their food.

The fishermen went to sea and the children resumed their schooling with new books and courses worthy of a democracy! Mado and Rose-Marie (teacher Nicodeme's assistants) had unpacked and installed a beautiful globe on a metal support custom built by Fredo. Throughout this day of school re-entry, most students had permission to observe the globe in groups of five in a limited time to allow a maximum number of students to discover the Earth! Each one was amazed discovering how small Kheo was compared to the vastness of the world! Nicodeme had stuck a sticker to the presumed site of their native island.

Tuesday, March 25

Athal had given me a workbook in which I had to store each card "Order of Service" and have it signed daily by Athal and Eglon. The teams were formed and the work was decided each day. The six diggers from Sunday had resumed their posts under the slab of the cold room. Athal, who had an eye for detail, brought to the edge of the trench too many blocks for building the facings of the unused well. Half of them were meant for the pillars to support the slab which would eventually had crumbled under the force of the digging below! The teenagers surveyed the comings and goings of the soldiers.

All agriculture was reorganized. On 1000 hectares of cultivable land of the island, 800 were devoted to poppy cultivation, the 200 remaining were left to farmers. Out of 265 parents in a family, 250 were designated officials of a poppy parcel of land measuring two to four hectares depending on the number and age of the members of each family.

From the quarry to the villa, a team began to cut fruit trees on either side of the trail to get the space required for the construction of a true pathway sufficiently wide for the passage of the truck.

In the villa, another team had to take down the rest of the old roof, take out the debris, clean the marble and prepare the openings for the future windows and doors. On the first floor, Eglon and Athal had ordered material via the Internet for the renovation of the villa and the equipment for the future laboratory.

Wednesday March 26, Thursday March 27,
Friday March 28, 1997

Most of the works were interrupted by incessant rain, a deluge which lasted three days. Farmers stopped, but not the diggers under the slab who made the pillars before continuing the excavation. Only the farmers and fishermen, bundled up in rain suits, continued to work. Athal took advantage of this awful weather to pour laxative in fifteen meal trays of the soldiers to demoralize them. Eglon decided to occupy his men by making them do collective interest tasks, like the laundry and cleaning. According to him, there was no question in letting a negro take care of anything in the inside of a bunker!

Saturday, March 29, 1997

Return of the sun. The land, filled with water resembled in places, to a swamp. On my fifth worksheet, the farmers that couldn't do anything in the fields received the order to gather all the available empty barrels and cut with chisels their lids. These metal barrels, imprinted *"Petroka"*, had been used to import fuel. Fredo informed me that Athal was waiting for me in his bunker to talk to me.

Arrived on place, I noticed that only one soldier was seated on a folding chair on the roof of Eglon's bunker. The door was opened and the dog was sleeping at the entrance. The guard, who seemed bored to death, didn't pay me the least attention and looked at the ground, stirring his feet.

I entered Athal's bunker, whose door was opened. Without electric light, the place was dark and gloomy. There reigned the smell of wet rags and old cartons. Seated behind a table crowded with radio equipment, Athal murmured:

'Sit down. I'm going to give you a walkie-talkie that will allow you to call me or receive my calls, but pay attention, Eglon hears all the conversations! He can also call you.

Alright.

I need to know if anyone you know in France will worry about your absence, as you can guess, you're risking not returning to your country for a long while.

Uhm… my parents are dead, I was an only child. The only person who will find it strange that I won't go back from my vacation will be my boss.

It's the reason you'll need to quit. Do you have an e-mail address?

Yes.

You're going to write him a letter of apology pointing out that personal reasons compel you to stay abroad and that you can't more work for him anymore. I will send this message via Internet as soon as possible without Eglon's knowledge.

But… My furniture? They're in a colleague's garage!

They don't matter, your boss will let your colleague know you're not renting anymore. We don't have a choice, I want to be sure no one will signal your disappearance to the French authorities, it's very important. When Eglon and his men will leave the island, you'll be able to move freely in the entire world with your passport that you're going to give to me.

Give you my passport? But why?

I need all the information in it for Kelia's future passport.

But... on what basis? Kheo isn't a country! Kelia has no name.

Don't you want to marry her?

Yes!

In that case, she'll take your family name, she'll live at the same address as you...

I don't live at the address on my passport anymore since I left my apartment!

It doesn't matter, your future wife will live at the same address, she'll be French like you and no one will go and verify. Only the validity dates or those of the visa will be checked on the passport.

So you're going to make a fake passport?

No, this passport will be true since it will have Kelia's true identity. We won't borrow someone else's identity.

Alright. I don't understand much but...

Don't worry, I know someone who makes excellent documents, truer than the real ones. His name is Jose and his workshop is on board the *Geometrix* tanker that often comes here. He worked for my father, he even made fake banknotes!

And if Eglon finds out about this?

Eglon will know nothing. Here is a compact camera loaded with a film of twelve poses. Take portraits of Kelia for her identity photo. Do this discreetly outside, in the shade or in front of a white wall. Not that white walls are lacking here! Tell Fredo to bring those three boxes of medical material to Linda for dinner.

126

6 – Disinfection

Sunday, March 30, 1997, Easter day

Easter was the longest and the most important celebration of the year. For sure, it wasn't the enemy occupation that would change anything! March 30, Sunday 31, and Monday, we celebrated the death and resurrection of Jesus according to the biblical texts, taking the holy dinner during the service. The equivalent of half a glass of wine was distributed to every baptized adult.

Eglon was furious to see that the people weren't working on Monday! Athal replied that the land wasn't dry enough anyway to work in the fields!

These two resting days allowed me to stay longer next to Kelia. Everywhere, the well-dressed people strolled under the courtyards and in the square. Nicodeme and all his chorists were trying to interpret new songs while others were learning the guitar and synthesizer around the rostrum. Hemerik played drums in the mechanical workshop. He was rehearsing, listening through headphones music recorded on a tape-radio. In the evening, after his rehearsal, he covered his precious instrument with a sheet to protect it from dust.

At the end of the first two weeks of the month, all was finished. The road had become passable from the porch to the villa. Even more, ditches dug on each side, a narrow trench was waiting for different electric and telephone cables to make the link between the village and the villa. The cultivable land was completely weeded. The farmers had spilled all the dunghill on their plots. The empty *Petroka* barrels were washed and repainted in black. We had only to wait for the delivery of the cargo scheduled for 15 or 16 April. But the weather took a turn for the worst, a violent wind and a relentless rain on the island from April 10 until the end of the month! During the last week, as the cargo still wasn't there, Athal took advantage of this moment of waiting and inactivity to further demoralize Eglon and his men through a series of meals infected with laxatives and vomitives. Athal made himself vomit in front of his bunker after having ingested a bowl of coffee in which he had poured the contents of an ashtray!

Later, he organized the staging worthy of a horror film with the help of Linda and her son Fredo. Three members of a family accepted to play ill, letting Linda sedate them with injections. Fredo, helped by three young men, pitched a large tent in which we put five beds. The three volunteers, two men and an eight year old, settled in this isolation tent, placed away from the buildings, at a hundred yards from the porch to avoid contagion. While the three "sick people" entered an artificial coma, Athal gave his last instructions before warning Eglon through the walkie-talkie:

'Fredo, you should put two bowls containing two inches of chlorinated water at the entrance to the tent.

Two bowls?

Yeah, and make a habit out of putting each foot in a bowl when going out of the tent to avoid transporting the virus in the buildings through your soles.

Good thinking! The young ones will come with me to look for them in the kitchen.

I'll also need about a bowl with egg white in a saucepan, it will be easier to carry.

OK… is this all?

Yes. Linda will give me a big needleless syringe.

What for?

You'll soon find out!

I don't like this, answered the woman taking her patient's blood pressure, I'm not in the habit of dosing this kind of sedative!

Trust me, everything will turn out well.'

Athal talked formally to Linda and Etienne. He had a lot of respect for them. In the enemy's presence, he

128

immediately went into the skin of a severe and pedagogue leader. He gave me his walkie-talkie just after having used it to invite Eglon and Gotran to come join us. The bowls were put at the entrance. Athal and Linda, holding the pans containing the egg whites came into the tent. Intrigued, we observed the scene in front of the entrance. Athal sucked the egg whites using the syringe for subsequent injection between the patients' lips. I was both disgusted and anxious. Linda looked at us occasionally, grimacing with disgust.

A dozen pickets delimited a security perimeter. A curious crowd gathered on the porch.

◆ ◆ ◆

Eglon and Gontran finally came twenty minutes later. The officer, with his usual contemptuous air, frowning, his pupils agitating nervously behind his rectangular eyeglasses. His semi-opened lips, always grimacing, let to show teeth clenched between his lower cheeks. He immediately questioned Athal:

'What the fuck? Is it that bad? What do they have?

We're trying to find out, we're keeping them isolated here and I'm going to disinfect their room.

What's with the bowls?

Chlorinated water, mandatory when you get out of here to not carry the virus anywhere.'

Gontran stood hunched and remote, tense and plagued by abdominal pain. His superior didn't spare him:

'Gontran!

Yes, my colonel.

Go in there and wake up those negroes! I want to question them to know what they ate in the last hours! Start with the child!

But, my colonel, they're contagious and I wouldn't want to…

So what? You're not risking anything since you're already sick!

Uhm... at your orders my colonel.'

Gontran walked awkwardly between Athal and Linda and waded in the bowls. Eglon cried:

'No, you moron, it's when you come out that you have to do that, not going in!

Yes... yes, my colonel.'

He grabbed the metal bars at the head of the bed where the sleeping boy was and shook him with all his might.

'He's not waking up, my colonel!

Continue!'

The feet of the bed eventually pierced the blue tarp that covered the ground, but the young patient remained frozen in his sleep. Gontran changed method and lifted the young boy by pulling his T-shirt to make him sit by force. The child's head bowed forward. Under the effect of the drug, his eyelids half-closed let appear the white of his eyes without pupils. A large egg white thread passed between his lips and wetted Gontran's hand who screamed, dropping his hold:

'Ah, my colonel, he drooled over me! It's disgusting!'

He hurried over to the bowls and washed his hand. Eglon spoke to Athal and me:

'It's fucked! We must finish them off with a bullet to the head and throw their bodies into the sea! Maybe like this we'll stop the epidemic.

Athal – Not so fast, these sick people will serve as guinea pigs to test the remedies that Linda will prepare, it's in the interest of the entire community, is it not Linda?

Linda – Yes, Mister Athal.

Athal – If this remedy is efficient for them, it will be for us.

Eglon – How much time will it take?

Athal – Tomorrow morning we'll be done. Max and I will assist Linda in the care room to better survey that the doses and the used products are identical to those that we'll

130

take when these sick people will be healed. We'll begin now and stay up all night, we absolutely must find a way to stop this virus.

Eglon – Yeah! While waiting, I'm not reassured at all.

Athal – My colonel, we must be extra careful and disinfect any suspicious place, starting with our bunkers and everything they contain: linen, bedding, dishes, utensils...

Eglon – What? But it's going to be night in less than an hour. Who will do this?

Athal - Tomorrow we will designate teams to wash everything from floor to ceiling with bleach. For now, my staff will give us some clean underwear and red suits, as well as blankets. We'll pass the night in the three empty containers near the pier, they have been washed. We'll carry the minimum of objects, previously disinfected.

Eglon – But, it's crazy, we're going to sleep in those cans!

Athal (ironically) – Would you rather sleep under courtyards or buildings in the company of niggas?

Eglon – Alright, fine! I demand a report on the health state of the three sick negroes tomorrow morning at seven! Gontran, go look for the whole troop. You'll only take your weapons. Gather in front of the containers.

Gontran – At your orders, my colonel!'

Gontran, still bent under the effect of the pain, went away muttering: "Damn virus, we'll all die!'

♦ ♦ ♦

Around eight o'clock, the wind stooped, leaving in its place a deep silence. The night enveloped the whole community with a heavy sleep. Eglon and his men kept watch around a fire in front of their new metal housing. They were weakened and pensive, some trying to sleep wrapped in a blanket on the floor of a container. Each time someone would go in or out, he would wake up all the others due to the creaking hinges of the heavy steel doors when they weren't slamming against each other! These brave warriors were suddenly feeling ridiculous in red suits belonging to the slaves. They were even borrowed undergarments! To finish this quiet evening, a stormy downpour fell on Kheo, a stinging rain that put out the campfire and produced a deafening crackle on the sheet metal roofs. These soldiers were relegated there, outside, herded like animals, while the niggas slept peacefully in their beds.

In the care room, Linda had finished storing solutions in the fridge, while Athal filled capsules with chocolate powder. Both of them had invented an efficient remedy against the imaginary mysterious virus: each sick person had to receive an injection of a morphine-based sedative to relieve the abdominal pain and two cocoa capsules...!

7 — The black cadet

Tuesday, April 29, 1997

In the early morning, the sun reappeared and chased away the last clouds. The squeaky doors of the containers were opened and breakfast was served to the soldiers that were stretching while grimacing. They were hurting everywhere and had had little sleep. The meals were infected one last time before Eglon and his men came to be treated in the infirmary. Many among them had migraines and fasted. Athal had passed the night in the care room, sheltered from the heavy downpour. He accompanied me to the new camp near the pier after breakfast. We passed the truck driven by Fredo returning to the kitchens. Eglon who eagerly awaited news came towards us to ask:

'Eglon – Then! In what state are the three negroes? Did you find a remedy?

Athal – Affirmative! I even tried it and I'm feeling much better, you can all come to the infirmary.

Eglon – And what is this remedy?

Athal – An injection in the vein of your arm and two capsules, that's all!

Eglon – He! She really knows medicine, the black woman!

Athal – I remind you that Linda is a nurse and she was formed by the doctors on the platform!

Eglon (sighing) – It's true, your father anticipated everything. All except that fucking submarine that destroyed everything! But we can't go back to the past. *(Silence)*

Gontran, assembly, I want to see you all in front of the infirmary and at attention! Execution and short strides! Let's do away with this damn virus!

Gontran – At your orders, my colonel!'

While the men were waiting in line in the square, Eglon, Athal and I walked towards the porch. Eglon made a detour to the tent of the three sick people to better assure himself of their healing. The child and the two men still remained lying, but had their eyes wide open, for they were coming out of their artificial coma.

The soldiers entered two by two in the infirmary to receive their care. Eglon was the last to arrive. While Linda injected his arm, for the first time, he talked to her with respect. Je played her role perfectly, answering with assurance.

'*Eglon* – Efficient this remedy! I passed by the isolation tent, the three sick people are waking up!

Linda – Yes, colonel, we passed a good part of the night working, but I have to warn you that certain side effects risk to appear during the day.

Eglon – What kind?

Linda – Drowsiness. Also, I think it would be best to rest today. Tomorrow, all those who received this treatment will be able to resume their normal activities.

Eglon – Are the three patients in the tent still contagious?

Linda – No, but we still have to disinfect their bedding and your bunkers because the virus can evolve and eventually become resistant to any form of vaccine.

Eglon – Really? This treatment serves as a vaccine as well?

Linda – Yes, but I will personally ensure that all the suspicious places will be correctly disinfected.'

Eglon folded his arms and after swallowing his capsules spoke to me:

'*Eglon* – Max!

Me – My colonel?

Eglon – See to it that this nurse doesn't miss workforce or means for disinfecting. Give her everything she needs. Absolute priority!

Me – Yes, my colonel.

Eglon – And I still want a report on the state of health of the three negroes at noon.

Me – Alright, my colonel.'

The morning passed peacefully. The star of the day brought up a small fog from the ground. The morphine contained in the sedative immediately comforted the soldiers who went to lie down in the shade of the containers. Joyful songs echoed in the bunkers where twenty men and women were disinfecting. We washed everything, even the foam mattresses that were put to dry on bushes and the lower branches of the trees around. I was supposed to monitor all the disinfection work, but I took advantage of the absence of my superiors to join Kelia and Nellie who were taking care of their breeding rabbits. Eglon and Athal had left in the truck for the villa to consult the Internet. Nellie still didn't understand why I refused to push the cart in which she loved to be walked. We were more distant than before due to the enemy's presence, but Athal constantly tried to reserve moments for me with my friend.

That morning, when I entered the clearing of the rabbits, Kelia put her fork aside and asked her sister to stop working to monitor the road from the villa. Then, she grabbed my hand, inviting me to snuggle against her in the hay under a sheet. How precious these moments were to me! She was so affectionate, smiling, full of life and... what to say? Nothing that surrounded us discouraged her. I never imagined to have such an effect on someone... and it was mutual! Her eyes closed, her braids brushed my cheek, her lips were barely touching mine, when Nellie's shrilly voice broke the silence: 'Hey, the lovers, we have company!'

Eglon and Athal, in deep discussion approached us. They seemed worried and Eglon was surprised to see me with Kelia, standing at my side, finishing to discreetly remove the last straws clinging to my clothes. Officially, I was supposed to be close to the bunkers. I improvised:

'I... one of the cold rooms is empty, I thought it would be useful to disinfect it. We'll then fill it with the content of the second one. Afterwards, we'll be able to disinfect the second one and fill it with the content of the third one to be able to disinfect the second one and so on.

Athal – Excellent idea! We'll make a note to organize the teams for tomorrow, isn't that right, my colonel?

Eglon – Yes, the nurse must have all the necessary means. But we have another worry.

Athal – We have received death threats through the Internet from the part of unsatisfied clients that my father owed money to or those who were waiting for an order stored on the platform...

Eglon – They want to send a commando here to put pressure and spy on us...

Athal – My colonel, we must reinforce the guards, training new recruits among my personnel.

Eglon – What type of training?

Athal – We have to make soldiers in our service to protect Kheo, teach them how to shoot...

Eglon – What? Entrust weapons to niggas?... So they can shoot us with them? What nonsense!

Athal – Trust me, let me choose six young men, this threat concerns everyone, so it's normal we recruite people from here to defend us.

Eglon – Yeah! Another one of your new methods! Still, trust our weapons to niggas, this worries me a little.

Athal – Do not mistake your enemies, my colonel, your true enemies are not on Kheo, but they risk to soon come here to kill us all. The people of Kheo, which is under my responsibility and your service. Stop underestimating them. Lately, you have seen who is among my servants? *(Silence)* Max, did you notice any sign of rebellion or negligence at the negroes?

Me – No, Mister Athal.

Athal – You see? You want to succeed in your projects here counting on us and taking all the benefits, right? In that case, train my youngsters that you will place in the first line if a threat appears. Thus, you'll limit unnecessary risks for your troops!

Eglon – Mmm... The weapons... Firstly, they'll carry weapons only during the shooting sessions, closely monitored by my armed men.

Athal – As you wish, it's you who decided the stages and the content of the training. Just tell me the necessary means.

Eglon - We must put in place an obstacle course and a shooting range.

Athal - I think the obstacle course should be on the beach and the shooting range in the quarry...'

The two men, absorbed by their projects forgot me, crossing the rabbit clearing to go down towards the quarry. The girls had taken their forks again during the conversation. When my superiors were out of view, Kelia invited me to resume my place next to her in the hay.

Wednesday, April 30

Athal chose six young men among Hemerik's "disciples". They were big, determined, wiling. Their hair was very short and their suits without sleeves let show their muscular shoulders. Rather than calling them by their name, Eglon gave each of them a serial number: B1, B2, B3, B4, B5 and B6. "B" for "Black" or "Blue"! Tables were installed between the bunkers where the *Blue* got their first courses under the amused eyes of the soldiers: knowledge of grades, the basics of military life and handling firearms. Disassembly and reassembly of the machine guns and adjustments, all without ammunition! The lessons, given sometimes by Eglon, sometimes by Gontran, lasted all morning, which allowed the teams to complete the installation of the obstacle course, following the Colonel's written guidelines.

We could see a fence to cross, a trench and tires to step over, a metal beam (recuperated from the platform) on which they had to walk, a portico with a rope to climb, clothes' lines (as barbed wire) tensioned at ground level under which they had to crawl.

I was charged to accompany the new recruits during all this day of training and then make my report to Athal who passed all his time on the Internet. No question of going to flirt with Kelia!

◆ ◆ ◆

After the noon meal was taken on site, the six young men had to go to the training ground. Eglon ordered his troops to try the new device:

'Eglon – Grontran, gathering. I want to see everyone pass, starting with you. It's time to resume operations. The *Blue* will pass the last. Execution!

Gontran – At your orders, my colonel.'

After the physical exercises, shooting session! They had to put in practice the morning lessons. At the end of the quarry, six pallets placed on the tranche, stood against the rock wall. On each of them a target was stapled, made from a piece of cardboard packaging painted white. The black silhouette of a human on his knees on the ground pointing his gun towards us had been drawn on them. The six *Blue* were at attention, facing the target. A rifle and a charger lay before each of them. Two meters behind them, six aligned soldiers, weapons on the shoulder, surveyed everything. Eglon, Gontran and me stayed on the side, Eglon's men were behind us.

As the evening was approaching, a hundred curious of all ages had positioned themselves in a semicircle at the entrance to the quarry to observe the scene. Gontran spoke:

'At ease! Before beginning to shoot, do you have any questions?'

The fifth *Blue* raised his hand.

'*Gontran* – I'm listening B5.

B5 - Sergeant, how much time do we have to empty our charger?

Gontran – You're not limited by time. Apply yourself.'

The second *Blue* raised his hand.

'*Gontran* – I'm listening B2.

B2 – Sergeant, what part of the silhouette must we aim?'

The soldiers began laughing. Eglon made them quiet and Gontran answered the question:

'Aim for the head, but if you touch the target, it will already be bad! Other questions? *(Silence)*. Section B, for a shot of eleven cartridges at a hundred meters, stock, load... Position prone gunman... Start shooting!'

Three long minutes of silence passed. We only heard the murmurs of the crowd of onlookers, then the soldiers started laughing and making fun loudly:

'Hey, guys, if the enemy attacks us, we have time to die!

We're having a wrong start with nigga soldiers, hello responsiveness!

Gontran - Close your big mouths and let them focus!

Eglon – They're here to learn!'

Other two minutes of silence and the first shot made everyone jump. In the white smoke, others followed, closer and closer together.

Once the shooting session finished, Gontran sent everyone to the square. We approached the targets. Gontran counted eleven holes at the center of each silhouette's head. Stupefaction! One of Eglon's warriors exclaimed:

'These damn niggas… they shoot better than us!'

8 – Achab industry

Thursday, May first 1997

After having passed a last awful night in the containers, Eglon and his men took their breakfast before regaining the disinfected bunkers. Athal was taking more and more freedom in coming to stay with us alone to talk. That morning, he found us at the back of a courtyard behind the sinks. Etienne was sitting on a stool, his wife Linda was cutting his hair with electric clippers. Hemerik, Fredo and I were waiting for our turn.

'*Athal* – Good day to everyone!

Hemerik (with a triumphant air) – Hi! Did you hear the news? My youngsters are elite shooters!

Athal – Yeah, Jerome told me everything.

Fredo – When will they carry guns?

Athal – Unfortunately, not right away, Eglon is too distrustful.

Hemerik – But why? What good will the training be in this case?

Athal – Be patient! I have to gain his trust first. It takes time. I did manage to gain yours the day I came to join you on this island, it just cost me an eye!

Hemerik – Sorry!

Athal – I also gained my father's confidence, he slowly let me take control of Kheo. I intend to operate in the same way with Eglon in order to conspire against him at the favorable moment.

Etienne – Am I to understand you intend to use firearms against our invaders? May I know what you're plotting?

Hemerik – It's true Athal, we trust you, but we ignore what you intend to do. What's your plan?

Athal – I'm looking for a way to find myself alone with Eglon to inject him an anesthetic, a kind of tranquilizer that will paralyze him without losing consciousness. Then I will make him believe he'll die poisoned and I'll propose an antidote that he'll obtain if he'll accept to order his men to surrender. Your youngsters will intervene in that moment with the guns.

Etienne – And if this doesn't work, if for example Eglon's men will take the chance to escape the colonel's authority, what will you do?

Athal – It's exactly what I want. Eglon is the only one his troops fear. If he loses his authority, his mercenaries will be left to themselves and we'll be in danger. I would love that Hemerik's youngsters continue to train at Eglon's school, the time we'll need to obtain their carrying guns.

Etienne (talking to Hemerik) – Be careful with your youngsters, they're easily influenced and some are immature. By being trained by our enemies, they risk being "warped" for us!

Hemerik – I'm watching over them, I talk to all of them in the evening before going to bed and they obey me.'

Linda, who had finished cutting her husband's hair, shook the towel, while Hemerik took his father's place.

'*Linda (talking to Athal)* – An anesthetic? Not simple, your plan! Not easy to dose. My three fake patients needed two days to recover from the coma in which I had immersed them. We can't accurately predict Eglon's reaction, who can fall asleep too soon, or on the contrary stay awake without any weakening in his legs after the injection. Not to mention these injections won't be an intravenous because it's too precise, but rather subcutaneously.

Athal – I thought of all this. I obtained injector pens from military packages serving to soldiers in case of deadly gas absorption. We'll adapt some of them and I'll use myself as guinea pig for the dosage.

Linda – Really? And how do you intend to explain this to your superiors?

Athal – No one will be surprised to see me suffering in the infirmary with all the imaginary viruses that loiter around here.

Hemerik - If this trick doesn't work, we'll use force!

Etienne - No matter how, it is essential to avoid a mortal conflict!

Fredo – You were waiting for a delivery of containers, how do you explain this delay?

Athal – Several reasons for this. First of all, it's not easy to obtain such a big quantity of poppy seeds to plant eight hundred hectares, then, the delivery of this seed across Africa is made difficult due to civil wars, in particular in Zaire.

Fredo – Zaire is at war?

Athal – Yes, it's not only here we fight against dictatorship, a wave of democracy took over Africa as well, and the Zairian people, supported by neighboring states organized a rebellion against their governor. A six-truck off-road convoy belonging to my father, regularly crosses the country to Dar es Salaam. That's where the containers that usually come to Kheo are formed. Beside materials and chemical ingredients, the containers were carrying more than several hundred pounds of latex bread from Colombia used in the manufacture of heroin in the laboratories from the platform. Eglon was appointed to liaise between Colombia and Kheo via Africa, with the consent of the Zairian and Tanzanian authorities. He has free passage in the air space of these two countries to move by helicopter...

Etienne – But these two countries let you freely convey latex on their territory for free without asking any questions?

Athal – Actually, they don't know about the presence of the latex hidden in the loading of the medicine in the trucks. We can see the mark of the black wheel gear with the inscription "Achab industry" on the flanks and vehicle doors. Officially, the Achab group denotes an independent humanitarian pharmaceutical company, secretly financed by drug money. The personnel of the group gives at each passing medicine to orphanages, to clinics and public hospitals for derisory sums in Zaire, as well as in Tanzania.

Etienne – Where does this medicine come from?

Athal – A part was directly bought in Dar es Salam, another was made in the laboratories on the platform, starting from base products, also bought in Dar es Salam.

Etienne – These people pass themselves as being a good humanitarian association?

Athal – Affirmative, and they give weapons and ammunition to the Zairian armed forces. Eglon offers his services to this government, his headquarter is based there. Moreover, the Zairian soldiers are still waiting for the guns promised by my father that remained on the platform when it exploded. Eglon and my father had known each other for a long time. They thought of all this to be able to go around anywhere with a good image. One day, *Achab industry* intervened in a mini bus accident in the middle of nowhere near Budjala. All the injured were transported by Eglon's helicopter to the nearest hospital.

Etienne - No one ever suspected anything wrong with this organization?

Athal – Yes. A few years ago, a true NGO got worried noting the comings and goings of the *Achab industry* trucks. It requested help from foreign journalists hoping to open an investigation. These journalists alerted the local authorities close to the Zaire border, next to Tanzania. But Eglon was known by all police stations and paid informants among the police of the two countries. Immediately informed, he bought six corpses that were ready to be buried in different places of the province and had them placed in the back of each truck. When the Tanzanian customs ordered a search of the trucks, Eglon explained that he had to evacuate the patients as quickly as possible to avoid a serious contamination of the country. The custom officers opened the back door of the *Achab industry* vehicles, they saw the sick people in question transformed into corpses, I'll let you guess the smell, so none of them dared go aboard to perform the search! The investigation was never completed and the dead were never found. The journalists couldn't prove anything. Their gesticulating only further exacerbated the local authorities who saw in the Achab group brave, dedicated, generous people, well integrated in the social network!

Etienne – But those six dead that Eglon served himself of, no family claimed them?

Athal – No, for those in charge had been paid to replace the bodies in the coffins with stones wedged with rags! As for the bodies, I assume they disappeared into the ocean!

Linda shook the towel again and tapped her feet to remove the curly black hair clinging to her boots. Hemerik gave the place to his brother.

Fredo – And the heroin, to whom was it sold?

Athal – The heroin left for Europe via the sea. The flow and sales related to another branch of the organization.

Moreover, it is with this that Eglon has problems. The last order of heroin destined for them burned in the attack.

Hemerik – Why should we occupy our good earth with a poppy plantation? Why not bring the Colombian latex as before?

Athal – For various reasons. With the destruction of the platform and my father's death, the entire organization will crumble. All unsold goods destroyed in the fire didn't report a penny in my father's bank in Mexico. Those who hold the bank money will not pay the farmers who harvest latex. The war in Zaire makes things worse, and the connection to the African continent may be cut off. The bank won't buy medicine in Dar es Salam anymore, it won't give salaries to the personnel and the truck drivers that were under Eglon's responsibility in Zaire and Tanzania. Consequently, Eglon anticipates this and will seek independence by producing his own latex on Kheo. He knows he won't go back to his headquarters in Africa. In a mafia like that, all the members are supportive as long as the money comes in, the day the chain breaks, each link will leak taking with it the maximum. Eglon will try to keep to himself the most lucrative market: the production of heroin. His potential buyers in Europe only know Kheo. They know nothing else concerning *Achab industry*. Moreover, Eglon's in debt, he no longer has a choice. He either erases his debts selling drugs made on Kheo and can hope to rebuild his life, or he loses everything and only keeps the permanent threat of being murdered by his creditors!

Hemerik – Why not?

Fredo – Why not what?

Hemerik – Why not let Eglon be murdered by his creditors? It's all he deserves, we won't manufacture latex just to save his life!

Etienne – I confess it's hard to understand. Why make heroine to save Eglon's life and at the same time harm the health of thousands of unfortunate addicts? This is our role?

Athal – Wait, there's no question of selling the drug to anyone!

Hemerik – In this case, why make it?

Athal – We'll make it to pretend to work with our enemies so that they don't massacre us! They need workforce for the harvest. I'm counting on this to manipulate them at the last minute. As soon as Eglon will be neutralized, this coveted harvest will serve as a bargaining chip to send the mercenaries in search of the women deported by my father. Once this mission will be completed, they'll be able to leave Kheo with the drugs and everything will come back to normal. I'll warn all the coastguards of the countries where it will be delivered. The heroin will be taken and Eglon stopped.'

There was a silence. Everyone was thinking, skeptical. Linda shook the towel for a third time and Fredo let me have his place. We only heard the children's voices in front of the school and the electric clippers that were beginning to cut my thick hair.

Athal resumed his speech:

'You can even act without me, spying Eglon through the audio visual equipment and the computer we're going to receive for the secret room under the cold room. Microphones and cameras will be installed in the villa. It will be possible to check the hard disk on Eglon's computer remotely and to know the content of his messaging. Eglon knows nothing about computers, I will compose the access codes myself. This way, we'll know the destination of the heroine.

Hemerik – Why should we act without you?

Athal – In the case something will happen to me, if for example, Eglon discovers I have been lying to him since the beginning.

Fredo – You're saying your plan might fail?

Athal – In principle, it should work, but you must never underestimate your enemy and I want to leave you with all the necessary means.

Fredo – How to install cameras in the villas without being seen?

Athal – Most of the cameras will be visible and destined to survey the surroundings of the villa. We'll also place them before the main entrances and inside each room to guarantee security. We'll capture their signals in our secret room. Only three cameras will be hidden behind one-way angled mirrors at the top of the walls of the control room where the computer will be. They'll be invisible and will have to be set with the utmost discretion. They'll transmit images only to us on monitors in the secret room, even if the electricity in the villa will be cut. We'll put microphones behind false air vents far away enough of the true ones where the air conditioning will circulate.'

Silence again. Linda shook the towel for the last time, and tapped her feet to remove my light brown hair clinging to her boots. Kelia, who had accompanied her sister to school entered to join us under the covered area. She made big eyes discovering my shaved head and spoke to Athal:

'Eglon is screaming like a madman, he's furious, he's insulting us!

Really? If he needs something, why doesn't he call me through the walkie-talkie?

He doesn't need anything, but he's complaining that the cleaned and ironed lattice we gave them became too light.

Too light?

Yes, they became white striped apple green.

This is because of the bleach used for disinfection, you should have put less.

What can we do?

Nothing at all. Let him scream and continue to ruin his life!

9 — Disconnection

Thursday, May 22, 1997

Still no cargo. That morning, in front of the bunkers, I received from sergeant Gontran's hands the fiftieth worksheet for the organization of the teams. Never had this form appeared to me so empty, Gontran's head so sad and the sky so dark. The morale of our occupants was at its lowest. The delay of the cargo imposed us all kinds of savings. The fishery was now banned because the boat used by our fishermen was a former modified tug with engines that consumed too much fuel. The generator had to be programmed to stop three times for an hour during the night. According to Athal, these nightly power cuts did not affect the food preservation in the cold rooms.

The training of the *Blue* had finished, still with no permission to carry guns. As it rained often, no one went to the fields anymore and the breeders drew on food reserves from the attics and basements of the technical rooms for the animals.

Around eleven o'clock, the wind blew more violently, Etienne suggested not to venture outside. The same message was sent to me by walkie-talkie from Athal: 'no one is to go outside, everyone in his quarters until new orders!'. We recovered the beds remaining in the isolation tent, dismantled the truck tarpaulin and put to cover anything we could. Life was organized inside the buildings. The family heads made provisions in the kitchens, we ate everywhere, we sang, we prayed, waiting for the end of the cyclone.

Friday, May 23, 1997

The wind calmed down around ten o'clock. Eglon ordered an evaluation report of the damages. Around noon, Athal, who was coming back after having checked the villa, joined us for the first time at our table. He had just gotten the authorization to carry guns for the new recruits. I had the list of damages made by the storm, composed by Hemerik and Fredo. Reading it, Athal told us that the Internet station was out of order, the satellite dishes broken away. Everywhere, twigs and branches littered the ground. Some trees had fallen, the roof of the south courtyard completely detached, the isolation tents and the disinfection ones from the entrance of the bunkers, flown away. The sun reappeared. No worksheet was written that day, the people organized themselves the cleaning and repairs after lunch.

Monday, May 26, 1997

After the end of the cyclone it didn't rain anymore and the autumn temperature was still mild. The people, seated in the dry courtyard to have lunch, like before. Athal had taken the habit of eating at our table at noon, and had dinner in his bunker in the evening. But that day, he had stayed in the infirmary to test an anesthetic, and according to Linda who had prepared the injectable solution, it was necessary to resume the experiment at a later date. I remarked to Etienne that Athal was taking a lot of risks and that his proximity to us could arouse a certain suspicion of the enemies in our regard. Etienne hesitated before answering:

'We're in a situation that is beyond us. Athal has fully committed to fight against our occupants in proposing us a way of conduct that we're trying to follow. But our enemies are unpredictable even if they seem to trust us. What will their reaction be when they'll learn the truth about our intentions? They'll understand at some point. Athal is

148

counting on the time that passes to discourage them, but this time also passes for us. We're starting to lack everything, our fields are barren and the radio isn't working and can't inform us of the cargo that still hasn't arrived, and then if Eglon is suspicious of us, so what? The situation won't be more explosive! May God prepare us to follow his will!'

A heavy silence accompanied this noon meal. No tension, no worries with this Christian people, but a long, strange wait was making the adults quiet, most of all the farmers who had never left such a large arable land fallow. Only the children were talking.

Nellie, seated at my left, had brought me her geography book. Kelia, at my right, hurried to open it at the page with *France* (this country was making her dream!), to comment on the colored photos. The Eiffel Tower, the Arch of Triumph, Champs Elysées... The text was talking about the different climates of the world and Kelia often asked me the same questions as soon as she found something concerning my country: *'Do you know this place? Have you already seen this or did you do that?'*

Nellie's attention was on another subject. She grew impatient, asking her big sister to turn the pages until the chapter with the *North and South Pole.* The young girl's eyes devoured the photos with snowy landscape. We could see igloos, European children were building a snowman and a winter sports resort. At each question asked by Nellie, Kelia tried to answer before me.

'Nellie – If we can slide on snow, how can we keep it and built walls for the igloos and statues?

Kelia – We don't say 'statue', but 'snowman'.

Me – Uhm... the snow becomes hard when we tighten it between our hands and this way, we can gather it to make walls or snowmen. If a mound is rolled on the ground, it becomes a ball growing larger which is used to build, but if we walk on it or is rolled over with vehicles, it becomes compact and slippery. It can also harden and turn into ice under the effect of freezing.' *(Silence)*

The girls looked at me with a thoughtful air. Visibly, my explanations weren't convincing!

'*Nellie* – Can we eat it? Is it good?

Kelia – It doesn't have any taste, it looks like the ice in the cold room.

Me – Yes, it tastes like water, since it's solidified water.

Kelia – It's like ice except it's white, powdery, sticky and slippery, while ice is just slippery.

Nellie – The ice in the cold rooms, it's not snow.

Me – No, it resembles it because it's white, but it's rather a sort of ice, harder and stickier than snow. This said, the more the snow is lighter, the more it sticks.

Nellie – If we mix ice, frost and snow in a bowl, what will it turn out? Everything will stick together?

Kelia – Yes, and if we warm this mix, it's going to become water!'

◆ ◆ ◆

The afternoon passed slowly, under a pale and timid sun announcing winter approaching. Time seemed to stop. The roof of the south courtyard had been half fixed with sheets found whole.

Fredo and his team were trying to make the Internet station work again after having found the satellite dishes that had been carried away. Behind the building near the beach, all the clothes lines were covered with clothes and materials hung to dry.

Life was frozen in Kheo, making economies with everything, even movement! We would often stop the generator by monitoring the gauge. Only one cold room was still functioning, the others were empty. The farmers had finished cleaning all the trenches, waiting. There was no radio contact with the outside anymore, no more fuel in the tank of the fishing boat, no more kerosene in the helicopters, no more rum in Eglon's bottles and no more motivation in his mercenaries!

10 – Dangerous delivery

Thursday, May 29, 1997

At the end of this afternoon, I found myself behind the building and I was talking to Linda and Kelia, busy hanging laundry from the last wash. I approached the cart being loaded with clothes as they advanced. A little further away on the beach, children were coming out of the school, were running towards the obstacle course which had become their favorite game field. Suddenly, two of them came towards us exclaiming: 'A boat!... Look, a boat is coming!' Beside the metal skeleton of the platform, a huge boat was waiting, immobile.

'*Linda* – But, for how long has it been there? No one saw it?'

I immediately informed Athal via the walkie-talkie I always had on my shoulder.

'*Athal* – A boat? Yes, I see it, it's a container carrier, I'll let Eglon know! It's unbelievable, the guard posted on the roof of the bunker didn't say anything! They're all sleeping in there! Let the others know, go to the pier!'

◆ ◆ ◆

Eglon climbed first in the zodiac, followed by Athal and myself. Athal gave my walkie-talkie to Fredo with some instructions:

'Put the last liters of fuel in the tank of the fishing ship, take a rope and shackles and join us near the platform. We'll maintain radio contact.

Understood.

You'll wait for Gontran and his team that will embark with you! Eglon added.

Yes colonel.'

We headed towards the ship and I could hear Eglon vociferating, while Athal was trying to convince him that the container carrier was too big to get any closer. Our *zodiac* stopped at the foot of the ladder, especially unfolded for us. According to Athal, this boat measured 240 meters long. On its rusty bank, you could read the inscription: "*SS Westward Venture*". A side opening in the middle of its hull was used for loading the containers through a ramp.

On the deck, a dozen men of the crew, of white race, were observing with stupefaction the remains of the platform. Some had binoculars. Eglon moved behind them screaming: 'Where is the Pasha?' At the same moment, the captain, in his fifties (also of white race) appeared and answered as dryly: 'I'm here Eglon, we have been waiting for two hours! Do you think I have time to waste in this shitty corner? Don't you ever answer to the radio?

It's broken. And don't start pissing me off, Michal, because I too am tired of waiting for my containers! What were you doing in Dar es Salam? Were you painting the giraffe? It's enough for me not to be there for everything to get ruined!

Yeah, and I return you the question, what happened here? Is it Beirut? Everything is fucked and we can't even contact you on the Internet!

A cyclone destroyed our station and a submarine attacked our platform! Achab is dead and three-quarters of his staff as well.' *(Silence)*

The two men calmed down, observing the pile of scrap with the other sailors. Michal continued:

'I know you were the victim of an attack, I found this out from a member of the *Geometrix* staff.

I paid them to shut up, and there was one who spilled the beans anyway!

I didn't even want to believe it!

My neither, it's the radio silence that pushed me to come here.

It's hot in Zaire, Laurent-Désiré Kabila took over, Mobutu is out of the picture, it's bad for our business. Still, when are you planning to return there?

It's not your concern, mine either! I won't involve myself in any insurgent movement. I don't want to hear talk of Africa anymore and I ask you to remain discreet on the event that happens, my men mustn't know!

Oh, yeah? And your colleagues that are waiting for you at Dar es Salam, what am I going to tell them? And where is the medicine and the weapons?

The Zairians don't need anything now that they have democracy!

I see. On the contrary, what I don't understand, it's how we're going to transship the containers without docking and without crane.

Our fishing boat will arrive any minute now. We'll fasten a rope on the two parts of the bottom corners of each container, to drag them to the beach.

You want to swing your containers just like that? Are you completely mad?

(The two men raised their voices)

I don't have any other alternatives since you refuse to approach the end of the pier!

Absolutely not, with an eight meters draft, I'm not taking that risk!

I'm sure it would be alright, the *Geometrix* always docks there!

Yes, but it's a tanker much smaller than my container carrier! I won't move from here!

So be it. My men are coming, we'll begin the maneuver!

Aren't you afraid your containers will sink?

They won't sink, they're waterproof. Goodbye! I'll leave you with my mercenaries, they'll know what to do.'

Eglon began descending down the ladder, for signaling us to follow. Without even turning, he made a last recommendation to the captain:

'I won't need your services anymore, be discreet about Africa.

What will you do now, you're abandoning *Achab industry*?

It's the war, Michal, and like in all wars, there are winners and losers! Me, I'm trying to limit the damages in recovering my things. Forget about me and forget what you see here!'

Our *zodiac* met the fishing boat on board which were Fredo, Gontran and his soldiers. Upon our arrival on the coast, Athal, Etienne and Hemerik organized the receiving of the containers. Athal borrowed me his binoculars to show me the containers falling in the water under the side opening of the cargo. It was surprising to see these huge metal boxes dive, disappear for a moment and then return to the surface, leaving a quarter of their height above the foam of the waves! The container was hoisted on the rocks of the jetty, then dragged across the beach by the backhoe loader where it sank into the sand. At nightfall, the delivery was completed and the SS Westward Venture rose anchor.

Friday, May 30

Exceptionally, that night, the Blue stood guard close to the beach to watch the precious cargo. At early morning, they returned their assault weapons at the entrance of the bunker and went to sleep. The sky was dim, but it wasn't raining.

The presence of this refueling gave energy to all and a glimmer of joy brightened the look of the cynical colonel.

We formed teams. For the first time, my name was written on the worksheet! I was invited to get my work order from Eglon himself, who was waiting for me with documents.

'Max!

Hello my colonel.

Here is the list with all the material you're going to take to Athal's bunker.

A specific material?

Absolutely, this concerns the future laboratory. Take two negroes to help you.

This material is found in what container?

You'll find this in the ones that contain fuel and food. Poppy seed bags are with the bags of rice. The remaining goods are stored in boxes mixed with other filled cans, dried fruits and vegetables.

Alright. What is in the other containers?

One contains electronic equipment, windows and everything concerning the villa and the other agricultural equipment including a partially disassembled tractor. You won't take care of this. Other questions?

Uhm… no my colonel, everything is clear.

Then get to work. Let me know as soon as everything is stored and check well your list!

Yes colonel.'

I wasn't impressed by Eglon and carefully avoided to answer him in the manner of Gontran: *'at your orders, my colonel'*. I didn't feel like a military man! As all my friends were busy discharging the other products according to their kind, I appointed two farmers at random to help me.

We opened the containers. About ten centimeters of water escaped without having done any harm, for everything inside was resting on pallets. Athal had predicted everything!

The two farmers put all the products from my list on a portion of beach not too close to the crowd:

Alcohol, ether, hydrochloric acid, sulfuric acid, anhydride acetic acid, sodium carbonate, ammonium chloride, chloroform, lime, activated carbon, poppy seeds, twelve gas stoves, pots, utensils destined for the future laboratory equipment. Everything was there, in accordance to my list and we were finished at the beginning of the afternoon. Two hours of waiting had been necessary to finally be able to have the truck with the driver!

Just before nightfall, our products were stored in Athal's bunker and I gave back my list to Eglon: mission accomplished! We were exhausted.

Crossing the quarry, we heard the rumbling of an engine resound under the porch. A motorcyclist approached us in a cloud of dust. It was Athal. He stopped right next to me to frighten me and told me: 'Look Jerome, this bike is for you! It's a *Yamaha Virago* of 125 cubic centimeters.'

A bike? But why?

You're going to need it to go to the different sites on the island.

But, is this really necessary?

Absolutely, there's room for two. You'll be able to take Kelia, but it's understood that this is your work vehicle, no question of leaving it to our occupants! Is it clear?

Very clear!

Hop up behind me, I'll take you home!

No, thanks, I would rather accompany my two friends who have helped me all day.

As you wish. I'll leave it in front of the infirmary. Good evening to everyone and see you tomorrow!

Good evening.'

Everything was discharged. The farming equipment remained outside and the half dismantled tractor rested before Hemerik and Fredo's mechanical workshop.

11 – Suspicion

As soon as the sun was up, all the community went to work. The unfolding of the events would depend on the setting of the agricultural equipment. It was a race against time before winter. Eglon would have wanted the earth to be plowed and seeded before the rains. He prowled restlessly in the square around the spare parts that stretched before Fredo and Hemerik's workshop. They were doing all they could, helped by a dozen farmers, converted assistance-mechanics for the occasion. Athal, who didn't want to see the pressure mount between the officer and Hemerik, tried to set them apart, suggesting to Eglon to come see the plans for the renovation of the villa. The colonel accepted after a short hesitation.

Athal showed himself reassuring towards our enemies, he organized a big barbecue in front of the bunkers and opened a case of tequila to cheer up the soldiers who had been desperately short of rum for a few days now!

In the courtyard, everyone was working. The mechanical arm of the backhoe loader was used to lift the tractor temporarily resting on ski-shaped ramps. The wheels and the cabin were mounted towards the evening. Even if the connections weren't finished, the machine began to resemble a tractor.

Sunday, June 1, 1997

Right after the service, the mechanical works began anew under Eglon's watchful eye and of some onlookers. Hemerik and Fredo finished alone the last preparations, late into the night.

Monday, June 2, 1997

At nine o'clock in the morning, the engine of *New Holland M135* began growling for the first time. All our occupants were present in full. Fredo was at the wheel and began working. An hour later, a true deluge fell on Kheo!

◆ ◆ ◆

It rained almost all the month of June! The few times when the rain stopped were too short to allow the land to dry. Eglon was furious. He passed all his days in the villa working on a computer, for the Internet connection had been restored. He wasn't interested at all in the village, which allowed Fredo and his small team of farmers to completely finish the audiovisual installations in the secret room under the cold room.

Hemerik and Fredo led the works in the villa and finished the connection of the telephone and electricity networks in the trench between their site and the village. Around the end of the month, the rain stopped. Three hundred people were assigned to take part in the renovation of the building, which also ended in late June.

At the beginning of July, the trench of networks was closed and the tractor began to work on Wednesday, July 8. The drivers were maneuvering the engine in turns, changing every two hours. The work lasted sixteen hours a day. The farmers approached the bags of poppy seeds and the planter of four meters was attached to the tractor on Tuesday, July 22. The seeds looked like black flour.

At the end of the month, after the planting, the family heads took possession of their plots, according to the consolidation plan established by Athal. Each plot was defined by 265 small alleys, fifty centimeters wide. We passed the rake to properly bury the seeds, we unrolled the water hoses...

Tuesday, August 5, 1997

This day was the coldest one this winter. The temperature grazed eight degrees at dawn and children were wearing hats and scarves. Each one had warmly dressed under their red suits. Eglon didn't want the people to have access to the Internet and the computers of the school only served for word processors and for teaching, using educational software. Thus, Athal and Etienne discreetly proposed to those who wanted the possibility to look at the world by using the material in the secret room. The news spread and all the inhabitants of Kheo wanted to be initiated in discovering the unknown through computer screens! To manage this crowd of curious people, Etienne asked for the help of Nicodeme's assistants, in order to make a waiting list. Half hour sessions per person took place all night, in all tranquility, since the *Blue* were the only guards allowed to take the night watch. Among all these new enthusiasts, some asked the organizers to print some pictures and documents that they carefully preserved from the enemy's knowledge. A limit had to be put due to economy reasons. Only Kelia managed to obtain a greater number of pages, insisting near Hemerik who cracked under her beautiful pleading look! Actually, the two brothers were in the secret room each morning at five o'clock to provide an update and check Eglon's email. Kelia, who loved to wake up early, had taken the habit to join them. As for me, I got up around five thirty only to take breakfast with them. After that, I went to look for my worksheet *service order* with my photo from Gontrant in front of his bunker.

One day, Kelia showed me her large collection of printed pages, arranged in a folder. There were a handful photos in black and white representing all the monuments of Paris and numerous French touristic curiosities! She also wanted to learn how to drive my bike. I accepted by suggesting the quarry site for training. I had a few scares

159

during the part of changing gears, for if she knew how to maintain the balance on two wheels, dosing the acceleration and using the commands was completely new for her. When her attention wasn't on these maneuvers, the bike's course was deviated and she sometimes ended the race in piles of sand or bushes. But the student had such a wish to learn everything, nothing discouraged her! Children observed the movements of this strange motorized bike as soon as they heard the engine backfire. When my friend mastered the machine, some toddlers had the privilege to mount behind her to do a lap in the square, but Nellie was still a priority.

♦ ♦ ♦

For some time, in the moment to sit down at the table, I noticed that Rose-Marie and Mado were wearing loose clothing and it was more difficult to straddle the bench. It seemed to me they were pregnant. As I didn't dare ask, I discreetly asked Nellie who answered in a loud voice:
'Yes, Mado and Rose-Marie will have a baby!
And they're not the only ones, added Linda who had heard Nellie's reply, other nine women are pregnant!'
I found out that Rose-Marie was 22 years old and Mado 38. Before, they had refused to have children, scared of having them taken. The dictator Achab sold them for adoption. Just after the tyrant's death, most families wanted to grow bigger!
Around the end of August, the poppy plants sprang up. Everything seemed to work perfectly, according to our occupants' wishes who had, it looked like, gained our trust! But behind this apparent quietness, a suspicion was germinating. Athal called for me on Thursday, August 28, at the end of the afternoon, near the pier to talk to me:
'Eglon worries me, he refuses to see me, he's drinking more and more, he isolates himself in the villa that he has his morons guard it like a fortress.

Do you think he doubts anything?

Yes, consulting his hard drive, I discovered a lot of worrying information in regard to my father's bank accounts in Mexico.

I thought Eglon had cut all ties with *Achab industry* to reclaim his independence?

At the beginning, yes, but afterwards he tried to reestablish contact with the Horsewoman to ask for financial aid, which was refused.

The Horsewoman? Who is it?

The head of the bank, a woman of my father's age that was his mistress for several years.

According to you, this woman refused Eglon's proposition?

Because she doesn't need him to get rich and she doesn't trust him.

Drug trafficking doesn't interest her anymore? When your father was still alive, the business was running well, no?

Sure, but without the platform, all current affairs were interrupted and as you already know, clients were still waiting for their orders and this could well lead to retaliation against Eglon. The Horsewoman doesn't want to get mixed in all this and Eglon's efforts will never allow what *Achab industry* knew before. Moreover, this woman has always dealt in traffic with my father, even if she didn't love him anymore. a certain loyalty still remained between them by remembering the obstacles that they had overcome together to set up their affairs.

A sort of code of honor?

In some way, but Eglon means nothing to her and as I told you, she doesn't need him.

The "Horsewoman", is it her true name?

It's a nickname. I don't know her real name. This is in connection with her questionable activities. She is the queen of cheating the financial markets. She built a pyramid scam based on lies that consist in paying the high interests of her existent clients thanks to the capital provided by the new ones, themselves attracted by the reputation of these hefty pseudo-investments!

But doesn't no one notice anything?

As long as no one claims the money they placed, this gigantic scam will go unnoticed. But the day her clients will need cash and they will want to remove them at the same time, this pyramid will collapse.

How does this concern us?

Eglon is investigating and sticks his nose everywhere. He's feeling more and more alone and threatened. He found out the transactions from his account in France, he knows for example that a certain Jerome Valentin received a large sum of money from the part of *Achab industry* and that I was the one who made it.

Is this the reason you wanted to call me Max?

Yes, and if Max was hired by Achab, why isn't his file found? Why would a submarine shoot our platform? What would their profit be after an attack? These are questions without answer that irritate Eglon. He may lose his patience.

You want to say we're in danger?

Yes, and my idea to find him alone in his villa to make him submit and we'll inject him the sedative, falls! It's not possible to approach him anymore!

What do you want me to do and why don't you talk to the others?

I want to give you the responsibility to take the people to shelter of our enemies, you'll explain yourself the situation to Etienne and all his family.

But why? You're abandoning your commitment? Why should I assume everything on my own?

I want to be honest with you: you're risking to find yourself alone in a short while. I know Eglon, he's a criminal. My father and him, before I was born, killed several negroes to make themselves obeyed. Then they began to build the platform in 1966. I know Eglon's path and his way of thinking. He'll neutralize me and you'll have to continue the fight without me.

You know everything, but you still made an error of judgment since your sedative project falls!

No, I also took this possibility into account!

Really? In this case, why didn't you tell me?

Because you would have never accepted to find yourself the only mediator between our enemies and the people, I showed you the sedative project to reassure you and not to leave you without any solution faced with the enemy. It's your and your friends' turn to continue the fight, you have all the necessary means and you all have the abilities that you underestimate! May God bless you!

But Athal, where are you going?

I'm returning to my bunker passing by the forest. Take courage, after all this is over, it's going to show I was right about everything. Later!'

Athal left me alone and headed towards the forest at the end of the beach, behind the training course. He wasn't his usual self, he seemed to sense really difficult days. I was shocked by all these words and decided to go inform Etienne's family during dinner. Back in the courtyard, I met Kelia who asked me to loan her my bike. A little surprised, I asked her:

'You want it to go where?

Uhm... Hemerik would like to borrow it so he learn to drive it.

Really? Why didn't he ask me?

Uhm... He would like me to show him the way to use it at the site of the quarry. He'll learn fast since he already knows how to drive a truck!

OK, you may take it, but be careful.

Thank you so much! After that, I'm sure he'll accept to print me new images of France!

I see! Later.'

Kelia straddled the bike and stopped in front of the mechanical workshop. Hemerik got out right away and took a seat behind her. Both of them disappeared by the porch.

♦ ♦ ♦

A little before dinner, when I was still at the table with Etienne, the bike, driven by Hemerik came back in all speed in front of the workshop, priming spectacular controlled drifts. Kelia, frightened and sitting behind Hemerik, clutched him, laughing hard. He stopped the engine in a cloud of dust and took his passenger's hand to help her descend and accompanied her to our table. Coming near me, he gave me Kelia's hand who was still folding with laughter, exclaiming:

'Jerome, the tourist, I give you back your fiancée in one piece!'

Me – Thank you. I appreciate the fact my bike also seems to be still intact!

Linda (finishing to bring the meal trays) – Hemerik, do you find it amusing, all this cloud of dust we now have on this table?

Etienne – You should be ashamed! That machine isn't a toy, it's dangerous to drive that way!

Hemerik – Bah! I control her well! It brakes much better than a bicycle, you should try it!

Etienne – Certainly not... in any case, not in this fashion!

Me – This bike came without a helmet. In France, wearing a helmet is mandatory, and a driving license is necessary to drive this kind of bike.

Nicodeme – A driving license to pilot a bike? It's strange!

Etienne – OK, if everyone is here, I'm going to say grace.'

No one found Athal's presence abnormal since he only ate with us at noon. Still, I was sure he wouldn't come back and towards the middle of the meal, I decided to repeat

164

everything he had told me near the pier. My friends listened to me carefully without worry.

After dinner, Etienne picked those he wanted to invite to an evening of prayer in the secret room. The chosen people were: Etienne, Linda, Hemerik, Fredo and me. The pastor wanted the information to stay between us as to not panic the people. Kelia stayed with us and asked Etienne to accept her in our group. The man refused, but my friend insisted, and cried: 'Pastor, don't leave me out, I know we'll have to conspire against these criminals, they killed my parents, I'm doubly concerned. I want to take part in your meetings, I will involve myself in everything we can possibly to do against these people! *(silence)* They killed my family, they're polluting our island with their filth of radioactive waste, cultivating poison, insulting us, mocking God!

Etienne stopped dead and turned towards Kelia. Without saying anything, he hugged her. Then, she gave me her hand and we continued towards the cold rooms.

Hemerik opened the hatch and we went down into the technical room. We had to go lower, as the secret room measured only five feet high for an area of six square meters. Three big computer screens and two speakers were placed on a high shelf, near the ceiling. Below, a table that had been built on place with pallet boards was covered with numerous devices, keyboards, computers, table for mixing, a smaller screen, a printer. Fredo was making adjustments, sitting next to his brother. Etienne, Linda, Kelia and I were also behind them on a bench fixed against the wall.

Fredo scrolled on the screen all the images from the cameras placed around the house and on the inside of the main rooms. Outside, everything was calm and lighted by neons that attracted mosquitoes. The electric shutters were all closed. Fredo made sure that our three screens retransmitted the signal of the cameras hidden behind the oblique mirrors in the living. We saw Eglon dozing, sitting on his leather sofa. A bottle of tequila, a glass, a walkie-talkie and files were on the short glass table in front of him. We could distinguish the whole room under different angles. This place was his headquarters that he left only to go eat and sleep in neighboring rooms. In front of the officer there was the control desk with eight screens that were in correlation with the external cameras. The desk and the computer, connected to the network of the one in our secret room was in front of the large bay window overlooking the terrace.

As soon as Eglon was away from his computer, it was possible for us to consult his inbox, his hard drive and connect to the Internet. It's what Fredo and his brother did each night.

Etienne started praying out loud and invited us to do the same. That evening, no decision was made on how to act against our enemies. But in their hearts, ideas started germinating!

12 – Confrontation

Friday, August 29, 1997

As was to be expected, Athal was absent at five o'clock in the morning. Scared, I took my bike to go look for the worksheet from Gontran, as usual. I was expecting to get stopped and be submitted to an interrogation any minute now. The sergeant gave me the sheet that had been simplified and I left without being attacked… and without delay! Passing in front of Athal's bunker, I saw in front of his closed door a soldier sitting on a folding chair. On road, I crossed the truck driven by Fredo, carrying breakfast to the soldiers.

I showed Etienne the sheet. It resembled more like a service note than a planning! We understood that the only important thing for Eglon was the poppy cultivation. Everything else had no interest for him now and we had white card to organize everything. Obviously, Athal's signature wasn't on the document!

Etienne gathered one last time our little prayer group in the infirmary before starting the day. I was becoming the only mediator between them and our enemies and we decided to submit by continuing the works like nothing had changed. Hemerik finished our little reunion by telling me: 'Do what you have to do and if you decide to plot against them, we're at your disposal to help you.'

Plot? In what way? The *Blue* didn't have the right to carry weapons anymore. Eglon was losing his trust in us. It was impossible for me to decide anything during the whole month that followed. I was worried.

♦ ♦ ♦

The winter rains flooded the crops during the two first weeks of September, before giving way to the first spring sweetness. The minimum temperature was of 12 degrees in the morning and could go up to 16 in the afternoon.

Consulting Eglon's e-mail, Fredo discovered a correspondence with a group of six Colombians. They had once worked for *Achab industry* on the platform and in a clandestine laboratory. But they had been "cut off" by the Horsewoman who didn't want to hear talk of them. Eglon knew this and had heard that these men were looking to be hired. He proposed them to go take them by helicopter at Mahe airport at the beginning of November.

The situation seemed to get worse faster at the beginning of September. Kelia was more distant towards me and passed all her spare time with Hemerik. They both cleaned the granary above the technical places destined for animal food storage, without informing me. Every day, Kelia accompanied Fredo in the truck to give the meals to the soldiers. They were rather idle.

167

Gontran was missing authority and Eglon wasn't leaving the villa anymore. The soldiers took advantage and behaved themselves terribly towards the people, allowing the *Blue* to come back (who were passing all the night to stand watch) at the bunkers in the afternoon to make them do all sorts of chores like cleaning and maintenance of chemical toilets.

◆ ◆ ◆

Around a month later, it was decided to weed the aisles that gridded the cultures. The poppies were beginning to flourish and measured one meter in height. I slowly crossed by bike the operation when suddenly, an elderly farmer around fifty years old motioned me to stop to talk to me. He seemed anxious.

'Jerome, the tourist!

Yes, hello.

Hello. Do you know about my girl?

No, I don't think I know her.

Two soldiers came to look for her to take her to sergeant Gontran. They claimed it was an order of the colonel and that you knew about it!

But... never in my life! How long ago did they leave and which way did they go?

About ten minutes ago, they took the direction of the quarry, but tracked back into the forest at the end of the central path! They're armed.

I see. Stay here, I'm going to look for your daughter!'

I didn't know how I would intervene, but I was driving with my head down, making my bike scream. The situation really escaped me and I was feeling guilty for not having tried to attack our enemies since Athal's forced departure.

Everything passed very quickly. I noticed a soldier who was pointing an automatic pistol at me displaying a

168

mocking smile. As I was heading towards him, he vainly went to the side to avoid me and slipped against the slope that ran along the road. My bike reared by climbing the slope and fell heavily on my assailant while I was thrown over the handlebars. The branches of a bush deadened my fall.

While the first soldier stuck under my machine was screaming in pain, I met the second one: the biggest and most muscled of all. He was a former legionnaire, so strong that everyone was afraid. His skull was bald and his small black eyes threw flashes at me. His mouth, topped with a small mustache, twisted with hatred. He leaned towards me with contempt. I saw the naked, scratched back of the farmer's daughter, sitting at his feet. She was standing there, still and hunched with her head against her knees. I tried to talk with this monster to attract his attention hoping the young woman would take advantage and run:

'Hey, big moron, aren't you ashamed to attack a girl without defense?

You should have never said that, you fucking Max!

What a man! Neutralizing a weak black woman, what a proof of virility!

I'm going to hurt you!

You're tough because you're holding a knife, but what do you know to do without it?'

His look landed on the knife in his arm, his brain was trying to think. His comrade stuck under my machine cried:

'Jo, what are you waiting for? Come get me out, hurry! I'm hurting! Damn it! Jo, never mind those two and come get me out of here!'

After a few seconds of deep reflection, the man put away his combat knife. He grabbed my clothes and threw me on the path like I was a feather. I landed face down against the ground so violently that I was out of breath.

I don't know how much time it took me to find my breath again. I spat earth. On my knees, I assisted, despite me, to a show I will not soon forget! My attacker slowly lifted my racing bike under the screams of his colleague whose thigh appeared to be attached to the motor! It pulled away in one go, revealing the axis of the bloodied speed changer! I understood the piece was strung in his thigh! The mastiff then threw my bike next to me. He hoisted the injured man on his back warning me: 'If you'll tell the colonel, I'll kill you, with or without knife! You got it?' He then disappeared between the trees.

The young woman hadn't moved one centimeter and didn't answer any question. I put my track jacket on her back scratched by the monster's knife. I noticed drops of blood were running from my nose and decided to go look for the farmer to take care of his daughter.

Straightening the bike, I felt a strong gasoline smell. I gave up firing the engine, for fear of fire. I went down the road, holding to the bars of my machine, when I heard the young girl approach behind me. She resembled Kelia, but her face was more round. She walked leaning a little in the front. Her arms, resting on her bare stomach, her arms were holding my jacket and the shreds of her red suit. She hurried and said her first words in a hoarse voice: 'They tore my clothes. I didn't want to get undressed!' Below, at the edge of the woods, her father ran to meet her.

♦ ♦ ♦

'The tank is pierced!' noticed Hemerik, removing the earth hanging to the flank of my *Yamaha Virago*. He returned to his workshop staring at me. 'And you must have the wounded face I advise you to go immediately to see my mother, it's her job!

Yes, my nose is hurting, but it could have been worse. One had a gun, the other a knife!

You should have called me! You took too many risks!

170

I know, but I had to act quickly. I was afraid for the young girl.

This can't go on, we'll have to act.

We have to treat the soldier who is wounded at the thigh.

Yeah, but first you have to treat yourself, we'll accompany my mother to the bunker, there's no question that those morons monopolize our nurse!'

♦ ♦ ♦

Linda noticed my nose was broken and she put a bandage that I had to keep for several days. She accompanied us in the truck to the bunkers to take care of my attacker. The wounded was waiting in his bed, someone had made a tourniquet to stop the bleeding. Stitches, dressings, injection, perfusion, instructions... Linda finished her work in silence. Gontran had evacuated the bunker and remained alone with us. I was afraid he would order the nurse to stay at the bedside of the wounded for several days. So, I proposed to Gontran to leave him my walkie-talkie so she could be alerted at the first sign of a problem. The sergeant accepted and told me I was called by his colonel on Monday, October 27 at ten o'clock. I found this very troubling and I tried to reassure myself by thinking that this convocation only concerned the organization of the harvest.

The treatments being completed, Fredo started the truck and we set off with a heavy heart, passing by the closed and guarded door of Athal's bunker.

♦ ♦ ♦

As each evening, our usual little group gathered in the secret room. Kelia was very affected by the dramatic events that she had heard about and cried against me. I wasn't unhappy she had chosen my shoulder rather than that of Hemerik to cry on!

The time had come to make a move, the enemy was becoming too menacing. I told my plan to my friends:

'I know I can count on you. I think Eglon is becoming dangerous, but I don't want to be impressed during this meeting on Monday. Hemerik and Fredo, I ask you to distribute a fuel container and a box of matches to each family head. That everyone waits in his plot. Hemerik will stay near the bunkers. If I don't come out alive of the bunker at the end of fifteen minutes, Hemerik will give the signal to Fredo who will honk five times from the truck. When the family heads will hear this signal, they'll pour fuel and light their plot. Attention will have to be paid so that no one will be trapped by the flames, let the plots above be lit first and then the others, progressively.' *(Silence)*

'If Hemerik will see me come out alive, he'll signal Fredo to honk only one time. Agree on the signals.

How many liters of fuel for family head? asked Fredo.

A liter minimum, three maximum, the poppy stems will be dry enough to ignite. With such a number of fires started, it won't be possible to stop it!

Yes, but I don't think they'll take the risk of losing the harvest. The threat of destroying it must be real for them. We have to show ourselves credible and determined. From here on out, the poppy will become our exchange coin to get from them everything we want.'

Monday, October 27, 1997, 9h45

The bike was fixed. I used it for all my travels. I was afraid this one would be my last.

All our plan was in place. The farmers were crouching in their plots. Each one had received a bottle, a bowl or a can containing gasoline. I stopped voluntarily close to the door of Athal's bunker to try to approach him. The guard, seated on a folding chair, intervened without even looking at me: 'No one goes in, no one goes out! Colonel's order!'

172

I heard Gontran's voice behind me, at the door of the bunker in front: 'Through here, Max!'

I stepped over the dog who was sleeping and saw that there was only Eglon sitting behind a table on which they had prepared a bottle of tequila and a single cup. I wasn't expecting him to drink with me!

He made me sit down and asked Gontran to close the door. The sergeant remained standing next to me and Eglon began the interrogation:

'Your friend Athal and you, you took me for a fool! There never was a submarine! I would like to understand what you're up to!...'

During the colonel's long monologue, I thought about everything Athal had told me: *'If you're afraid in front of your enemy, he mustn't see it, if your enemy is stronger than you, make him believe the contrary, show him you're in charge of the situation, that you know everything about him and that he needs you.'*

As I wasn't answering the questions, the tension mounted. My silence confirmed Eglon's doubts, who said he didn't need me or Athal anymore. The moment had come to "tighten the screw" with the negroes, like in the good old time of Achab and eliminate the parasites like me. I felt the barrel of Gontran's automatic pistol against my temple. I realized in that second that my faith in God banished all fear of death, but I also deplored my lack of a reply! With the energy of someone who has nothing to lose, I began screaming as loud as Eglon:

'You know, Mister Eglon, the poppy isn't yet harvested. A little flame, it comes quickly! And hop! Goodbye harvest! What do you think?

Ah-ah! A little bullet in the head, it also come very quickly!

Come on, Mister Eglon, kill me, and if I don't come out of here in three minutes, eight hundred hectares of poppy will go up in smoke. While I'm talking, 500 liters of gasoline are waiting with 265 matches, my personnel is ready!' *(Silence)*

'He's bluffing, my colonel, screamed Gontran, I'm sure he's bluffing to save his skin!

Lower your arm, said the officer, put your gun away and make him go out.

Yes, my colonel.'

Once outside, Eglon saw Hemerik a little lower, as he did the truck at the entrance of the crops. Walking towards the poppy, I continued to convince my enemies that were seething with rage behind me, unsheathing their weapons:

'Calm down, Eglon, if something happens to me, goodbye harvest! Do you see there, I left my walkie-talkie with Hemerik. If you'll borrow me yours, I can tell my negro friend to cancel everything, but if my friend doesn't hear my sweet reassuring voice, he'll risk getting annoyed by starting the fire!

Yeah, ok, replied Eglon, stop everything and tell me what you want!'

I stopped walking half-way between the bunkers and the crops. Eglon held out his walkie-talkie, addressing Gontran:

'Where are your men?

But, my colonel, you yourself gave them free time!'

After having contacted Hemerik to wait for my signal, I told Eglon my plan:

'Mister Eglon, starting now, you'll have to have faith to continue together. You only have two alternatives. The first is to kill us all. In this case, goodbye harvest. You'll find yourself alone, completely ruined in the middle of an island ravaged by flames and littered with corpses. The second solution, you keep Athal in good health, we'll start to gather the latex. You do what you have to do and you'll get out of here with your harvest after having given Athal back to us. What do you chose?

The second solution! But I don't want your negroes to not get out the poppy right now, with this heat, the gasoline could ignite at any minute!

174

A moment…

What else? For the name of God!

Give me all your firearms!

No way, if we're attacked, I don't want to be without weapons!' *(Silence)*

'So be it, the poppy is in bloom and the earth was sufficiently watered. While my personnel will come out of the field, I'll order to plug the sprinkler pump on a barrel of gasoline out of the sun. Starting now, I forbid you and all your mercenaries to approach the crops. I'll install a string and stakes to limit the plantation, it will be our demarcation line. I'll put up a tent that will serve as guarding post, as well as a camera and projectors. If one of you will mistreat us, or if you hang out in the area… In short, any misstep on your part, and I'll burn everything! Is it clear, Mister Eglon?

Yeah, alright!

Kid, put it on hold, if not…!

I haven't finished! Starting now, the *Blue* won't keep the night watch, they'll remain under my responsibility and if you want sentinels to watch the bunkers and the villa, you have your great, armed warriors. I'm sure they'll also know how to accomplish your chores and clean their toilets themselves! Isn't that right Mister Eglon? *(silence)*. Questions, Mister Eglon?'

The officer fixed me with a hateful look. His forehead was dripping, his jowls quivered with rage and his mouth twisted even more. He launched me his walkie-talkie exclaiming: 'OK, you win! Make your negroes come out of the field and go away! I saw you enough for today!'

A radio message to Hemerik, a horn sigh and all the crowd of farmers moved in the direction of the truck containing the barrels of gasoline. Eglon watched them for a moment with his binoculars, then, after having ripped his walkie-talkie from my hands, turned tail to regain his bunker.

13 – Taking over

Before going to join my friends, I was in a mood to take a little tour on the bike in the forest, on the heights of the island. I left the road between the rabbit clearing and the villa to hide in the bushes. I stopped my bike and walked a few meters. Leaning against a trunk, I breathed deeply, my legs were shaking. I still felt the cold barrel of Gontran's gun against my temple. Even if I wasn't scared of death anymore, brushing against it was impressive! I thanked God, I had found the necessary words to avoid dying. But I didn't think of it as a complete victory! As long as our occupants were armed, the danger was still there!

Upon leaving, I met three women, each having a bucket on their heads. They were very shocked and the youngest one was crying! The oldest called me before even giving me time to question them:

'Jerome the tourist...

Yes, hello, what's happening?

What we saw is unbearable!

What have you seen?

The soldiers, they're mistreating our young ones, they're threatening them with their guns!

What young ones?

Hemerik's young ones, those who stay on guard all the nights.

Where are they? Did they see you?

No, but we, we saw them, they're a little higher, hidden close to the villa.

Don't stay here! Is your farm far from here?

Lower, under that of Kelia, but further back in the forest.

Good, go, don't come back here this morning.'

The two young girls went away, but the oldest seemed to want to talk to me. She gathered her courage to tell me:

'It's terrible, they're making them walk nude, on their knees, all kinds of positions. They're making them cry like animals, they throw earth on them...

Listen, I promise you this will soon end. I ask you to not talk to anyone, not even to the pastor, I'll take care of this!

But when will it end? Until where will these people go?

They won't go any further, if they'll try to begin again, we'll burn the poppy.'

The woman let a tear fall before going to join the two young girls.

◆ ◆ ◆

During the noon meal, Hemerik made me a report with the morning actions. All the gasoline from the containers had been returned in the barrels, the demarcation line was in place. My friends thanked me for the intervention with our enemies. They ignored the content of my negotiations, but they felt reassured. We had accomplished a victory, but the war was not over. Kelia found her smile again.

◆ ◆ ◆

After lunch, Hemerik helped my fiancée wash the dishes. Nellie took advantage to play in the yard. Linda asked me drive her on my bike to the bunker to treat the soldier wounded at his thigh. While she was preparing the materials at the infirmary, Etienne took me aside to talk to me:

'Jerome, look, he told me while giving me an automatic pistol, my brother gave me this!

Where does it come from?

He confiscated it from a student who was showing it to the others during class! The boy pretends to have found it in the forest.

It must be my attacker's gun, the one with a whole in the thigh!

Really? He had lost it that day?

Yes, it was certainly found at the place where my bike was in the accident. Moreover, it's loaded, fortunately the children didn't shoot!

Yes, and I would like my sons to not see it for the moment. If we could still use firearms, I would be pleased. Could you keep it away from the view of others?

Yes, thank you, pastor. I also have something to ask you.

I'm listening.

Now that the demarcation line is finished, I would like the women and children not to go outside the yard and the buildings as long as our enemies are on Kheo and the harvest hasn't begun.

You're right, only the men will go take care of the breeding.

I also have to tell you that the *Blue* have been mistreated this morning by the soldiers. I told Eglon: our youngsters will not keep the night watch anymore and they'll stay with us!

I'm so happy to hear this, those poor boys were like slaves! I don't know how you negotiated all this, but I'm very grateful to you. Thanks to you and thanks to God who grants our prayers!

Thanks to God! We're safe and sound... for the moment!'

♦ ♦ ♦

When the treatment was over in the bunker, Linda and I went back to the infirmary. Gontrant and the few soldiers present kept silent during the whole time of our intervention. I think Eglon made a nice speech! I kept the automatic pistol with me. I was wondering where the *Blue* were and in what state we would find them!

The emotions of the day had exhausted me and as soon as I regained my room, I fell asleep on my bed. Linda was working in the room next door, made into a laboratory.

At the end of the afternoon, I was woken up by Hemerik playing the drums. He hadn't put his headphones on. The loud music attracted children who were dancing in front of the open door of the workshop. Going closer, I saw Kelia wiggling in front of an armchair between the speakers and the drums. I had never seen her dance with such energy and the most surprising, was that she had high heels on. Her red suit was roughly folded at her calves.

When she was nearly exhausted, she fell in the armchair. Hemerik stopped the music and immediately went to take her shoes off. She fell asleep and the children, with no more music to listen to, returned to play a little further away.

Hemerik put the boots on Kelia's feet, who woke up gently. He whispered some words in her ear. She got up from the armchair and noticed me at the entrance of the workshop. They both looked at me surprised and embarrassed. After a long moment of hesitation, Hemerik stammered: 'Jerome, my friend, come in... I invite you to try my drums. Do you know how to play?'

I settled on the round stool behind the drums as if I hadn't seen anything unusual in my friends' behavior. Hemerik rewound the tape and put the same rock music on, then took Kelia's hand to ask her to dance. The discomfort between us disappeared.

A little after, Kelia turned off the player and Hemerik sought my help to cover the instruments and the chair with sheets.

◆ ◆ ◆

The *Blue* entered in the infirmary. Etienne and Linda were encouraging and comforting them. Hemerik and Kelia were dismayed in learning about the humiliation endured by these youngsters. Fortunately, there was no question for them to return under the reign of our enemies and it was a subject of joy that brightened our whole evening.

◆ ◆ ◆

After our usual little prayer in the secret room, I was in a hurry to sleep. No need for guards outside, but an extra camera had been placed under a projector in front of the demarcation line. We had buried a 200 liter drum of gasoline really close by, a device ready to spit on crops by means of a pump activated by a remote control. Volunteers agreed to monitor in turn this new facility overnight.

On the point of falling asleep, I thought again about Hemerik and Kelia. It seemed to me that Hemerik was influencing my fiancée, but the presence of romantic feelings between them seemed unimaginable to me. Despite appearances, I was convinced Kelia loved me. My two friends had known each other forever. Their childhood, their lives were scattered with dramatic moments. Wasn't it normal a certain complicity to appear between them? You could have a big brother taking care of his little sister. I think my loved one was preoccupied and that she was putting our relationship on break. I wasn't jealous, but I was hurting. I was convinced she was hiding something…

14 – Little Red Riding Hood

Tuesday, October 28, 1997

Everything had calmed during the night and Eglon's e-mail told us that the six Colombians would arrive at the Mahe airport on the morning of Monday, November the third.

A little before breakfast, I noticed Kelia occupied in arranging her wet hair, she had removed all the braids. She ate nothing that morning and I found my friends abnormally calm and thoughtful. A strange atmosphere reigned…

I took the bike to inspect the crops. I crossed a man holding a basket. He was coming back from the plot of breeders. On our enemies' side, nothing had changed: a guard was still keeping watch in front of Athal's bunker. Gontran didn't give a worksheet, claiming the independence of our respective camps. According to him, each had to organize their own work.

I was about to leave when I saw the truck with food come. Fredo was doing this with two people, replacing Hemerik and Kelia.

It was at the infirmary that I found my two friends. Linda was also there and had just finished developing an injectable solution. I had some difficulty in recognizing my fiancée, with a completely new look! Her hair was brought up in a bun, placed high on her head. Several small thin strands emerged beneath a broad red headband. A woman was finishing the last makeup touches: orange eye makeup, a light golden foundation that brightened her cheekbones and a pink lipstick made her smile shine. Her dress with short sleeves, smooth stitch and corduroy was red, matching her headband. Her deep neckline in a V was highlighted with a golden belt under the chest whose black and shiny buckle strangely resembled Achab's gear wheel. The base of the slightly flared dress stopped at the knee, black stockings, high-heeled boots, earrings, bracelets, matching watch. She took my breath away! But I was more troubled when I heard Hemerik say: 'You came at the right moment, Jerome, your fiancée needs your bike to go see Eglon! *(Silence)*

Is this a joke?

No, it's time. You must know what we'll do. It's a mission Kelia will accomplish voluntarily and willingly!

You all agree to send my fiancée in the clutches of that madman, don't even think about it! Don't tell the pastor agrees!

My father doesn't know anything, but he'll soon see on the screen in the secret room where we all have to go.'

I crossed the embarrassed looks of Linda and Kelia. The nurse bent in front of my fiancée to put a pen in each of her boots between her legs. Kelia then came towards me to try to convince me. She seemed very determined: 'Jerome, forgive me for having hidden this plan from you. I love you and I didn't want you to worry. The day Athal was sequestered, I decided to do everything in my power to stop these people who are destroying our lives. Hemerik thought of this mission. Trust me and come look for me at the villa when Eglon will be neutralized.'

What could I answer? I was devastated. If I had married her before, I would have dared stop her! I wanted to kiss her, but Linda, faster, approached to hug her. Hemerik got out to prepare the bike and put in the back the basket of the man I had crossed in the crops who was coming back from the breeding plot. We all got out. Hemerik wanted to kiss Kelia who refused saying: 'That's enough! You're going to end up making me cry and it's bad for my makeup!'

She tucked up her dress and climbed on the bike. Folding the stands for a quick heel kick, she gave me a wink and drove slowly to spare her hair. She disappeared by the porch. I heard my friends call me to invite me to join Fredo and Etienne, already ready in the secret room.

Fredo had set the left screen on the new camera under the demarcation line, the one in the middle showed the soldiers keeping guard in front of the entrance gate of the villa and on the one on the right, we saw Eglon putting the food tray on his desk. He had finished his breakfast. Etienne protested: 'You dared throw this poor little one in the arms of that monster!' Then, he turned towards me: 'I'm sorry Jerome, I knew nothing!

Me neither, I answered him, I just found out, like you.

Shhh! said Fredo, shut up!'

Left screen: the bike passed the demarcation line to stop in the middle screen. The two guards approached Kelia and warned Eglon by intercom. The image from the middle passed on the left, the one in the middle and right ones showed the interior of Eglon's living room. Fredo increased the volume to catch all the conversations of the soldiers with their superior:

'My colonel, you have a visit.

I said I didn't want to see anyone!

It's a magnificent black woman who came by bike. She wants to see you.

I don't give a fuck! Make her leave! *(Silence)*

If it's your last word, my colonel, are we authorized to pass a nice moment with her? You should see this, it's not every day we encounter little Red Riding Hood! She insists in offering you two freshly picked pineapples that she brings in her little basket. Too bad for you!

What's this crap! Are you making fun of me?

Not at all, my colonel, see for yourself, I'll position her in front of the camera.'

<u>Left screen</u>: The soldier pushed Kelia under the entrance portico dominated by a surveillance camera.

<u>Middle screen</u>: The image taken by that same camera showed in plain view the angelic face of my fiancée.

<u>Right screen</u>: Eglon got close to his control panel to discover the image transmitted by the camera.

'What does she want? Did she come here alone?

She insists in giving you the fruit with her own hands, my colonel! *(Silence)*

Alright… Before letting her come in, check the content of the basket.

Two pineapples and a large knife, my colonel.

Yeah. Keep the knife and search her as well.

With pleasure, my colonel!

(Two long minutes of thorough search)

It's ok, you obsessed fools, there's no need to search her several times, let her enter and be done with it!

Yes, my colonel, one is never too careful, you know!'

Our three screens showed the inside of the living room: Kelia planted in the middle, holding her basket against her. The guard who had accompanied her hurried to get out while adding:

'She's well curved, the black woman, my colonel, have great fun!

Shut your mouth and close the door behind you, you fool!

183

Yes, my colonel. If you need anything, we're here!

Exactly, I find it odd that she would venture here all by herself. Call Gontran and four armed guards to patrol the surroundings of the villa around two hundred meters round. The others will reinforce the bunkers. I don't trust these negroes, I feel they're preparing a great coup.

Right, my colonel.

Make me a report through the intercom when the surroundings of the villa will be secured!

At your orders, my colonel!'

Eglon sat comfortably on his couch, serving a glass. Kelia, immobile, determined and straight as an i, seemed to peacefully wait for the reactions of her worst enemy. I thought back to that moment with governor Achab, when she had so bravely rejected him. The officer began to question her while tasting his tequila:

We're alone! What the fuck did you come here for?... What do you want?... I think you've got guts to come here!

Guts?

Ah ah! It's true you negroes have a rather limited vocabulary, just like your brain!

Why did you lock Athal? Why hurt my people so much? Can you really not make the choice between good and evil anymore? How can you live without having any fear of God?

Ah ah ah! You make me laugh, little black woman, with your childish vocabulary and your straight morality...

I presume my parents' death makes you laugh as well! Remember, an opened barrel of radioactive waste, a couple tried to close it with their bare hands. This doesn't tell you anything?

I vaguely heard about this story. The nuclear waste, it was Achab's idea. Personally, I thought this storage wasn't profitable. But Achab wanted to be well seen by the industrialized countries who were paying for this. He would lead his affairs peacefully, legally, on the platform. Brandishing the specter of radioactivity, it is very effective to keep the curious away!

All these poppy crops, they're poison, aren't they?

Let's not exaggerate, they're medical plants that allow pain relief, it's not my fault if certain clients abuse it and don't use it correctly!

Doesn't it bother you that people of white race, like you, die? You're poisoning people who are of the same race as you! I don't understand!

Bah, I'm not a racist, a client is a client, I'm not the one to look at the color of the hand of the one who pays! Ah ah ah! And so, little black woman, I don't poison anyone. I only sell pure heroin to importers. Once paid, it's not my problem anymore. I know it's cut several times before reaching the consumers, I'm not responsible for the abuses the intermediaries do, who blithely sweeten the passage!...'

The conversation was interrupted by an intercom included in the control panel:

My colonel!

Yes, answered the office, suddenly getting up to go answer.

My colonel, it's Gontran, my platoon operates on the excavation perimeter of the villa according to your orders, we have yet to find anything. Everything is normal. No one in sight between the demarcation line and the villa.

Alright, continue to search and inform me if you find anything.

Yes, my colonel... but... what are we supposed to find?

Negroes who are threatening, it's obvious, isn't it?

Yes, my colonel, it's obvious.

I don't want to be bothered anymore. Only call in case of extreme necessity.

Alright, my colonel.

If I need you, I'll contact you on your walkie-talkie.

I always have it with me, my colonel.

Over and out!'

Eglon returned to his couch, facing Kelia. He poured another glass of tequila and questioned the girl.

'OK, my dear, should we pass to the serious things! The room is electrically locked and soundproofed. Interesting, no? Don't stay planted there, put your ridiculous basket down and go look for a glass at the bar on your right, I'm offering you a drink.'

Kelia took a glass and came back to the same place. Eglon continued:

'Have some tequila!

I'm not thirsty.'

Eglon got up suddenly and put his automatic pistol at my fiancée's temple. I felt my heart beating 100 km per hour!

Etienne began screaming near me, in the secret room:

'Hemerik! We can't let him do that!

He won't kill her!

What do you know?

He won't kill her before having raped her first!

It's very reassuring!

He has no reason to kill her since she's no danger to him.

These people don't need reasons to act!'

Kelia tentatively dipped her pink lips on the edge of the glass. As Eglon found her too slow, he holstered his gun and pulled back her bun to force her to drink. She fell on her knees as the drink spilled on her bodice. He then threw the glass and pressed the barrel of this gun on his victim's temple saying:

'And now, doll, your good God will come help you? Will he stop me from burning your sparrow brains? *(silence)* You see, I have the power to keep you alive or give you to death! Your trashy God doesn't care about you... of us neither, as a matter of fact! Bang! he screamed to make her jump before starting to laugh.

Your only powers are the ones that my God deigns to give you!

186

You respondent little bitch, you didn't come to me in that outfit just to bring me pineapple! Up! You wanted to inflame me, now you're going to have to take the responsibility until the end!'

Eglon put his weapon on his desk, Kelia took advantage to get her pen out from her left boot and hide it between two cushions from the couch. Eglon rejoiced by exclaiming: 'Good, darling, we're going to have fun the two of us!' He took a seat on the sofa, pushed the glass table with his feet and grabbed Kelia's both hands to pull her to him. She tried to resist, grimacing with worry. Eglon, hypocritically, wanted to reassure her:

'Come on, little black woman, have no fear. It's true you're well shaped. You resist? I love it when they resist me! It excites me more!

I don't understand!

You can't understand, since you're a black woman!... Miam, here's a nice belt buckle soaked in tequila!'

After having rolled up her dress, the man hugged my fiancée violently. During this forced embrace, we saw the hand of the woman sink between the two cushions where the pen was hidden. Everything passed very quickly. The officer got up suddenly while screaming. Once upright, he tried to free himself, but she remained hung like a leech, to pierce his neck well. As she was completely stuck to him, the man, at the end of his strenght, fell hard on Kelia, whose back banged the glass table. All of a sudden, she got away and took refuge behind the desk. Eglon was writhing in pain in the middle of bits of glass:

'You dirty beast! What did you sting me with?

Venom, Mister Eglon. It's useless to scream, the place is soundproof.

Ah!... I don't have any force anymore... in my legs!

It's normal, Mister Eglon, it's the venom who's taking effect! Don't get agitated. The more you move, the quicker the venom will spread in your body and reach your heart, but don't worry, I have the antidote in my other boot.

(Silence)

What do you... want?

Here is the question I wanted to hear! It's very easy, Mister Eglon, tell your men to immediately shut themselves in your bunker to escape a dangerous virus, it's the reason for my presence here... then I will give you the antidote.

Gontran! Screamed Eglon in the walkie-talkie that Kelia held to him. Gontran... answer!

My colonel?

Go back... to the bunker... a dangerous virus... execution!

A virus, my colonel! We haven't seen anything of the kind.

Gontran... you all go... in the... bunker. It's an order!

You want us all to go in the bunker, my colonel, you confirm?

I... confirm... it's an order!

Alright, my colonel... is everything alright, my colonel?

Yes... get the fuck away from here... group of idiots!

Now I understand better, my colonel!

Call me... as soon as you're... settled... there... over!

Received, my colonel... over!'

In the secret room, we began organizing. As my walkie-talkie was set on the same frequency as our enemies', we could hear their conversations. Hemerik wanted to block the door of the bunker with the backhoe loader and Fredo proposed to take us all to the villa in the truck. On the screens, we saw Eglon on all fours, vainly trying to get up. Kelia, upright near him, was carefully surveying him, while extending the conversation to keep him awake.

'The antidote... quickly!

Calm, Mister Eglon, as soon as your men will be locked, I'll give you an injection in your shoulder. In the case in which you'll die first, take the chance to repent for all your sins. You can still be forgiven while you're still on this earth. Pardon is also for you!

188

Stop your mystical delirium… and give me… the antidote!'

Kelia took from the wall a large gilded frame representing the black gear on red background. Below, could be read: *Achab 1967*. She delicately put it on the ground under Eglon's nose, whose head was inexorably getting closer to the ground.

'Ah, Mister Eglon, 1967! The year in which the platform started being used, I wasn't born then!

The antidote… I'm having… trouble… breathing!

Oh come on, Mister Eglon, a little dignity! The big bad wolf who's crawling at the feet of Little Red Riding Hood, it's not very glorious! You love it when they resist you, Mister Eglon, this excites you, right? And well, here you are! This is what you're going to like!'

Kelia put her feet in the center of the gear wheel from the gilded frame that she had put on the floor. She put all her weight on it and the glass shattered completely under the impetus of the heel of her boot. She continued to taunt her attacker.

'Oh, please, Mister Eglon, don't make that face! It's an honor to die at the feet of a woman like me, don't you think?

Poor bitch… do you think you're… intelligent?

Mission accomplished, my colonel, declared Gontran in the walkie-talkie, we're all in the bunker! My colonel? Can you hear me?

Yes, spluttered Eglon… over!'

15 – New government

The antidote Kelia injected in Eglon's shoulder was in reality, only a second dose of anesthetic. When we entered the living room, the officer was completely asleep. I found Kelia lying unconscious on the couch. I carried her to the truck. Fredo helped me get her up in the arms of Linda, seated against the side panel. It was when I let her go I saw the blood on my arm and left hand. I was horrified. Linda immediately reassured me.

'We're going to treat her, Jerome, she hurt herself when she fell on the glass table.'

The truck crossed the rabbit clearing. Hemerik and Athal were walking towards the villa and greeted us. Our vehicle rounded the backhoe loader parked against the door of the bunker in which all our enemies were locked.

As we were approaching the porch, Linda asked for our help: 'Jerome and Fredo, as soon as we arrive at the infirmary, you'll put an intervention table in the middle of the care room, you'll put Kelia in a side position. Etienne, you'll go look for Esther and a blood donor. To choose him, I must first consult the files to know everyone's blood type.'

Esther had clothed and put makeup on Kelia. She sometimes helped Linda in the infirmary. The nurse got everyone out and closed the door. Outside, all usual activities had stopped and Etienne went to look for his speaker to explain to the crowd the latest events.

Linda and Esther were wearing a mask over their mouths and noses and talked in a low voice at Kelia's bedside: 'Local anesthesia... Under the right shoulder blade... at least seven stitches.' Then she told me in a loud voice: 'Talk to her, Jerome, reassure her, I would like her to stay awake.' She continued while whispering: 'Her blood pressure is low, I want her to remain conscious.' Under the table, a bucket was filling with compresses and cotton soaked with blood!

Sitting on a stool near the table, I was confused, not knowing what to say. The back of her right hand was pricked by an IV. I touched her right one, cold and without reaction. Her eyelids quivered as if they weighed a ton. I finally managed to get some words out: 'Kelia!... Kelia, it's going to be OK... I love you... I'm here!'.

The side of her doll face sank deeper into the pillow. Her eyelids closed. At the end of a moment that seemed an eternity, her brow furrowed under the red headband, I heard a whisper: 'Eglon... Eglon... we... managed to...

You did it. You alone neutralized Eglon!

I... Jerome...

Yes.

I would like... to tell you...

I'm listening... ' *(Silence)*

I would have really wished the end of her phrase to be: '*... tell you I love you too*' or '*... tell you I want to marry you*'. But I still had to be patient while carefully surveying her pink lips that weren't moving. To get a reaction, I let out a: 'I love you Kelia!'. Immediately, her orange eyelids opened, her numb mouth blurted pieces of phrases that made my ear tender: 'Jerome... will you... will you... do you want to... ?' I desperately waited for the word '*marry me*'. But my sweetheart's eyes closed again. A long time after, in a last effort, she said a complete request: 'can you... will you... get my boots off?'

◆ ◆ ◆

Around noon, Kelia was sleeping in "my" medical bed. Going out of the infirmary, I was feeling ill and sat against a wall. The man who had given his blood also got out. He encouraged me by putting his hand on my shoulder: 'Don't worry my boy, I gave good blood to your fiancée and she's going to be fine soon!' I didn't have the courage to answer.

I was rubbing mechanically Kelia's dried blood on my arm and hand, when suddenly, I saw Athal sit next to me.

'I knew you would make it, Athal rejoiced, this little one, she's not afraid of any dictator!

Athal, I'm so pleased to hear your voice!

I'm also happy to see you all again. And our heroine?

Linda doesn't want us to bother her, she's sleeping in my bed... well, the bed of the infirmary! *(Silence)*

I'm sorry for your fiancée, all this violence...!

It's not your fault, but of those brutes. Now, these people are our prisoners. Since you're back, take care of them!

You're right, Etienne is also counting on me. I heard six Colombians will land here on Monday.

What do you plan to do?

We'll let them accomplish their mission. They're specialists in heroin. They usually worked on the platform, they were on leave with their families in Colombia the day of the attack. They don't know my father's dead.

Despite our victory, we'll still help our enemies make heroin?

This drug represents our prisoner's salaries. Their mission will be to look for the women my father deported.

And the Colombians, how are they going to react when they'll hear about what happened here today?

For the moment, they know nothing. They're also working for us. If they want their part of the spoils, they'll have to produce the heroin. They need us to gather the latex. The harvest needs a big quantity of workforce, well-formed and conscientious. It's a delicate operation.

Our prisoners are still armed, how are you going to get them to obey?

They'll have to completely give us their weapons, by passing them through the ventilation grille that we'll dismantle on the bunker roof.

If they refuse?

They won't eat. Prohibition to bring their food as long as they're armed! Etienne agrees, he said fasting is conducive to meditation. This evening, Eglon will be up, he'll order his men to surrender their weapons!'

Linda got out of the infirmary and invited us to follow her to go eat. I refused the invitation. Kelia remained alone with Esther.

♦ ♦ ♦

Half an hour later, Linda and Nellie came back with a meal tray for me: 'Up, Jerome, Nellie said, come eat!' Linda dragged me to the room in which Kelia was sleeping. At her bedside, Esther watched over the transfusions and instruments. 'Thank you very much Esther, Linda told her, you can go eat lunch.'

Linda was used to handling emergency situations. She refused to see me depressed and made me stay close to my fiancée, saying my place was there! She told me the parameters to watch out for on the instruments: cardiac rhythm, blood pressure rhythm, body temperature… She planned the schedule of the afternoon: 'In half an hour, Nellie will leave the room taking your tray with her, then, my husband will come pray for your fiancée. Those who wish, will be able to come, but one person at a time for a quarter of an hour for each visit. At five o'clock, you'll go join the others in front of the bunkers and I'll come replace you. Any questions?

None. Thank you for everything Linda. I'll keep this walkie-talkie.

Absolutely, Athal will give me Eglon's. Don't worry. I'm going to the villa to take care of the colonel. He's going to start to wake up.'

Nellie stayed with her arms crossed, leaning on the edge of the bed to the right of her sister. She observed her with a thoughtful look. Kelia wasn't wearing makeup anymore and her headband had disappeared. Her disheveled hair was spread out across the pillow. Her bare arms were connected to infusions and probes.

Etienne was talking to the crowd through a speaker. I heard songs outside, prayers and the bike's engine stop in front of the infirmary. People came during the afternoon to visit my fiancée: Etienne, Nicodeme, Mado, Rose-Marie, Athal, Hemerik, Fredo... but the wounded still slept. Linda took my place before five o'clock so I could go with the bike in front of the bunkers.

♦ ♦ ♦

The crowd was spread from the demarcation line until the military zone. On the roof of the bunker, I saw Fredo take apart the ventilation device of half a square meter to take out the weapons and some ammunition. Eglon had his hands tied behind his back. Hemerik and his six youngsters were recovering the weapons.

From where I was standing with my friends, it was impossible to hear the conversations. When all the weapons were taken out with some ammunition, we removed the backhoe loader to open the door and let our prisoners out, hands on their heads, ordering them to line with their backs to the wall. Facing them, the six *Blue*, in a firing position, were pointing their machine guns. Hemerik and Athal had assigned ten men from the people to search and other ten to verify that no handguns had remained in the bunker. All the arsenal was stored in Athal's. Hemerik took the speaker to make himself heard by the soldiers as well as the surrounding crowd:

'Before letting Athal speak, I want to warn you that each time we'll authorize you to come out of the bunker to go look for your meal trays behind the truck, my six guards will watch you like they're doing now. These youngsters know how to use their weapons since you trained them yourselves. I want to specify that my guards only obey me and they have the order to shoot you at the slightest try of escape, even in my absence! Is it clear? *(Silence... Hemerik gave the speaker to Athal who continued the explanations)*:

'On Friday morning, we'll give you a complete mission order, telling you how to find nine women deported in different countries during these last ten years. You'll leave Monday afternoon, without arms via helicopter, destination: Mahe airport. We'll give you the addresses where the women were sold, money for your plane tickets and your travels in the concerning countries, as well as your passports. I'll give you two months to find all the women and bring them to Kheo. Upon your return, you'll receive a good hundred thousand dollars to deduct from the sale of the heroin that will be manufactured here in your absence. If you'll come back without the women or if you won't come back, you'll receive nothing. Colonel Eglon will organize all the logistics of this mission with sergeant Gontron's assistance. They'll answer all your questions as soon as they'll know the necessary information. Any questions?' *(Silence)*

One of the soldiers raised his hand while screaming:

'I have questions! What if the black women no longer work in the whore network or if they refuse to follow us…?

It's up to you to lead the investigation. Your superiors will send you in pairs. Those who will succeed will get their reward. The others that will not have found them, don't even need to come back here! If the women refuse to follow you, don't force them, you'll get your reward, but less. Tell them a nice story to make them follow you, as in manipulation, you're experts. I specify that it is a kidnapping and that it is not a question of negotiating with pimps or anyone else. If warriors like you aren't capable of taking weak women without defense, then rather go get hired as a guard in a supermarket and don't come back here! *(Silence)* Any other questions?

(Another soldier) – Yeah! I also have a question! Who is to say we'll really get paid? What's this story of a hundred thousand dollars? We, we want real dough, not a piece of paper!

He's right, cried another, we don't have any guarantee, after this stupid mission, will we really get paid?

Calm, answered Athal, to be able to pay you with true dollars, first we'll have to sell the heroin, and before selling it, we'll have to make it! If you would rather, we'll give you the corresponding quantity of heroin to the promised sum and you'll go sell it yourselves, it's for you to choose! Understand well that this mission can get you a hundred thousand dollars. As soon as you'll leave Kheo Monday afternoon, you'll be free. You can keep the travel money and disappear, or you can come back with the women and get the hundred thousand dollars! The ball is in your court! It's to take or leave!' *(Silence)* Hemerik took back the speaker:

'I repeat you have two months to accomplish this mission. We'll keep the weapons. Anyway, a firearm will only pass on the containers, never in planes. In two months, mission accomplished or not, my guards will throw down all of you who venture here! If you have any other questions, ask your superiors. Finished!'

16 – The Colombians

Tuesday, October 29, 1997

For the first time, I passed the night in my sleeping bag put at the end of Nellie's bed in the pastor's apartment. The little girl was thrilled and left me little time to sleep, she talked so much! Linda had slept in the delivery room, next to Kelia's room to watch over her.

During the night, no one stood guard outside or in the secret room. Was there any reason to worry? Hemerik and Fredo were only watching Eglon's inbox.

Those who wanted to consult the Internet could do so in plain view during the day. Nicodeme asked Fredo to connect the computers from the school on the same network. The wiring was already ready and the connection was made the same day.

A freedom wind was floating in the air, despite the presence of our prisoners with all their disturbing current projects!

In the moment to sit at the table to have the first meal of the day, Linda gave me good news concerning the health of my loved one. She proposed to take her a meal tray. I gladly accepted!

◆ ◆ ◆

Kelia was standing upright in her bed. She only had one IV and the machines were disconnected. 'Hello, Kelia, did you sleep well?... As you can see, the roles are reversed! It's me who's taking you your meal to the infirmary!

Ah, Jerome… hello… thank you!

How are you feeling?

As someone who has three wounds on the back. Linda sewed up again the deepest one under the shoulder blade. I won't be able to raise my right arm for a while!

I was very scared when Eglon threatened you with his gun.

I knew the risks, I'm sorry to have hidden everything from you, but I didn't want to worry anyone. Even the pastor didn't know anything!

I don't want to lose you. I love you!

I love you too!

Her smile lit up the white room. I put honey on her bread. While she was biting her bread, I put my lips on the fingers of her left hand to cover them with kisses.

'It was an idea of Hemerik, she continued, he wanted to use the anesthetic used by Athal. I thought about governor Achab on the platform. He made me wear a dress. I tried to seduce Eglon to be able to approach and trap him. (Silence) The other day, you also took risks in stopping those two soldiers from raping a girl. You see well that the white people are all the same: they despise us and want to rape us!

Kelia, I'm also white, but I'm not like that!

I know. You and Athal, you're different. I would love to stop talking about this. Is it ok? Eglon is no longer a threat, it's the main thing. Where is he now?

In the bunker with his people. We kept their weapons. We're out of danger.'

◆ ◆ ◆

During the days that followed, I helped Nellie and Etienne with the rabbit breeding. The pastor told me that a baptism would take place on Sunday. I was well decided to follow the other three people who had taken this commitment.

Sunday, November 2, 1997

Kelia spent her last night in the infirmary. Her right arm was on a sling and the bandages on her back stiffened her and certain gestures sometimes made her wince in pain. After having had breakfast with us, she turned her back to her sister who began braiding her hair.

In the yard, the crowd, well clothed, prepared for an hour and a half of peaceful march. The baptisms always took place on the north beach on the other side of the island, without doubt, by habit. They preferred to be baptized outside the field of view of the platform!

Every morning, I accompanied Hemerik and Fredo in the truck to serve the meal trays to our enemies. Our six armed soldiers were already waiting in the military zone. They formed a "fence of honor "between the door of the bunker and the back of the truck. Gontran served first his colonel who never got out, then he sent his men, two by two. Contrary to other days, we gave the prisoners additional crates and baskets to last the whole day, as we needed the truck to transport our own picnic for lunch on the beach.

Hemerik and Fredo came to look for Kelia and helped her climb aboard the truck. Athal suggested I go to

198

the beach by bike, so I could come back to the village as fast as possible in case of emergency. As the population was going north of the island, our young soldiers received the order to guard the whole area from the bunkers to the village. No question of leaving empty buildings and our prisoners alone, without surveillance. They were happy and proud to serve their native island and contribute to the good going of this special day. Nellie, seated behind me on my bike, was holding my backpack. We drove slowly in the middle of the crowd who was walking on each side of us, singing songs. The road was new until the villa, but we had to turn left at the end of the quarry to take the rutted track leading to the north beach.

I recognized the beach on which Franck's helicopter had left me the day of my arrival on the island. The people sat on the sand dune that ran along the sea. Below, Etienne was holding his megaphone waiting with Nicodeme, his choir and three other future baptized people. The lowest point was not formed naturally. It was the result of all the sand needed for the mortar used for the construction of the buildings and bunkers. The old rutted track used for transportation of the truck. It was the time and the successive torrential rains who had made it. Between the crowd and the forest, a huge pile of dead wood prepared the day before was burning to later form a large bed of coals for cooking the lunch meat.

At the end of the service, Etienne made us go into the water. We had water reaching our knees and the waves wetted our stomachs. The man next to me seemed to be about thirty years old. I later learned that his fiancée was part of the list of the deported women. Like me, he was clothed with shorts and a T-shirt for the occasion. Further away, a teenager and a little girl of about ten years old were waiting their turn, dressed in a pink bathrobe.

Etienne began to baptize the youngest saying: 'On the confession of your faith, I baptize you in the name of the

Father, the Son and the Holy Spirit.' I was the third one to be submerged. A new life was beginning for me. I was truly entering God's family. I briefly thought about my parents, I would have wanted them to see my commitment. The memory that remained of them wasn't as painful as before. I was certain I was going to see them in Heaven! I let myself be carried in the water by this unexplainable peace. It didn't leave me and stayed underlying in difficult times.

Nicodeme directed the choir, the water from the shore was carrying the songs, making the whole crowd on the dune sing:

Into Thine hands I surrender, everything that I call mine.
Lead me, O heavenly Father, let Your face upon me shine!
I surrender all, all I have with joy, into Thine hands I surrender,
All I have with joy.

In Thee, O Lord, I put my trust; ashamed let me never be;
O save me in Thy righteousness, lord give ear and rescue me.
I surrender all, I surrender all, into Thine hands, I put my trust,
I give Thee my all.

No one was worried about the radioactive waste floating on the sea at thirty meters deep!

◆ ◆ ◆

Hemerik had asked the kitchen team to prepare everything from the day before. A tent was put up to serve as changing rooms for the new baptized. The fire, lit from five o'clock in the morning, was just finishing burning the huge pile of branches whose embers were spread out in a brick rectangle of 8 meters long and 4 meters wide. Around eleven o'clock, this gigantic barbecue was ready to receive the metal device made by Fredo to maintain 28 sockets. The Cooking of the 200 big chickens and 80 rabbits ended in the early afternoon. We were seated or lying on the sand in the shade of palm trees. I served my fiancée who only had one hand to eat with. I would have wanted to hold her in my arms, but her back pains forbid me from doing so.

Monday, November 3, 1997

During breakfast, we heard three helicopters take off. At the same moment, Hemerik came with the bike in the yard by the porch.

'*Hemerik* – Gontran chose a pilot and a copilot to go get the Colombians. They'll be there in the middle of the afternoon.

Etienne – Gontran? Why not Eglon?

Hemerik – Eglon never comes out. I don't think he's in good health.

Linda – Really? Did you try to find out what ails him?

Hemerik – He drinks too much tequila! And he's not the only one!

Fredo – How are you going to manage the situation when the Colombians will find out you took control of the island? The pilot and his colleague may tell them everything.

Hemerik – So what? If they're not pleased, they'll go back to where they came from. But don't kid yourself, when they'll see 800 hectares of white flowers, they won't hesitate to take the chance to stay among us! Athal will know better how to explain it to them. On another subject, we decided to lock Eglon in the villa. We'll bring him by truck and we'll be able to watch him with the camera. We have to let him communicate with his potential clients.

Athal – I'll sleep in the small room of the villa. My bunker will be arranged as a laboratory and the one in front will serve as housing for the Colombians in the place of the soldiers who will be away on mission.

♦ ♦ ♦

After lunch, Hemerik got out all our enemies to allow Gontran to organize the preparations for their leaving, waiting for the Colombians. The men divided into three groups: one for each helicopter. Each group was watched by two of Hemerik's soldiers. The soldiers loaded their luggage and stayed seated near their respective aircraft.

◆ ◆ ◆

Around three o'clock, the helicopter landed in the middle of the quarry following Hemerik's directions. In the shade of the trees, close to the back bags, we prepared a kerosene barrel and "Happy" pump to fill up. The six passengers, in city clothes descended from the helicopter and timidly approached the "welcoming committee". They vainly waited that the negroes come take their luggage. Dismayed, they looked at each other, crying:

'¿Qué pasa aquí ?

¿Esta permitido que los negros porten armas ?

¿Quién manda aquí ?

Calm, amigos, answered Athal, approaching the only Colombian who spoke French, I'll clearly explain things. As you have certainly found out, my father is dead, victim of an attack. There's nothing left of *Achab industry*. So it's me who took control of Kheo. Gontran will leave in a mission with his men, I named Hemerik responsible of security. You'll have to train the negroes to harvest the latex and put it in place in the laboratory for the heroin fabrication.

As soon as it will be packaged, we'll evaluate and discuss your share.

But where are Gontran and his team going? What is this mission?

It's a long local history that concerns the people here.

What? Listen to me well Athal, don't mock us! Everything that happens here concerns us! We want to know what you did! Where is Eglon? I want to talk to him!

Perez, I'm not going to split things! Here, I decide everything! There are several million dollars at stake. You either collaborate according to my directions and you'll get your share or you go the fuck away! I'll find someone else to help us make it. It will pass without problems at prices negotiated by Eglon himself. His agenda with orders is full! *(Silence)*

I want to see Eglon. I want to know why the mercenaries are leaving!

I'm replacing my father and I decided that you'll not move from here. Give me an answer. For the last time, do you want to work here under my orders?

Don't get smart with me Athal, I worked for your father before you were born, don't think everyone ignores what happened on this island, there are satellites that monitor all square meters of this world and…

Do I take it your answer is no?

Your father would have never acted like you're doing! Tell your negroes to stop pointing their guns at me, it's inadmissible! I want to see Eglon, it's him who made us come here!

Very well, Perez, there's no point in getting your bags, my people will fill up the helicopter and you'll leave!

¡Me lleva la fregada !'

Perez threw his cap to the ground and went into a rage. He turned towards his five colleagues who didn't understand French and who didn't stop asking him:

'¿Qué pasa aquí ?
¿Qué estas diciendo ?
¿Qué quieres ?'

The tension was escalating and at the end of a few minutes of tough discussions in the group, Perez questioned Athal again:

'Who can assure us you're not going to throw us out when the drug will be finished? Who will prove you'll give us our share?

It's a risk you'll have to take Perez, it's not the first time you're taking risks in this kind of business. You pretend to have worked for my father for over thirty years. In this case, you know very well my father always honored his contracts with you. So you have nothing to fear!

Yes, but you're not your father! He would never have given military weapons to macaques! You're completely oblivious, how can we work like this?

You're right, I don't act like my father. Moreover, I forbid you to disrespect my soldiers! Hemerik is in charge to watch you and he's authorized to get you if you try to harm anyone. You'll work for us according to my conditions and in my way! 800 hectares of poppy, you'll have your share, it's take it or leave it!'

Perez got really close to Athal, pointing his index finger and mumbling: 'We'll stay, but I warn you, amigo, if you try to scam us, I'll find you even at the end of the earth, me or someone else!'

He took his cap and asked his colleagues to get the bags out.

17 – Mission accomplished

Tuesday, November 4, 1997

Athal asked me to stay with the Colombians to assist them in their work. He wanted things to be forgotten and ordered Hemerik's soldiers not too get too close to them in order to "lower the tension". As I had stored the products and instruments myself in the future laboratory in Athal's bunker, the inventory was finished more easily and these men showed themselves to be calm and satisfied. All of them had mustaches, two of them had beards in addition to the moustache. The dark color of their skin prevented me from giving them a specific age. The ones with the beards were the oldest. They were dressed with a red blouse with the sign of the gear wheel of *Achab industry* inscribed on the back and a red cap, whose visor was marked with the same symbol. They were thorough and very organized. They talked a lot and their language, that I didn't understand, sang and resonated gently under the roof of the bunker. One of the mustached ones, Perez, their leader, invited me to follow them to the building opposite to sit around the table. A bearded one served us a little glass of tequila. A few sips later, Perez spoke to me in French:

'We're thinking: it's not good here for the laboratory. We're going to be too hot with the twelve lighted stoves and no running water for filtration, so, it's preferable to put it outside under a covered area that I saw this morning in the yard, close to the sinks. Can we do this?

I don't think it should be a problem. When?

A little before the harvest that we estimate to be at the end of the month.

Understood, we'll use the truck for the move and I'll designate some people for the handling.

We'll have to train your very numerous personnel for the harvesting technique.

205

I suggest you begin tomorrow for the group of ten family heads.

Alright, amigo, we'll do as you say.'

♦ ♦ ♦

The following days, the poppy petals began to fall. Etienne sent groups of ten family heads in the military zone to receive training. Tables and cardboard equipment were lined up before ten folding chairs. Perez explained to the farmers the method of incision of the poppy capsules using a cutter by simulating the action on a small green mandarin. Then, he pretend to peel the fruit with a wooden scraper shaped like a tiny sickle to show how to remove the latex drops, then place them in a plastic bowl. The container should be closed as soon as possible to slow evaporation and limit the hardening of the product. Bowls, cutters and scrapers were distributed to all participants.

Wednesday, November 12, 1997

For a week now, Linda had removed the stiches of the back wound of my fiancée. Her arm wasn't attached in a sling anymore and she could gently do some rehabilitation movements.

All the poppy petals had disappeared and had let the capsules appear, which began growing in the following days.

In that sunny morning, Athal asked me to accompany the Colombians on foot until the villa for a reunion in the living room. Those present were: Athal, Hemerik, Fredo, Etienne, Eglon and myself. This meeting was the first one between the Colombians and Elgon. He was worrying everyone by showing himself to be taciturn and embittered by the alcohol. He indicated with a trembling hand the shipping sectors of the heroin representing the Mediterranean naval chart. Places of landing and trans-shipment at sea were listed. Athal talked more often to overcome the lack of insurance from Eglon. Etienne and his two sons were seated on the couch, covered with a red bed ornament, doubtless intended to hide Kelia's blood trace. Fredo had replaced the glass table by a wooden drum, which had supported the telephone wire in a container.

Athal explained that the drug would be packaged in metal cans of powdered milk for babies, hidden in waterproof barrels, painted black. Perez translated the main phrases to his colleagues and exposed a summary of the different stages of labor in the laboratory regarding the latex: boiling in water, filtration, concentration... He asked Etienne for a certain number of people worthy of trust to help them and estimated the latex quantity between thirty and forty kilos a hectare. Before the end of this meeting, the Colombian leader expressed his disappointment towards Athal and Eglon: 'I hope you know what you're doing, both of you! No more threat toward us with your negro welcoming committee! Understood?'

♦ ♦ ♦

It was decided to begin the incision of the still small, green capsules the next morning. Two days later, every family head split his team into two parts: one third of the group was to continue to scarify the capsules, the others had to recover the latex flowing from the incised bulbs the day before.

♦ ♦ ♦

The harvest lasted until the end of the year, a little after Christmas! It was a true nightmare. We worked twelve hours a day under a summer sun that shone will all its force! I had to empty the plastic bowls in a bucket using a spatula and return the motorbike at the laboratory in the courtyard. Children were waiting for me at the end of their family plots along the trails to give me the freshly harvested opium. Linda and her sons were sharing water and sweet drinks. The nurse made each worker wet his hat or cap to protect themselves against the sun.

♦ ♦ ♦

At the beginning of December, the bulb growth ceased and the drying opium made our task more difficult. Eglon and Athal had planned too big and three quarters of the crops became unusable. The Colombians barely calculated just over four hundred kilos of pure heroin! We would have needed ten times the personnel to hope to manage such a surface! I thought Athal knew it but said nothing so he wouldn't have to enhance the teams with foreign workforce.

Linda invited me to leave the infirmary to put my sleeping bag in the dormitory of the teenagers, among whom were Hemerik's soldiers. We had to free the care rooms and prepare the delivery room to receive the eleven babies that were born only in the month of December! The nurse and her assistant, Esther, had a lot of work on their hands!

◆ ◆ ◆

For New Year's Eve, Hemerik, Fredo and I stayed in front of the courtyards housing the laboratories. Perez proudly showed us the fruit of the harvest: 'Look amigos, it's the purest in the whole world! Nothing to do with the *black tar* of the Mexican peasants. We prefer to lose a little amount by making it more refined! It's better than that of the Gold Triangle or the Gold Crescent!'

While he was still talking, three helicopters of *Achab industry* landed in the middle of the quarry in a cloud of dust to cut with a knife! The six guards grabbed their guns and ran to meet Eglon's soldiers, returned from the mission. Athal and Hemerik took the truck and me the bike to join them. The soldiers, tired but satisfied, came out of the aircrafts, stretching. They put their bags on the ground between two cases of tequila. Hemerik asked Gontran as soon as he saw him:

'Where are the women?

They'll arrive at the end of the week aboard the *Geometrix*.

Are there nine women?

Yeah… nine women and a kid!

There's a child with them?

Yeah! You ask too many questions, I also have my own! Where's the drug? Where's Eglon?

The drug is under cover in the courtyard, it's in the packing phase. Eglon awaits you in the villa.'

♦ ♦ ♦

The night of the new year was calm. The tired people only had one wish: to see all those strange evildoers disappear forever. While Hemerik's soldiers kept watch around the village, Eglon and all his group celebrated with the Colombians in the villa. The inside pool was empty and the men improvised a game of football on its floor. Everywhere, rum and tequila bottles were taken out of the cases imported by the helicopters. These men got drunk all night and slept even on the floor until morning.

Thursday, January 1, 1998

After breakfast with all the community, Hemerik and Fredo put the meal trays in the deserted bunkers by the occupants, then they finished preparing the black barrels under the watchful eye of Perez, the only foreigner to hold himself up at that hour! The precious boxes were hidden in metal barrels and stowed in hay. A plastic sheet was closing everything under one layer of wet sand a few inches thick. Fredo adjusted everything by blocking the cover with five or six points of welding. The sealing was achieved by putting sealant around the lid.

'*Perez, talking to Athal* – I don't understand your distrust of Eglon's men. Why not give them their weapons back? Why give them to the negroes? We have never seen this. Your father didn't operate this way! I'm amazed.

Athal – In the absence of my regretted father, I became governor of Kheo and I secure my territory as I see fit and with whom I want! It so happens that the colonel's mercenaries don't know how to do anything else but drink and rape the women from the people.

Amigo, these men have been here for months, away from their families, in these unhealthy bunkers and in this difficult climate. Most of them have ill stomachs. They need a little distraction

They're going to have some distraction on the same boat as you! I wish you much pleasure!

What do you mean?

I don't trust them. Eglon is very sick, consumed by the alcohol, we can no longer rely on him. Gontran has no authority over his men as soon as his superior has his back turned.

Mmh… It's in their interest that the drug is sold and that all goes well. Why are they dangerous?

Very well, Mister Perez, I see you have compassion for them. So I will give them a part of their weapons and ammunition in the moment when they'll embark with you, but I'll keep the other part, for I have to fight back, faced with possible enemies of Eglon who could come here with ill intentions!

I think to understand you're not coming with us? What will you do here? More heroin?

No, no more heroin, but I have some little things to settle in Dar es Salam. It's there you'll leave me before heading for the Suez Channel.

As you wish, this is your business. When the drug will be sold, how will you get your share?

I trust you, Mister Perez! I'll give you my account number to deposit the sum that's entitled to me and I'll also give to each member of your group an automatic pistol to protect yourselves during your travel.

Good, amigo. I hope Eglon will be able to succeed with our business!

I also hope so. Max and I have to leave you for a moment to organize the work. Please excuse me.

210

Later, amigo.'

Athal signaled me to follow him to get away from the enemy's ears. He told me about his next projects, while we walked toward the beach:

'As you have just heard, I'll leave with them in two or three days on board the *Epiphane* freighter, which will leave me in Africa. From there I'll leave for Europe by plane.

You want to leave to do what and go where? When are you counting on coming back?

Jerome, I want to remake my life. If this community will agree, I will leave Kheo to live elsewhere. I finished my mission by bringing back the deported women by my father. When I'll board the *Epiphane*, I would have achieved my goal: rid Kheo of its enemies without bloodshed and repair the damages caused by Achab... at least, in part!

In part? You're thinking of the taken babies sold for international adoption?

Yes. Unfortunately! These children were scattered around the world and have new names. Impossible to find them. *(Silence)*

But this drug, still, you said that...

Don't worry about this. I met a correspondent on the Internet who accepted to warn the authorities of our enemies' passage on the Suez Channel. They'll be trapped and stopped after the search of their freighter... but...

But what?

I doubt they'll end up there without a fight. They may kill each other before reaching the Red Sea!

They'll fight to not split the drug money?

The *Ephiphane* captain, a certain Gerd Doldinger, isn't an innocent! In this moment, he's finishing a long journey to come here. Until now, he always operated in the Atlantic Ocean and his main owner was *Achab industry*. He handled the latex from Colombia to Zaire...

Then Gontran and his men took this latex to take it to Dar es Salam...

211

Where it was loaded on board the *Geometrix*, destination: the Kheo platform.

This Doldinger knew your father well?

Yes, but they didn't meet often, Eglon was the main mediator between my father and Doldinger, who accepted all the contracts. They were hidden aboard the *Ephiphane*, the children of Africa and of Kheo were taken on the American continent for adoption and organ trafficking. Eglon asked of Doldinger to carry heroin in Europe. He ignores that my father is dead and believes that it's the war from Zaire from last May that prevented the usual convoy to cross Africa!

Why did Eglon hide your father's death from him?

I think he didn't want to risk worrying him. By pretending to act under the usual orders of governor Achab, Eglon would ensure total confidence of the devoted Doldinger, ready to do everything to serve the *Achab industry*!

Won't he act badly when he'll hear the truth as soon as he docks on Kheo?

No. Four hundred kilos of heroin, it calms!

Aren't you afraid of boarding this freighter in such bad company?

Yes, but I'll take the risk. I want to make sure these criminals go away from the island!'

I was surprised by the sudden decision of my friend to leave us. I would never have imagined such a hasty departure. I was wondering how the others would act when they would find out.

18 — Liberation

All the ones at my table were carefully listening to Athal's words during the noon lunch. No one had expected to see him leave and no one seemed ready to assume to following of the events without him! We could feel sadness invade our hearts, but the son of the tyrant Achab had decided to remake his life! He had first given all his youth to work on the platform, while undergoing humiliation. Then, conscious of the ignominy of his father, and after risking his life conspiring against him, he promised to release Kheo. As usual, he had carefully prepared his leaving and a project for our future. The *Ephiphane* wasn't coming only to take our occupants and their 21 black barrels containing the heroin, but they brought materials coming from Canada: wind turbines, solar panels, a handheld submarine...

'*Hemerik* – A submarine? To do what?

Athal – At first, you'll use it to refloat the nuclear waste to store it in the bunkers. It's equipped with articulated arms with pliers to grasp and handle objects underwater. It's very easy to handle. Then, try pearl culture starting with a flat oyster farm you'll place in suspended grids supported on rafts. The submersible will be used to develop this site and will protect it from potential predators. All the explanations are in the computer.

Nellie – At what will these pearls serve?

Athal – You'll sell them to foreigners. You can't live self-sufficient eternally, you'll need to trade with the outside to import what you need as your needs increase.

Etienne - And we deeply thank you!

Athal – I'll work together with you by maintaining Internet contact. Jerome will daily check the electronic inbox. But before finding a clientele, you'll have to produce the pearls first!

Nicodeme – That goes without saying!

Mado – These pearls, we'll have to find them a name.

Athal – Of course. You could name them: *Jewels of the Indian Ocean* for example, or: *Pearls of Kheo*.

Me – Or: *Kelia Pearls*, it's more beautiful!'

Friday, January 2, 1998

We passed the day preparing our future projects and Athal's trip. Families were working in the field at the edge of the forest. I asked Fredo who was next to me:

'What are they doing in the field there?

They're mowing the poppies. All that remained dried.

They'll manually mow such a big surface? It's impossible!

No, they only clean a strip of ten meters wide at the boundary of the field. Then, they'll work this strip and will set fire to the whole arable land. Once burnt, the earth will be entirely workable and ready for cultivation. We'll put fruit and vegetables like before. The farmers prepared the seeds around the breeding!'

Athal showed me all the files in the computer. He wanted to train me to make me his replacement on Kheo! He packed his bag and the evening meal took longer than usual. Etienne prayed for him and we sang some songs. The last radio call to the station confirmed the arrival of the *Ephiphane* in a few hours. Gontran informed us by walkie-talkie from the villa.

Saturday, January 3, 1998

Day "J"! The silent people hurried on the beach and on the pier. Everyone wanted to see our invaders leave after more than nine months of occupation! Athal was wearing his Sunday clothes. With his bag, he really had the air of an European tourist!

The precious black barrels were loaded first with the mobile crane of the vessel whose gantry was moving on rails arranged on each side of the hold. According to Athal, the *Ephiphane* was a small bulk carrier converted into a general cargo vessel. Its captain, Ger Doldinger was a racist. He was on good terms with the members of Achab's mafia. As we were staying away from the ladder, I could hear the conversations between the crew and Eglon's mercenaries. He appeared lying on a stretcher carried by two soldiers. Athal explained: 'Eglon is sick, he vomited blood last evening. It was to be expected, too much alcohol!'

No one seemed to worry about the colonel's fate who they hoisted aboard without care. The truck drew back to distribute to the soldiers and the Colombians the weapons and ammunitions in a reduced quantity, as we wanted to keep a part of this arsenal to ensure the defense of the island. The crane placed the single container on the pebbles from the pier and Fredo immediately climbed on it to unhook it. Once the hold was closed, the three helicopters were put one after the other on the deck. The crew strapped them securely. It was in that moment Athal saluted as all. Some hugs, the women tried not to cry. He tapped me on the shoulder: 'We keep in touch, he told me, I want a weekly report of all your activities and I will also tell you about my new life. I'll come back one day to steal some beautiful pearls!'

The *Ephiphane* disappeared on the horizon and the crowd scattered in silence. Peace and freedom on Kheo! Could we believe it? Should we fear the arrival of new

215

enemies? The people began its work, leaving its fate in God's hands, like it had always done!

Ten men among which were Etienne and his sons opened the container to get the out materials. Kelia, who wanted to visit the deserted bunkers of our enemies, climbed behind me on the bike. The place where the soldiers had slept seemed like a battle field! The beds were overthrown, the bedding was scattered, empty bottles and garbage littered the ground, all in a foul odor! Outside, we heard Nellie followed by a group of children cross the place in the direction of the quarry.

Without losing a minute, we began taking the tables out, on which we put the mattresses.

◆ ◆ ◆

A little before noon, the children came back between the bunkers. Nellie stopped me, proudly holding the leash of the German shepherd abandoned by the soldiers:

'Look, she exclaimed, he was attached to a tree in the forest! He wouldn't stop barking!

Weren't you afraid? You dared approach him?

At the beginning he scared us, but when we talked to him, my friends and me, he calmed down and we detached him without him biting us! Do you think dogs understand our language?

A little… some people manage to train them so well that they're capable of making many incredible things.

Colonel Eglon trained him well: each time we throw him a piece of wood, he brings it back!

No, this act isn't the result of a particular training, but it's something all dogs have naturally. All dogs do this without being taught. It's in their instinct!

You want to say they do this as soon as they know how to walk when small?

216

Yes, it's a type of game, dogs love to play with their masters. *(Silence)*

If he wasn't trained to do this, then it's God who programmed him this way!

You could say that.'

The animal suddenly entered the bunker and nervously sniffed the beddings. Then, he got out and stopped in the middle of the road, while a dozen children's hands were petting him from all sides!

'There's the happiest dog in the world!

We have to give him food, answered Kelia, children, you'll watch over him!

Friday, January 9, 1998

Around noon, we saw the imposing silhouette of the Geometrix approach the pier. The people hurried forward to greet the nine women and a child of about eight years old, without luggage, at the foot of the ladder. I couldn't get near as the crowd was dense, and I preferred to let the people directly affected by this joyful reunion pass. During almost an hour, the families slowly dispersed and the Geometrix raised its anchor. I suddenly saw Hemerik leave alone on the beach with an energetic step. Intrigued, I went to the pier at the end of which were Fredo and his parents, as well as black woman, seated on the ground next to a little boy. As I was approaching the group, I imagined a terrible scenario: she had to be Maryse, Hemerik's fiancée, and the little boy was her son. Hemerik, upset to find out she had had a son with another man, had left to isolate himself on the beach. I crossed the embarrassed look of my friends who were keeping silent. The woman and child had bare feet and were shabbily dressed. Tired and staring into space, they seemed to wait for someone to decide their fate!

At the end of endless seconds, I dared say a word in Etienne's direction:

'Maryse?

No! *(Silence)*

But…'

Etienne grabbed me by the arm to continue the conversation a little further:

'These idiots haven't found Maryse. They took this young Malagasy to get their bonus.

But what will happen to her? How will she return to her home?

That's just it, she speaks our language a little and I could hear her story.

And so? What's her story?

She lived alone in the bushes with her son, her partner abandoned her. So she would like to live on Kheo. What do you think?

What do I think? Now there's a question! Is it me who decides the fate of these people?

Athal chose you to replace him, so you have your opinion to say!

Well… I… honestly, it would be a crime to send her back from where she comes from. And you being a pastor, I'm sure you think the same thing!

Yes, but you're managing our island, so it's your material responsibility to do or not do a particular project.

Alright. On the material side, at the risk of being cynical, I declare nothing stops us to feed two extra mouths. So this mother and son are welcome here.

Bravo! It's exactly what I was waiting from you!

Well, look! If I had said no?

These people would have been sent away with the next cargo!

Well. I confess my feelings have strongly influenced my decision.

What does it matter, the main thing is to make the right decision. Tell this Malagasy she can stay.

But, why me?

I insist, you're a senior in our community.

So be it. Madam, you can stay with us with your son.'

The woman got up like a spring and grabbed my hands:

'Thank you! Thank you Mister!' Etienne sighed:

'All this won't solve Hemerik's problem. He'll finish by accepting his situation. We're going to prepare a big party to celebrate all the marriages simultaneously, yours too, I hope, even though Kelia still hasn't told me anything!

No.

No? Why not?

We can't just leave Hemerik aside and behave as everything enters normality!

Jerome, I'm touched by your compassion towards my son, but we should do what?

I'm going to talk to him.'

After a quarter of an hour, I found Hemerik sitting on a rock, busy throwing stones into the sea.

'Your father explained everything, Eglon's mercenaries didn't find Maryse. In my opinion, they didn't search enough!

Didn't search enough? Misinformed, the result is the same! You're all going to get married and I'm going to end up alone.

You're not going to end up alone, we'll just have to find Maryse!

Really? We're not even sure she's still in Madagascar. And even if she still lived there, how are we going to find her? It's like looking for a grain of sand in the ocean.

I have a passport. I'll go look for her myself. I won't come back here without Maryse or I won't come back at all!

You're raving? And your marriage? My father wants to organize the nuptials next week! You'll refuse to get married for this?

Absolutely! I refuse to marry Kelia if you won't marry Maryse!

It's crazy! You have no right to do this to Kelia. I forbid you to hurt her. I think of her like my little sister!

And I consider Maryse like mine!

Jerome, you don't even know her. Why ruin your life for nothing? Let this project go!

Come with me, we'll find her!

No! It's a lost cause! *(Silence)*

Very well! Continue your weeping. I'll go look for Maryse myself!'

19 – An unexpected visitor

Since the departure of the *Ephiphane*, I lived alone, cut off, in the villa. I only got out for the meals to find my friends.

Every evening, before dinner, I visited the sites where the families worked. Hemerik and Fredo, helped by their six young soldiers, organized the work on the three sites simultaneously! The crops, the construction of the new hall of worship, for which the works had been interrupted during the whole time of enemy occupation, and the north beach where the nuclear waste barrels were piled, they were being refloated by the handheld submarine. Fredo perfectly mastered the submersible and had asked me several times to accompany him to admire the seabed, but my head wasn't into that because I was looking for a way to go to Madagascar. Hemerik continued to courageously do his work and his father quashed any marriage project because of me.

All the cultivable area of the island once occupied by the poppies had been burnt and the tractor was plowing the blackened earth. The happy and motivated farmers could finally plant fruits and vegetables as before!

I occupied my days thinking, reading and discovering different websites on the Internet. From time to time, Kelia and Nellie came to pay me a visit. On the surveillance cameras, I sometimes saw children approach to play in the vicinity with the dog.

Each day began with a meeting with the pastor and his two sons, during which we thought of ways to work and the technical data of the equipment to install. We weren't in agreement on the choice of where to put the two wind turbines, still in pieces, scattered between the bunkers. Whatever the place chosen to build them, we wouldn't have enough cables to connect them electrically with our existent network, so it was decided to suspend the works momentarily.

I appeared reluctant to lead these projects because I was too absorbed by my investigation into the disappearance of Maryse. I had found the diskette copy of this woman's folder. The mission order given to Eglon's men, charged with finding her only contained a part, Athal had added more information. All he knew about the company and the connections of his father was registered on this disk. Athal had, in this way, saved everything before Eglon didn't format the hard drive of his computer on which I was working.

It was like this I learned Maryse's story: after having been raped (as with the majority of the women destined to be deported), she had been sold to a certain Gwladys Venceslas, posted in Madagascar. Venceslas, with Achab's financial support, had built a hotel in Manakara in the south of the island with intention to develop tourism. But this business failed because of the insufficient ways of communication and the difficult access to receive potential clients. The questionable morals of Gwladys Wenceslas and his odious behavior towards the Malagasy in that region eventually exacerbated the local authorities. They politely invited him to leave that place. The hotel remained empty and this gentleman was forced to run in the capital where he became the manager of four other bar-hotels. It's in one of them that Maryse was force to work as a "waitress". She found herself implicated in a network of sexual tourism, more profitable then the hotel industry itself! Athal had pointed the name of the hotel and the one of the street in the mission order. Why hadn't Eglon's men found Maryse?

That morning, as I was seating in front of the computer, I heard the rumbling of a helicopter! With fear in my stomach, I hurried outside to try to recognize the aircraft through the trees. Who was it? Mercenaries of *Achab industry*? Enemies of Eglon coming to take revenge?

The craft slowly scanned the sky of Kheo like taking the time to examine everything before landing. At the third passage, I sufficiently noticed its silhouette to find the smallness of its size and the lack of distinctive sign on its fuselage. He landed in the center of the quarry by raising a thick cloud of dust. I recognized Franck's helicopter! Happy, I ran to the cockpit door which opened with hesitation.

'Hey, Franck! Is it you?

Jerome?

Yes! Welcome to Kheo. I'm happy to see you again!

Me too. No danger here anymore?

No, the way is free. But what made you decide to come here?

Well, it's a long story…

Come with me to the villa to tell me everything!

Uhm… my aircraft…

No worries, no one will damage it, just close the door and follow me!'

I was in a hurry to hear Franck's story. I was convinced inside myself that he would lead his investigation to try to understand the events surrounding the mystery of this lost island on which he had left me ten months earlier. On the way, he looked everywhere around him, surprised to find me alone in this surreal setting free of any military presence.

◆ ◆ ◆

My pilot took a seat on the red ornament of the sofa, while I served him a small glass of tequila. He discreetly observed the screens behind me and the corners of the room, stroking his index finger around his mustache. I read in his look and his small smile that he knew something concerning my new life. His words confirmed my suspicions:

'I met someone you know well in Dar es Salam!

Really? Who?

Athal! He told me everything. I know everything that happened since you have been living here!

Yeah, since the day I made the acquaintance of the helicopters of *Achab industry* who almost shot me dead in the place I was waiting for you!

Sorry, but I didn't measure up to them! I'm not armed, and when I saw them head towards Kheo...

I know Franck, there was nothing you could do for me.

Next, there was war in Zaire. Damn war! When I think your father worked there for many years without doubting anything! He bought medicine from this mafia for his humanitarian mission.

He knew nothing of the hidden activities of *Achab industry*, fortunately the medicine was in general of good quality. But tell me about my friend Athal. How is he? How did you meet him?

Everything happened at the port of Dar es Salaam during the operations at the bay of *Sirius*, *Geometrix* and a little freighter: the *Ephiphane*, one that no one had ever seen. Athal came towards us while I was talking to the members of the crew of the *Geometrix* that I knew very well. It's through them I learned of the existence of the island of Kheo from where certain medicine came destined for the humanitarian missions, like your father's, stationed in Zaire. Everyone was surprised to see him there. Jose, who worked on the *Geometrix* gave him an envelope, excusing himself of not being able to come to Kheo in the next days.

The word "Kheo" made me react. I questioned your friend, talking to him about you and we hit it off.

Did he say what that envelope contained?

No, but here it is, it's for you.'

Franck gave me the document taken from the pocket of his aviator jacket. He carefully fixed me with his look while stroking his moustache. I took out two passports from the envelope: mine and that of Kelia, more real than the original. Inside, there were even Malagasy tax stamps on an expired visa as if Kelia had already visited Madagascar! I recognized my fiancée's photo which I had taken in front of a white wall of a building on the island. Franck exclaimed:

'Passports! This doesn't surprise me. Jose has his lab on the *Geometrix*. One day he even succeeded in making fake dollars that he sold to dealers!

I know, Athal told me. So he asked you to come here to give me this envelope, isn't that right?

Affirmative. He assured me there was no risk anymore. He told me everything that passed here since the conspiracy against his father, until today. That boy, he's got guts! He's really extraordinary! And you all by the way, not easy to maintain your cool and conspire against that kind of armed and dangerous scum!

Yeah...'

At the bottom of the envelope, I discovered a scribbled paper by Athal, writing this:

'Jerome, hello my boy!

As you notice, I survived! Gontran and his two brutes took control of the Ephiphane, mastering the crew – The other soldiers, the Colombians and me got off at Dar es Salam!

Eglon died during the crossing.

The Colombians and the others found the fallen members of the Achab organization to make an alliance with them. At the time I'm writing, the Ephiphane was raised its anchor. The Colombians with their new accomplices have

224

just finished equipping heavy weapons on a fishing boat
with which they will embark in pursuit of Gontran.
Me, I'm staying out of this.
Destination Somalia, then Europe.
See you soon, my boy!
Athal.'

After having read the letter out loud, I invited my visitor to go down to the village to introduce him to my friends. He accepted, reading Kelia's passport:

Your fiancée? Cute!

Yes, she's an orphan like me.

Did her parents die a long time ago?

No, they were contaminated with nuclear waste while storing the waste in the bunkers.

Damn waste! Athal told me there's no risk today, but he told me nothing regarding your fiancée's parents.

It's in the past.'

We walked in silence until the quarry with rabbits where Franck spoke again:

'I can't stay for very long, I won't have enough kerosene to join the *Cirius* who set sail for Madagascar.

Don't worry about it, I know the place where Athal hid two barrels of kerosene.

Your invaders left it? In that case, I'll buy enough to fill my tank. Regarding this fuel, I owe you a return voyage, I didn't forget. When are counting on leaving?

I have to go to Madagascar to find someone, it's very important.

No problem! Do you have any family there?

Not really. It's about one of the deported women that Eglon's men weren't capable of bringing here.

Athal also told me about this, but I don't understand. There were nine women on the *Geometrix*, one is still missing?

The duo responsible to repatriate Maryse didn't find her and replaced her by a randomly selected Malagasy!

225

Unbelievable! And you put it in your head to find the true Maryse.

Yeah.

Well, considering the circumstances, I'll finance and completely organize your travel, I owe you this!

Ah?... Thank you.

But once there, I won't be able to stay with you. I'll give you ten days before coming to get you, is it ok?

Yes, it's ok!

Take off at the beginning of the afternoon after having filled my tanks! You'll find your cabin on the *Cirius* again!

At your orders, Mister Franck!

20 – Looking for Maryse

Tamatave, Monday, January 19, 1998

During the stop on the *Cirius* container carrier in the port of Tamatave, Franck talked to me in my cabin. He had just passed his morning in town, asking me to wait for him aboard. He gave me a huge bundle of cash containing two million Malagasy francs, warning me:

'Stash them well, watch out if you walk into town at night. Do you have your passport?

Yes, but no visa!

No matter, here's your card as a member of this crew, I made it up for the occasion. You're a mechanic on the *Cirius*. You have the captain's authorization to go out.

But what if they search me?

Pft! Calm down, I'll accompany you to help you get out of port. Don't take any luggage so you won't attract attention.

Are you sure I'm not risking anything?

I am well placed to tell you that we don't become rich by transporting bananas, rice or charcoal! You only have to look at *Achab industry.*

What report?

Just an example, president Clinton just authorized a Chinese company to control the Long Beach port in California to facilitate arms trafficking. Most democratic countries close their eyes regarding the handling and surveillance of their ports. All this is to tell you that we're in a lawless state area!

Let's not exaggerate, this is not America!'

Franck greeted some sailors and dockworkers. He seemed to know everyone. Container-terminal, stockyard, tanks, parking lots, warehouses... After half an hour of walking, we finally got out of port among the general indifference.

Is it still far? I asked.

No, only this path to cross. My taxi awaits at Lambert Street.

The taxi driver that Franck introduced was black, thin and had a minuscule moustache, corduroy trousers and a light colored shirt. He seemed peaceful and smiling and answered to the name of Jacques. Franck sang me his praise and gave him some last recommendations:

'My friend Jacques, it's been ten years since I know you, so I will trust you with a trusted mission. You'll take good care of my "nephew" Jerome. You'll take him everywhere he wants, you'll serve as guide and interpreter and you'll bring him back here in exactly nine days, safe and sound and certainly accompanied by a woman. Understood?

(Affirmative nodding of Jacques's head)

That day, your mission will be finished and I'll give you another million! And if you'll find the person he's looking for, I'll give you another million! Understood

(A more affirmative nodding of Jacques's head)'

Franck greeted me as my driver was starting his cab. He tried to reassure me:

Don't worry, you'll give him the address and he'll find the place you're looking for. Sorry for not being able to accompany you. Safe journey and see you here in nine days! Stash your money well!

Thank you... thank you for everything!

It's nothing, it's normal, your father would have done the same thing!

I opened the squeaky door of the Renault 12 which had to have my age, to sit on the back seat. I gave to the young Malagasy a page from my pocket book on which the complete address of the hotel where Maryse worked was written:

Bar Hotel "Moonlight"
Batimad City, in Ankorondrano
Antananarivo

Without the slightest hesitation and after a last affirmative nodding of his head, my driver launched his *Renault 12* on the asphalt road heated by the white summer sun. I didn't risk falling asleep because the car zigzagged to overcome crowded minibuses, carts of all kinds pulled by zebu or men, bicycles and potholes. I had no idea how long the road we had to take was. Should I ask my driver? This would have allowed me to hear his voice. If he had to serve as my interpreter, it would be best he was not mute!

♦ ♦ ♦

We arrived in the suburbs of the capital about three hours later. The anti-sagging board under the seat in black leatherette had become very hard and I couldn't wait for the ride to finish. Suddenly, the car climbed a median in the middle of a boulevard. Horror! A policeman in a beige uniform motioned for us to stop. Would he ask for my passport which had no visa? Anxious, I put my head between my shoulders, awaiting inquiry. My driver, very calm, stopped the engine and got out to meet the agent who was approaching behind us. I watched them in the mirror. The two men exchanged some words, then my driver got out his wallet, no doubt to show him his papers. I saw a plated banknote against the driving license that he handed to the policeman. As he wasn't reacting, I saw a second banknote slip over the first one. The agent took the license, looked at it and gave it back to my driver... without the banknotes! Jacques resumed his place as natural as could be, pressed a switch and grabbed two electric ends folded under the dashboard to put them in contact one with the other and, some sparks later, the engine started.

The *Renault 12* resumed its wild ride. But it had to slow down because of the population that was becoming more and more dense. After having crossed huge tracts of vegetation, rice fields and red dust, we went into the crowd that moved in all directions on the pavement while the sidewalks were completely congested with stalls and merchants. Everyone sold everything. Some displayed their meager harvest on the ground. Oval tomatoes, bean pods, fruits, poultry... and stuff I didn't know. Jacques often honked to clear a passage.

I was a stranger, a clandestine that was slowly sinking in that unknown country. In the midst of this human tide, I thought about what Hemerik had said about his fiancée: 'It's like looking for a grain of sand in the ocean!' I was worried. Despite the crowd around me, I felt terribly alone. This solitude was good for meditation and gave me the desire to confide myself even more in God. There was no question of abandoning, it was inconceivable that Maryse and Hemerik remain separated, no matter what it cost me! After having driven slowly for half an hour in crowded avenues, we reached an elevated road, dominating rice fields on either side of us. There, no more sidewalks or displays, just an endless line of pedestrians traveling between the road and the water. Far below, strange brick buildings, like huge graves were spitting smoke.

'What is it? I asked my driver, who was not so talkative.

Brick kilns. The earth is baked to make bricks.'

At the same time, I noticed stored bricks for sale piled beside the road.

'In how much time will we get there?

Soon!'

I was exhausted, thirsty and I was hurting everywhere. Suddenly, the car left the road to stop on a trail near a district of shacks. Intrigued, I immediately questioned my driver:

'Where are we? Is it here?

No. We drove for a long time, the engine too hot!'

The young man got out to open the hood and blocked it using a stick from under his seat. Then, he told me:

'I'm going to look for water for the radiator. You must you stay here to watch the taxi. I'll come back quickly!

But I'm thirsty, is it possible to have some water?

Yes, me, I bring. You, watch the taxi.'

He disappeared among the shacks.

I was disappointed: the journey wasn't over! Everything I knew was that we would "soon" arrive and I had to "watch" the taxi. But why watch over this old vehicle? Someone would want to steal it?

Paradoxically, with my clandestine status, I felt safer in the middle of this slum than on a highway. The police, for sure, wouldn't come pick me up here!

◆ ◆ ◆

As Jacques was late in coming, I began baking in that taxi. I tried to open the window of the left door, but it remained blocked, the one on the right opened two centimeters. Two young children approached, a hand outstretched to ask for money.

'Mister please... Mister please...'

They were dirty and their clothes had holes. Persistent, they repeated calmly in a thin voice:

'Mister please... Mister please...'

Behind us, an older girl carrying a baby hooked to her belly also approached by repeating the same litany. I was troubled, crossing their pleading looks.

The minutes passed with an unbearable slowness. What was Jacques doing? I was getting increasingly uncomfortable. These poor kids had to be really hungry to insist that way! How to get out of this indescribable adventure?

I decided to give them some money. I took a wad of cash that I hid between my knees, out of sight. I would have liked to give them some Malagasy francs, but I had no coins, nor any banknotes of less than ten thousand francs. I didn't know the value of the local currency and I had the idea to get rid of the most damaged and dirty ones. I folded one in four so it wouldn't be torn in the scuffle and I slipped it through the narrow glass opening. The boy who caught it first, widened his eyes, screaming:

"Manome vola antsika ilay vazaha !". (The white stranger is giving money!)

I continued my distribution: a second banknote, then a third one. At the fourth one, I realized that it was darker in that suffocating car. Twenty children came out of nowhere, surrounding the taxi. Wanting to remain discreet, I had formed a noisy crowd around me!

When I understood my mistake, the right window opened completely, falling inside the door! I vainly tried to put it right again using the handle, but it turned in nothing. Supporting myself on my legs, I then seized the glass with my hands using all my strength to put it back. During the maneuver, my left foot sank abnormally in the floor. Under three layers of carpet, I discovered a hole surrounded by a rusty metal lace.

Outside, a boy shoved another one, smaller than him to take his money. I could see their legs and bare feet fighting in the red dust under the other kids. The crowd turned into a riot, and while I thoroughly replaced the carpet shreds on the floor, the glass fell again inside the door! Five arms took the opportunity to penetrate and small black hands tried to grab me like tentacles! What a nightmare! Was I to die of thirst and suffocation in this piece of junk?

"Mandehana ! Mandehana ! Lasa ianareo mandeha any !" (Leave! Leave! Come on, scram!) my driver screamed, finally back. He gave me a bottle of fresh water. The group of children went away quickly. That water must have the best in the universe! After having drunk half the bottle, I read on the label: *Living Water.*

Jacques slipped his hand behind the inner panel of the door and put the glass back in place in less than three seconds, warning me: 'No touch!'. Then, he spilled a liter of water in the radiator once the steam completely dissipated. He closed the hood, put his stick under the seat and started the engine of the taxi that left the track to embark on the paved road.

As night came, we stopped in the courtyard that was on a slope of a hotel in the town of Talatamaty. Before going in the building, Jacques explained that according to uncle Franck, he had to pay for the gas and guide me wherever I needed to go. However, hotel and food expenses concerned my wallet.

The staff was very welcoming and understood French. Our hosts were surprised to have no suitcase to get out of the trunk of the car! I reserved a room with two beds and covered the cost of the evening meal. The shower was hot and the room modest, but comfortable. As on Kheo, the night was very dark and life began again at five o'clock in the morning.

Talatamaty, Tuesday, January 20

After breakfast, my guide proposed to go on foot in a market not far away to buy some spare underwear. In the afternoon, he refueled and undertook a first approach to the bar Moonlight, ten miles from our hotel. When he located

232

the hotel, Jacques began to slow down voluntarily to properly give me the time to observe the building. It looked like a big villa, colonial style, with a four-sided roof covered with corrugated iron sheets, it had three floors, a large terrace overlapping on the sidewalk. A woman was sweeping the terrace surrounded by solid wood in which something resembling ferns grew.

We had no photo of Maryse. Jacques proposed he come himself on foot in the evening to question the personnel while I waited for him in his taxi, parked at the other end of the street. The idea seemed good and gave me assurance.

♦ ♦ ♦

Evening came, my driver stopped his vehicle as discussed, a hundred meters from the building. He asked me for money and began his investigation. When he returned two hours later, he told me no one knew Maryse. The same failure in the morning and the following evening.

Ankorondrano, Thursday, January 22

I decided to go myself, in my turn, at the same place, leaving Jacques in his taxi.

On the terrace, I found that the hostesses were more numerous than the customers. Three Malagasy waitresses, very friendly, welcomed me and invited me to sit on a wicker chair before a small coffee table. The two younger ones asked permission to sit at my table, while the older one (around forty years old) proposed she go get me a *Coca Cola* from the bar. She came back holding a tray on which were three other drinks for each of them! On the receipt, the bill amounted to 22,000 Malagasy francs! I began to understand why my driver asked me exorbitant sums to have a drink at this bar.

I felt bad at ease between these two teenage girls who ogled me. Jacques had no doubt already questioned everyone. The older waitress had just sat down in front of me, smiling. I began the dialogue:

'My name is Jerome, and you?

Here, I'm Valse Kely, and these are my two colleagues, Nadia and Rosa.

Valse Kely, for how long have you worked here?

For at least twenty years.

You have no doubt known Maryse.

No, no one with that name. *(Silence)*

Listen well, I'm going to ask you something, it's a secret.

A secret? I have no secrets.

If you tell me where Maryse is, I'll give you one hundred thousand francs!

One hundred thousand francs? It would be nice to know this woman. For as long as I have worked here, I haven't known anyone with that name.

Are you really sure?

Yes. I can't say where a woman I don't know lives, not even for one hundred thousand francs!

Very well, I'll pay my bill and I'll leave.

You don't want to pass the evening with us?

No, I'll come back tomorrow evening. If from now until then, your memory will come back or if you know someone who could tell me the place where Maryse is, I'll give you lots of money. But don't forget, it's a secret, Mister Gwladys Venceslas mustn't know.

You know the owner?

Yes, but I don't want to see him!'

Ankorondrano, Friday, January 23

On the terrace, the three women were waiting for me. At this end of the week, the clients were more numerous in the main hall. As the evening before, Valse Kely was wearing a new pink blouse with a deep V neckline. She

234

proposed I sit, but knew nothing of the place where Maryse was. I refused her invitation and went to the bar alone. The bartender was also Malagasy. As soon as he finished serving a client, he came to me:

'Good evening, Sir! What will you have…?

Good evening. A *Coca Cola* please.

Here you go.

Thank you. I'm looking for a waitress named Maryse. I know she works here. Do you know where she lives? *(Silence)*

I know Maryse, but I don't know where she lives. I wonder why a lot of people are looking for Maryse!

Really? Who are these people?

It was a few weeks ago, two white men in uniform. They wanted to give me money so I would tell me them where Maryse is. Me, I said nothing to them. I don't trust them.

Why? Did they threaten you?

They weren't polite with the girls, I didn't want them to hurt Maryse so I said absolutely nothing to them. They asked to see the owner, Mister Venceslas and I said: he's traveling.

Your owner is traveling?

Yes, and I don't know where Maryse is. There came a young man yesterday to ask the same thing. Maryse left five years ago, she didn't like working here. She ran and Mister Venceslas was very angry.

If Maryse worked here five years ago, why didn't Valse Kely know her?

It's normal, all the girls who work here have a nickname for the clients. Maryse's nickname was "Miora". Valse Kely doesn't know Maryse's real name, she only know the nickname Miora.

I thank you. How much do I owe you?

Four thousand, but why you are looking to find out where Maryse is?

To invite her to come back to the island of Kheo where her fiancé awaits her.

Kheo? Don't know.

I'm not surprised, there are many island in the Indian Ocean!'

Valse Kely came to sit at the bar, right near me. Without losing a second, she demanded I offered her a drink. I remained silent to make her ill at ease. The bartender, who was waiting for the order and who seemed to understand I wasn't there to have fun, asked his colleague in French:

'Kely, do you remember Miora?

Yes, she left. Four or five years ago... why?

This gentleman wants to know where Miora lives.
(Silence)

The waitress took a disdainful air, lighting a cigarette. She pulled on her mini denim skirt to position herself in her seat and tapped the heels of her boots on the bottom of the bar stool. Then, looking at the roof of the bar, she ironically replied, in the blue smoke of her cigarette:

'This Mister Jerome wants to know where my friend Miora lives! Well-well. And me, I know where my friend lives.

She lives where?

This Mister Jerome is going to offer me a beverage and drink a little with me.'

I understood I had to play her game if I wanted to get this precious information out of her, supposing it was true! The ball was in her court, I had no other choice but to give in to her whims. After having served his colleague, the bartender went away to take care of another client, on whose shoulders were Nadia and Rosa. Valse Kely quietly finished her mango juice and her cigarette and put her right index finger on my lips, smelling of nicotine. She whispered:

'This Mister Jerome will follow me where I'll invite him in my room, the silence, more quiet to talk about where Miora lives!'

236

We crossed the big main room, divided into six boxes, separated by massive artificial plants. Businessman and tourists of white race and mature, sprawled on leather sofas, were sipping rum and other exotic drinks. Teenage "waitresses" huddled against them. Red light spots, blue smoke brewed by fans, golden atmosphere and sequins, rhythmic and languid music... as I was hesitant, my waitress took my hand to pull me down the aisle that led to the stairs. Stuck on the back wall, a stuffed crocodile, two meters long "decorated" the place.

Valse Kely locked the door behind her and sat down on the edge of the bed, crossing her long feet, sheathed in black stockings. She pushed the button of a cassette radio set in her nightstand. German waltzes could be heard, played by a grand orchestra. Standing against the door, I asked the woman without further ado:

'How much?

To sleep with me?

Only in your dreams! I note that here, the age difference isn't a problem, and you would have an unique opportunity to do that with a guy like me, fifteen years younger than you!

Pft! You think me too old?

How much to tell me where Miora lives?'

The waitress was late in answering, without doubt to irritate me. She applied a layer of lipstick, fixing her eyes on her pocket mirror.

One hundred thousand francs.

Only this? Do you know how to write?

Yes.

Write Miora's address in my book and I'll give you one hundred thousand francs.

Give me the money.

Here they are. If the address is right and I'll find Miora, I'll come back and I'll give you another extra hundred thousand francs. This sum will go directly in your pockets, without leaving three quarters to your employer.'

The woman wrote slowly, moving her red, shining lips.

Private estate between Talatamaty and Mandriambero Ambohidratrimo

I don't know where she live, but I wrote where she work. Give all the money, address is right!

No way, I'll come back only if I find Miora.

You won't come back.

I will, I gave my word.

Where are you going?

I'm going back to my hotel.

No, don't leave right away. The clients downstairs will believe you no slept with me, and it's not good for my business. Stay a little more, please.

I understand, I'll sit in this armchair to wait.

No, it's broken and you'll fall!

Why keep a broken armchair?

I put my clothes on it, sit next to me on the bed.'

I had to wait, rocked by the joyful rhythm of a large Philharmonic.

The woman dared put her head on my shoulder. If someone had told I would one day find myself in a prostitute's room, listening to waltz by Johann Strauss in Madagascar…! My curiosity pushed to ask:

'Why are you listening to this kind of music? It's not very known here!

It's a gift from a Mister of the German country in Europe, he used to come here two years ago. I love his music, so he gave me this. Then my colleagues gave me the nickname: *Valse Kely*, it means: *Little Waltz*.

What's your real name?

Irene. The Mister there still left for his country.
(Silence)

238

And you're sad because this Mister left. You loved him, didn't you?

Yes... and me... Pft! Who loves me? No one! Miora has a lot of luck: her fiancé sends men to look for her, her fiancé loves her very much!'

She threw her red tube of lipstick against the wall and began crying against me. Taken aback and after a brief hesitation, I hugged her. And me, who thought that these prostitutes were hardened and obsessed with money!

Time passed until the click of the button "Start" that rose to stop the tape at the end of the track.

Saturday, January 24

Jacques parked his *Renault 12* on the side, a hundred meters away from the entrance to the private housing estate indicated by Valse Kely. A guard opened the gate to let people in or out of this fully fenced and gated neighborhood. As there were only passing cars, I wondered how to recognize Maryse, whose photo I didn't even have! My papers weren't in order, so there was no way I was going to question the guard.

At the end of the day, my driver proposed he go himself to question the guard, set on giving him money, but I refused to take this risk. The fact of parking there all day had to be enough to intrigue these peaceful people.

Around evening, I saw a group of Malagasy pedestrians exit. Jacques explained that most residents living in this neighborhood were of white race, coming from different foreig countries. They hired servants among the local population to make them work at home during the day. In the evening, all these domestic workers returned home, somewhere in the surrounding municipalities. Some stayed longer or stayed the night at their bosses' house to look after the children. This allowed the parents to go out in the city.

As soon as the pedestrians arrived at the level of my taxi, I approached them:

'Good evening sirs, ladies!

Good evening! They replied, staring at me.

Have you seen Miora or Maryse?

No.'

The group walked away, chatting in Malagasy.

Fifteen minutes later, a woman with a bicycle and a small backpack passed us by, ignoring my calls. I was sitting next to Jacques, asleep at the wheel. I sent him to question the cyclist.

My driver took several long minutes to start the old engine. I wanted him to hurry to catch the cyclist before she got lost in traffic.

I waited, standing against a tree in the twilight. When the *Renault 12* disappeared, another woman in a long, multicolored dress, holding a shopping bag, passed the guard's station. Arriving where I was, I noticed she corresponded somewhat to the description made by Kelia. My heart began beating faster, I dared approach her:

'Good evening, Mrs. Miora!

Good evening, young man, she answered, slowing her pace and fixing me with a look like she was trying to remember my name.

My name is Jerome, I said, walking next to her.

Jerome? I don't remember you. From where do you know me?

You don't know me, but I know you, your real name is Maryse!'

Miora hurried her pace, looking straight ahead. She seemed to be afraid and retorted.

'If it's Gwladys Venceslas who sends you, tell him I'll never go back to work in his establishment!

It's not your old owner who sends me, I come from the part of your fiancé Hemerik who's waiting for you on the island of Kheo!'

240

The woman stopped short and dropped her tote on the ground. She remained still for several seconds and then turned to me. Her hands tightened on her mouth and her wide eyes filled tears. I had difficulty holding mine! The taxi made a U-turn at the gate and stopped behind us. Jacques saw Maryse planted and motionless before me. He understood what had happened and opened the doors of his car.

It was getting dark and the lights emitted by the taxi were flickering light on the stony ground of the dam. Our new passenger showed us the way to her home in the neighboring village. She lived in an old container she shared with one woman and her three children near a truck frame. A canopy made of a metal sheet and four rafters, stood against an opening and served as a kitchen. This is where Maryse's roommate was cooking a pot of rice on a stove where charcoal was heating. Her children were playing with the rim of a bicycle wheel that they were rolling like a hoop.

We talked for an hour, seated in the car. Hemerik's fiancée told us about all her life. She had been the first deported woman, at the age of 26 and had been living in Madagascar for 9 years. She had run away five years ago from the *Mooonlight* hotel where she had been employed by force. It was there that a customer noticed her perfect speech and encouraged her to seek other employment. This is how she had found a place as a maid in a French family of residents in the private housing estate. I offered her a room at the inn where Jacques and I were staying, but she preferred to spend her last twenty four hours with her misfortunate neighborhood friends:

'Come get me tomorrow evening please, tomorrow's Sunday, I'm not working for my employers and I'll be ready. I'll also write them a letter to explain my sudden departure.

Understood, Maryse, I answered her, we'll be present for the meet. Until tomorrow!'

Sunday, January 25

Rest day! Free reign for Jacques who left his taxi in the hotel's courtyard to go walk in the city. As for me, I had decided to go to the religious service in the church of the village. I didn't understand Malagasy, but I loved finding myself in the middle of these faithful ones. The fervor of their songs reminded me of those of Kheo. Shortly before dark, Jacques went for Maryse. I reserved a room for her in our hotel. During dinner, she wanted to know my past and we chatted until midnight!

Monday, January 26

After strolling all day in the markets where I bought a bracelet for my fiancée, we returned to the hotel. Before spending our last night, I asked Jacques to take me to the Moonlight to meet Valse Kely, to whom I had promised one hundred thousand francs if I found Maryse. Jacques stopped his taxi in his usual place and as I didn't want to return to that bar, I decided at the last moment to send my driver to take the waitress her money. Around an hour later, when I was falling asleep in the back seat of the *Renault 12*, I heard doors slamming and voices. I opened my eyes and saw Jacques putting a bag in his trunk. Valse Kely was close to him and waited for a door to be opened for her. She had definitely quit her workplace to join us! I didn't have the heart to refuse her, I only hoped Franck would accept.

Tuesday, January 27

Destination Tamatave! After I paid my hotel bill of more than a million francs, we went aboard the taxi who started on the track. We arrived at Lambert Street, near the harbor at the beginning of the afternoon, at the same place from where we had left nine days earlier. Franck joined us a

242

little after. He paid Jacques, asking him for a last ride: to take us, the girls and I, on a beach a few kilometers from there, where he could come get us with the helicopter.

Franck embarked us by helicopter on board the *Cirius* that evening. The captain made the two new passengers visit the wheelhouse, while two old sailors offered them to visit their cabin! Seeming me come after them, the two sea wolves retraced their steps!

21 — Wedding on Kheo

Khéo, Friday, January 30, 1998

The captain of the *Cirius* agreed to get close to the island of Kheo to take us back. I had promised to offer him the two empty containers left on the beach. They would be repainted and available in the Dar es Salam harbor at the end of the year.

This Friday morning, around nine o'clock, the container carrier cast anchor close to the carcass of the platform. All the crowd, warned by radio of our arrival, gathered on the bank and invaded the pier and the cliff.

Hemerik and Kelia arrived in the *zodiac*. I thanked the captain and Franck who refused to stay a few days on Kheo, then, I hurried to the ladder, carrying the two women's luggage. I was euphoric at the idea of snuggling against my fiancée and asking her to marry me!

There are no words to describe such moments. Hemerik took Maryse's hand to help her climb into the unstable vessel. He kissed the one he thought never to see again. I saw him cry for the first time, tears of joy, erasing the years of service and deprivation.

During our hugs, Valse Kely waited on her knees at the prow of the *zodiac*. I invited her to come to us so we could make the introductions. Without hesitation, Kelia hugged her hard in her arms, like she had known her forever: 'Welcome to our home, Kely!' The latter was breathless and moved to tears.

Etienne, Linda, Nicodeme, Mado, Fredo, Rose-Marie, Nellie... The joy of reunion, introductions, vibrant songs from the crowd, my triumphant return... this is how this beautiful Friday passed, the last day of January, the first day of a new era on Kheo.

Etienne announced nine marriages and eleven introductions of children for Sunday! Why wait? During our absence, the seamstresses had crafted orange robes for the brides and tunics of the same fabric for the eleven babies. That of Maryse was created the day after her arrival. Everything was ready for Sunday.

Sunday, February first, 1998

Worship, introduction of the children, marriage, the ceremony began at nine o'clock and ended around one. From above, I saw the crowd, filling the yard until the porch, sing a last song in this unforgettable celebration.

> *On those spouses, Everlasting Father,*
> *throw in this solemn moment a favorable look.*
> *Protect them in your goodness,*
> *let them shine the light of thy lovely face...*

I was the only white among these people whom I considered family. I was feeling good in the middle of this people. Next to me, my wife looked at me discreetly, smiling. With her hat with flowers and her long orange dress with a round neckline, she resembled a doll. She wore white gloves and a white ribbon around her bun and another around the waist. I found her even more desirable! Anyway,

I always found her beautiful, even with her red suit and her rubber boots!

The communal meal was a veritable banquet. Tables overflowing with food lined under the courtyards. We could serve as much as we wanted. Many were eating while standing, others carried their trays and sat down under branches made especially for the occasion in the middle of the square. They had crafted an ephemeral shelter with fishing nets held by iron metal cords on poles. The vegetation on the ground alleviated the heat. Nicodeme had trained some musicians to interpret some rhythmic pieces.

The festivities lasted until late in the night. Kelia had no intention of waiting too much before returning to the villa. She had planned to escape the crowd around nine o'clock by hiding the bike on the outside of the place, close to the porch.

At "H" hour, I started the bike. Not easy for my passenger to position herself behind me with such a long dress. She held her feet on the left side and grabbed my waist with her right arm.

The night was warm, dark and light from the lighthouse caressed the ground, still hot. Plantations, bunkers, quarry, the clearing of rabbits... everywhere on our road, the spluttering engine broke the silence of the sleepy hill.

There were only two rooms in this huge villa, I chose the biggest one for our wedding night. The walls, the color of apple-green gave a relaxing atmosphere. Above my bedside tablet, a small keyboard with a few lights and a tiny screen allowed me access to the main computer of the property. Without losing a minute, I ordered the closing of all exits and electric shutters and I dimmed the power of the spotlights embedded in the ceiling to give a soft, white light. To cover the slight hum of the air conditioning, I programmed a languorous music to accompany our lovemaking. We were cut off from the world and decided to spend a... steamy night! I had just finished these settings when Kelia climbed over to hug me and came to lie on me. I loved the taste of her lipstick and the softness of her makeup.

She got up to make herself comfortable and removed all her jewelry.

'Stop! I said.

What?

Let me undress you, please!

Uhm... yes, if you want.'

She stood motionless, closing her eyes while I untied her white belt. I unbuttoned her dress, taking my good time to better appreciate it...

My wife was wearing only her underwear when suddenly, a buzzer sounded behind us!

'What is it? she asked with a start.

I'm going to see, I answered, approaching the minuscule screen, I see someone in front of the entrance door: I think it's Nellie...

Oh, no! What does she want?'

Kelia grabbed a robe and ran to the entrance. I followed her, staying a few meters behind. She opened the door and questioned her sister in an annoyed tone:

'Nellie! What's happening?

Nothing, I'm not well...

How come you're not well? It's ten o'clock in the evening! What did you come here for? Did you come alone in this darkness?

Yes, I want to sleep here... in the villa.

Nellie, I already explained. You won't throw a fit during my wedding night! There's no question of you staying here!

But, in the small room...

No, Nellie, and I'm sure no one knows where you are, neither Linda, nor the pastor!

No, but...

Don't insist, I'm going to take you back from where you came from on the bike!'

Nellie let a tear fall and added in an imploring voice:

'Please...'

Kelia turned towards me, embarrassed:

'I'm going to accompany her try to make her see reason. Dressed that way?

Bah… it's night, I'll leave her a little before the porch!'

Alone, I waited in the living room, seated in front of the surveillance camera screen to see the return of the bike.

Kelia came back around an hour later. With a jump, she took a seat on my knees without leaving me time to react. She stood huddled against me and seemed even more upset than before. After a long moment of silence, I dared ask her:

'Upset?

Yes. I thought I had prepared her to face this separation.

She still needs her big sister.

She's exaggerating! She's going to be ten years old soon, she's capable of understanding this.

She might understand this, but the break is too abrupt.

Still, she's blaming me as if I'm abandoning her. We can't let her sleep between us, she has to become responsible!

Easy to say, she has been sleeping in your bed since she was born, you should have gotten her used to sleeping alone before our marriage.

It's true, I didn't have the strength to do it before, but now, I'm paying for my mistake. The loss of our parents strengthened our connection.'

The evening passed, the body of my beloved seemed to relax against me. Then, her head slowly toppled backward: she had fallen asleep! Should I wake her? Her day had begun at four in the morning to help the other women prepare the party. Moreover, she was worried about her little sister. Here are two good reasons to carry my wife to the marital bed… and watch her sleeping! This wise decision forced me to turn off the soft light and the languorous music. After which, I decided to go take a cold shower!

For some days, Fredo had let the inside pool gradually fill at the level of the water in the wells. A floating system, connected to the computer regulated the flow rate to prevent damage to the groundwater. As the pool was almost full, I read the instructions concerning the devices for the filtration of the ground level and the solar water heating. I felt the sleeve of Kelia's bathrobe touch my neck. She sat on the stairs next me and laid her head on my shoulder. She had just gotten up and... noting the slowness of her movements, I guessed that her moral had not improved since yesterday! I had the honor of delivering the first words of the first morning of our married life:

'Did you sleep well?

Bah... sorry for yesterday evening...

You're worried about your sister, aren't you?

My sister, and also Linda and her husband. How are they going to handle this situation? Who'll take care of my sister? I feel responsible, if she behaves bad with them, do I have the right to let her bother these people who have already done so much for us?

Are you hungry?

No.

Me neither. In this case, this is what I suggest: prepare yourself and we'll go find our friends to think about all this. We'll find a solution.

You're right, I'll take a shower and we'll go.'

Kelia had put on her red suit, climbed behind me on the bike.

Already in work clothes?

Yes, I didn't feed the rabbits yesterday, I don't want them to starve!

I'll help you.'

Fredo had put vegetable peelings and pails with the truck and all those who were raising rabbits helped themselves.

248

We took what was left to bring them to the clearing. Suddenly, two children arrived by bicycle behind us, accompanied by the dog. I recognized Nellie and Rene, the little Malagasy who had disembarked from the *Geometrix* recently with his mother.

'Hello, lovebirds! Nellie cried, sparkling with joy, Fredo is going to build me a bed-house!

A bed-house? Kelia asked, what's this new invention?

It's a bunk bed for me and Rene, with walls, windows, door at the bottom to be able to go in with a ladder. It will be built in the place of your old bed where you used to sleep with me. Rene will live below and I'll live on the first floor.

There's a good idea, like this, you won't be alone. My husband and I can't wait to see it!

Fredo says he'll finish building it this evening! They put a curtain to separate the room. Rene's mom and Kely will also sleep in bunk beds on the other side of the curtain.'

◆ ◆ ◆

Around the afternoon, Etienne invited us to lunch, while we were in front of Fredo and Hemerik's workshop. When going to the table, Kelia wanted to help Linda and Nellie set the table, but the pastor's wife refused, saying: 'No, Madame, you stay seated with your husband! You no longer live with us and you're our guests. Let yourselves be served!'

Linda, who knew well my wife, did everything to make her comfortable. During the meal, she whispered some words in her year. She surrounded her like a mother watching over her daughter. Nellie seemed satisfied with her new environment, which reassured her sister. Life on Kheo was more beautiful than ever...

◆ ◆ ◆

Back to the villa, Kelia wanted to rest at the pool which occupied the entire center of the ground floor. This space was so big that the air conditioning was ineffective and the temperature didn't go down below thirty degrees during the hottest period of the day. Moreover, many windows let in the warmth of the sun. The filling of the pool was finished and I maneuvered some valves to activate the filtration system. The chlorine injunction was made. The solar panels hadn't had time to warm up so much water, but my wife begged me to take a bath with her. I hesitated, saying:

'Take a bath in a fifteen degree water? You're brave, Moreover, I don't have a swimming suit.

A swimming suit? What for?'

She undressed in the room next door which had to be a room for gymnastics or bodybuilding. The floor was covered with a thick, soft carpet, similar to those fitted to dojos. For some reason I do not know, no weight machine had been delivered to Kheo. Not only had this room remained empty, but the openings giving to the pool had never received no door or window. In the background, the shower cubicle was also devoid of a door, but the showers worked!

I accompanied my wife, also undressing next to her. Our clothes fell on the carpet in front of the entrance to the showers. We hesitated in the moment of taking off our undergarments.

'We should close everything, remarked Kelia, someone could see us from the outside!

You're right, I'll do the necessary.'

From the wall control panel (the same was in each main room of the villa), I ordered the closure of all electric shutters and a red light to illuminate our bathing time. We were completely naked. My wife swam better than me, a true fish! She then invited me to take a shower with her in the same cubicle! She poured too much shampoo on us and we were completely covered in foam. We were washing each other with circular movements. Suddenly, my hands stopped on the back scars of my loved one, who immediately assured me:

'Don't worry, they don't hurt anymore!
Still, I was so scared that day!
Bah, it's in the past! Fredo made his excuses.
Fredo? What's the connection?
He made that table with a plain sheet of glass recovered prior to construction, very sharp when it breaks!
I see! He hadn't planned on you falling on it!'
Our foamy massage session resumed with more energy. At rinsing time, we were so excited, too impatient to go back to our room at the other end of the property, we fell on our scattered clothes on the floor at the entrance to the shower cubicle! It's there we made love for the first time! We were soaked, and even though the place lacked comfort, it was very spacious, leaving our bodies full freedom of action! We were like two starved people, and the energy expended by my loving wife swept all my worries about it. The trials and tribulations of her past hadn't affected her feminine instinct. This defining moment made me forget my very bad wedding night!

We then fell asleep, entwined... then shower session... pool... shower foam. Our bodies talked again in the same place. We slept some more, then ate some fruit, slept... shower... pool... shower... slept on the floor... ate dried fruit! As we felt some aches, we ended up back in our bed. Time passed without us knowing if it was day or night as the shutters were still closed. I had never stayed completely naked for so long!

By mutual agreement, after a long sleep, we finally decided to go back to reality by taking a look at the bright numbers marking the time in a corner of the control panel: twelve fifteen. I gathered that it was a quarter past twelve on Tuesday, February 4th. The period during which we had been locked had lasted for about twenty two hours! I announced this to my wife, who replied: "Fortunately, Linda assured me she would designate someone else to take care of the rabbits!"

22 – Immigration

A new stage in my life was beginning. A dream life in a haven of peace? Not so sure! Waiting for the uncertain return of Franck or Athal, I had to manage the island. The whole community was counting on me and even if I was well assisted by the pastor's family to study the technical solutions for the development of Kheo, I was worried about finances. Money remained taboo and it was imperative we established trade with the outside. I was also waiting for news from Athal via Internet, who was supposed to put me in contact with a trusted person in the Dar es Salam port to access a bank account to make our purchases.

At the same time, we had to choose a team to learn the technique of pearl farming, according to Athal's idea: harvest the oysters, suspend them on rafts and implement in them a nucleon. A project programmed for the month of April.

Tuesday, February 6, I discovered the files of *Achab industry* on the computer. On the platform, beside the true or false medicine destined for the Africans, they were also making viruses and vaccines for the flu for the Europeans! "Missionaries" were responsible for contaminating industrialized countries to trigger a pandemic, others found a way to sell the vaccine especially developed to protect against the same virus. Actually, *Achab industry* had ramifications discretely applied throughout the juicy global pharmaceutical industry! I had shivers down my spine. This poison had probably been destroyed in the fire of the platform!

And it's not all: for the first time, I discovered the word "computer virus". The dictator's engineers had developed a virus meant to destroy computer systems linked to the Internet. According to the same principle as the one for the flu, they made "antiviruses" to sell them to Internet users and develop this way, a big business on an international scale!

Friday evening, February 7, I received Athal's first message on the Internet:

'Hello my boy! I hope you're doing OK without me!

I'm in Mogadishu, staying with someone. I met your friend Franck again! We settled that you'll be able to deal with him directly to get in contact with the different owners and suppliers you'll need. It's him who will take care of the bills (within the limits of my available money!) I took the chance to prepare a wedding trip for you and your loved one in Paris at the beginning of July (summer time in France). The Geometrix will go to Kheo to go look for you and deliver your future order of that moment.

I don't have any news of our enemies. My correspondent who was supposed to notify the authorities at the Suez Channel to intercept the Ephiphane takes me for a liar, for the Ephiphane never passed through there! Did it sink in the Red Sea? I have no idea. The only information I have so far concerns three helicopters of Achab industry found empty and out of gas in the Djibouti desert.

Give my greetings to everyone! Bye for now!
Athal.'

A vacation in Paris, France! Kelia's dream would come true! Around the end of the month of July, something unbelievable happened: three ships stopped on Kheo in the space of eight days, from July 23 to 30.

Friday, July 23, 1998

An old fishing boat, carrying thirty Ethiopian refugees, wrecked on the beach. These people had tried to find refuge in all the surrounding islands, but as no one wanted them permanently, they finished their journey on the

253

sand of Kheo. Alerted by the children playing there, we went to their encounter to greet them. As a "member of the government", I had no room for error. Etienne, Linda, Hemerik, Fredo and me stood before these refugees that were fleeing the war that had begun in early May between their country and Eritrea. They were waiting, seated on the sand, that we decide their near future. Only one man, of an older age, kept himself upright. He was no doubt the chief of this tribe and knew our language. Seeing them, I felt deep nausea, so terrifying was their appearance. Their skin was very dark and burned by the sun and sea salt. I was ashamed of this disgust I defined as a reflex, an uncontrollable reaction which was quickly replaced by a sense of compassion.

These people were desperate and we were their last hope. Men, women, children in rags were waiting, seated on the sand. After having exchanged some words of greeting, we went back a few meters to talk about the situation and agree on the decision that had to be made. Etienne insisted to welcome these strangers without the slightest condition:

Etienne – These people need us, we have to help them.

Me – Yes, but if they ask to stay with us for good, what will we answer them?

Hemerik - You're the manager, it's for you to tell us what we must answer!

Etienne – Do we have the means to keep them here?

Me – For the moment, I would say yes, but in the years to come… We have to take into consideration the population growth, it becomes a limit, we can't provide for all the refugees who venture here. Our children have priority, right? What do you think?

Etienne – We'll certainly not send these people back to where they came from! Let's propose a delay of a month, for example, to leave us time to find a solution.

Me – Yes, let's host them for a month and let them decided their future. If at the end of that month, they'll ask for permanent stay, we'll decide to accept or not their request.

Linda – First, they'll have to heal. They only have skin problems, a medical examination is required, beginning with the children, I hear the younger ones cry!

Me – As soon as they'll be better, everyone will work. What will our families think if they learn that strangers we haven't invited, are eating for free the people's supplies?

Hemerik (talking to his father) – He's right. We can't allow any injustice, it would create tensions among us.

Fredo – It's well thought all this, but what kind of work do you want them to do? We don't even know what they can do!

Me – I propose they clean all the paths delimiting the plantations, and also the abandoned plots around the villa. There is good topsoil just waiting to be cultivated!

Hemerik – Good idea, I'll organize this work!

Linda – Have you seen their clothes, they're falling to pieces, we have to give them new clothes.

Me – Not now. We'll give them clothes only if they stay here, which hasn't been decided yet. Moreover, if these people wish to leave us before the end of the month, would you find it normal they take with them the clothes destined for our community?

Hemerik – You're right!

Me – Let's welcome them for a month and we'll think about it. Personally, I would love for them to stay, but we can't decide anything on the spur of the moment.

Etienne – Understood. Enough talk, I want to accompany these people under the courtyards and give them something to drink. Linda and Esther, you'll give them the first care. Hemerik, you and your youngsters, take care of the rehabilitation of the bunkers. Jerome and Kelia will go look for linens for the beds. I think the soldier's beds remained in place.

23 — Epilogue

Saturday, July 24, 1998

Two hours before the arrival of the *Geometrix*, I received an e-mail from Athal:

"¡Holla ! Jerome the tourist. Are you bags ready for you wedding trip? (a little late in coming!)

Still no news of the Ephiphane! I hope the whole community is well.

I live near Barcelona and I found a collaborator who helps me set up a business in real estate. Demand for housing exploded a year ago, I think I chose the right investment.

I also found a little church in the surroundings of Barcelona that resembles the one on Kheo. They received me well and I took the baptism last week. A Christian woman (single!) translated the pastor's preaching. She's thinking of teaching me Catalan! That's not going to be easy, but I have to know the local language for my new job here. I think about you a lot and I plan to continue working with you, helping you financially if business is good.

Franck will come at the end of the month with the Cirius to deliver a second container from your last order (the one containing a kilometer of electric cable!) After that, no more money! We'll have to wait a year to make it again. The real estate, it brings in the money, but one mustn't hurry!

I'll come back to Kheo to celebrate the day of the year 2000! At that time, I hope to find beautiful pearls and see the blades of the wind turbines turn!

Sincere greetings to everyone!

Have a nice holiday, Kelia and Jerome the tourist!

¡ Buen viaje !'

I read the letter to Kelia, adding: 'Too bad that at the end of the month we won't be able to see Franck, for we'll still be in France.'

As planned, the *Geometrix* docked in the usual place. It stayed for a few hours. The container wasn't ours, so it had to be emptied right away to be taken back as soon as possible.

That day was special. We had a cabin booked on the tanker. For the first time, my wife went aboard a floating metal monster to leave her native island... destination: unknown! I felt her worried and tense. She constantly clung to me as if she feared everything around her, which made the sailors smile.

During the crossing, Jose, the talented forger, took our passports to add a few tax stamps and various annotations, according to Athal's plan. He also gave us a plane ticket "one way" to Paris, departing from Madagascar. Officially, we were two married young French, back from vacation, after a three week stay in Madagascar. We docked in Tamatave, in all "legality", since our fake visas weren't yet expired. I didn't know how Jacques, the taxi, had been warned by Franck of our arrival, but he was waiting for us in Lambert Street to take us to the airport on the outskirts of Antananarivo. The drive was already paid. Kelia discovered the continent of which she had heard talk forever, but she hadn't expected to find such poverty. In places, the Malagasy resembled the Ethiopians who had recently come to live on Kheo.

First flight for my wife, who grabbed my arm during takeoff!

I had a cold sweat when we arrived at the airport in Paris, where a hostess checked at length Kelia's papers, who answered all the questions calmly. She had already learned by heart the content of her passport! The hostess gave the document back, saying: 'Welcome to France Sir-Madame. Madame, don't forget to sign your passport!

Why did that woman ask me for information already written on the passport, asked Kelia while getting out of the airport, can't she read?

She knows how to read, she wanted to make you talk.

Why?

She was doubtful of the authenticity of your passport and wanted to hear you talk to check you're really French. As you perfectly master French without any accent, she ended up believing that the information concerning you written on that document was true.

You didn't tell me I had to sign, what does it mean "to sign"?

I'll show you at the hotel.'

Hotels, restaurants, walks on the Seine with the riverboat, visits to museums, shops, the Eiffel Tower, cinemas… our touristic vacation lasted for three weeks. My wife wanted to dress and get her hair done in the European style. Tireless, sometimes amazed, sometimes astonished, she proudly walked beside me, she wanted to see everything, know everything, understand everything... she was insatiable! Nothing escaped her and in the vastness of the city and the crowd, she noticed that Asians and Africans also lived in France. She was stunned by discovering beggars and homeless people in some street corners! Inconceivable, she said, to see this in the most beautiful city in the world!

We booked our airline tickets to Madagascar at the end the first week. We had to buy our visas (the real ones!) in the airport in Madagascar upon arrival and then get to Tamatave in Jacques' taxi.

◆ ◆ ◆

Strange events happened on Kheo during our stay in France. Two French journalists, on board the *Cirius* dared go on the island while Hemerik's youngsters were emptying the loading of the container on the pier. They had written an article in a newspaper I bought while boarding the return plane:

'We're just finishing our trip in the Indian Ocean, through the route of the tanker "The Cirius" on which we embarked. Stops for half a day allowed us sometimes, short visits in ports and close surroundings.

Pemba Island, Zanzibar, Farquhar... among all the coasts we have covered or avoided, the one of Kheo attracted our attention the most: an island of 32 square kilometers, little known and shunned by tourists. It was declared forbidden military zone for a long time. We thought it was uninhabited or private property where access was restricted to a handful of scientists coming from we don't know here to hide and observe who knows what! Big was our surprise when we discovered a sectarian community, closed on itself, busy with tasks as mysterious as its environment!

First of all, one kilometer away from the shore, we passed close to a heap of scrap, a hectare wide, fully deformed and plagued by sea water! It resembled the remains of a platform or an artificial island that you could have thought burned. Neither the crew on the Cirius, nor the inhabitants of Kheo we asked, wanted to tell us what it was about!

On the beach on which we walked a little, there was an arrangement that could be called an "obstacle course" used in the army.

More in the center, we saw buildings whose appearance made us think more of barracks than a monastery. These more recent buildings were surrounding a courtyard in the middle of which stood a white cross, ten meters tall. The members of this strange sect were dressed in red working suits with an inscription on the back: a symbol resembling a black circle, like a big ring corrugated on its periphery.

None of them wanted to tell us anything and all preferred to send us to their guru who made himself be called "pastor Etienne". He didn't show himself to be talkative or cooperative. In the absence of the manager, he

259

refused to let us visit the buildings and didn't want to reveal anything concerning the past of the island. No explanation on the pile of charred scraps protruding from the water that we had bypassed to reach the pier.

Nonetheless, we continued the tour along a path that led us to different crops and livestock. We found a set of concrete constructions, a type of bunker, all closed except for one which was inhabited by women and children in a well sad state. They were skinny, barefoot and wearing torn clothes. They, it seemed, didn't have the right to wear red suits. They were surviving like animals, away from the monastery and took shelter in this horrible concrete block without windows. None of them understood our language.

Following our road, oh surprise, I finished by discovering a luxurious villa, bristling with radio antennas and satellite dishes. For sure, it had to be the "humble home" of the manager.

Braving the surveillance cameras, we rang to doorbell. As no one answered, we made the tour of this huge building and saw, through a bay window an indoor pool! A little further, ten slaves were cleaning the garden of the property. These men, were no doubt the fathers of the tribe in the bunkers. They were in the same pitiful state, one of them accepted to answer our questions in a hard to understand French. It's through him we found out that the villa was usually inhabited by a "nice white man", who had left for a trip in Europe. As for a salary given to these poor slaves, they answered that there was no money going around on the island!'

I hope that after the spreading of such stupidity, the International Community will not meddle in our affairs!

Table of contents